PRAISE FOR

Moonlight and the Pearler's Daughter

"A sensitive and compassionate book, admirable in its engaging synthesis of multiple strands of history. It is alive to the complexity of how things must have been, and its consideration of race, gender, and sexuality invigorates the era with a freshness that feels organic. . . . At its heart, this is a story about family—whether it can survive in an inhospitable environment—and whether it is possible to be a good person in a corrupted world."

—*The New York Times Book Review*

"With the spirited Eliza at its heart, Pook's evocative debut novel spins a tale of intrigue and deception with a deft combination of gripping pacing and emotional restraint. Travel writer and journalist Pook's heightened observational skills are well employed in this lavish tableau showcasing Australia's vast and exotic natural treasures and fraught history."

—*Booklist*, starred review

"Lush . . . Pook casts an intoxicating spell."

—*Publishers Weekly*

"Beautifully evocative prose describing landscape and people intertwine in this bittersweet story of love, family, and courage. The small cast of characters, each wonderfully fleshed out, and Eliza's quest are what propel the story. Alongside the characters, it is place that is the book's focus: the ocean and the land complement and enhance Eliza's investigation. VERDICT: Readers will delight in the descriptive language that the author employs, so much so that they themselves will hear the sea and feel the desiccation of the heat and loneliness of the land."

—*Library Journal*

"[*Moonlight And The Pearler's Daughter*'s] atmospheric, evocative descriptions of the Western Australian landscape are an absolute masterclass in place—as well as being a proper, page-turning adventure."

—Ellery Lloyd, *New York Times* bestselling author of *The Club*

Moonlight
and the
Pearler's
Daughter

Lizzie Pook

Simon & Schuster Paperbacks
New York   London   Toronto   Sydney   New Delhi

Simon & Schuster Paperbacks
An Imprint of Simon & Schuster, Inc.
1230 Avenue of the Americas
New York, NY 10020

First Simon & Schuster trade paperback edition June 2023

For information about special discounts for bulk purchases,
please contact Simon & Schuster Special Sales at
1-866-506-1949 or business@simonandschuster.com.

The Simon & Schuster Speakers Bureau can bring authors to
your live event. For more information or to book an event, contact
the Simon & Schuster Speakers Bureau at 1-866-248-3049
or visit our website at www.simonspeakers.com.

Interior design by Lewelin Polanco

Manufactured in the United States of America

1 3 5 7 9 10 8 6 4 2

Library of Congress Control Number: 1982180498

ISBN 978-1-9821-8049-2
ISBN 978-1-9821-8050-8 (pbk)
ISBN 978-1-9821-8051-5 (ebook)

For Rose

AUTHOR'S NOTE

I acknowledge Aboriginal and Torres Strait Islander peoples as the First Peoples of the land on which this story takes place, and I pay my respects to Elders past and present.

Full fathom five thy father lies;
Of his bones are coral made;
Those are pearls that were his eyes:
Nothing of him that doth fade,
But doth suffer a sea-change
Into something rich and strange.
Sea-nymphs hourly ring his knell:
Ding-dong.
Hark! now I hear them—ding-dong, bell.

—William Shakespeare, *The Tempest*

"Seaward ho! Hang the treasure! It's the glory of the sea that has turned my head."

—Robert Louis Stevenson, *Treasure Island*

PROLOGUE

Bannin Bay, Western Australia, 1886

Eliza has never seen a land that looks so very much like blood. From the deck of the steamer it glistens, stretching wide in a lazy, sun-blurred smear.

She raises a hand against the glare, taking to tiptoes to squint over the polished guard rail. Before her, red dirt jitters in the heat and the sea is a boisterous, blistering green. There is something unsettling about the weariness of the breeze, hot and filled with the mineral stench of seagrass.

"We made it, my loves, we did it. Marvelous." Her father's oiled mustache lifts upward as he grins. He turns from his family to look out across the strange landscape—mirrored bays and shadowy crags the color of crushed insects.

This journey will be what saves them. Father had told them so over mutton and gravy back home. He regaled them with tales of pearl shells first, their shining nacres of champagne, silver, and cream. He was to work with his brother to launch a fleet of luggers, hauling shell to sell in bulk to the Americans and the French. The world was already lapping up the spoils of Bannin Bay, turning mother-of-pearl into buttons and the prettiest pistol handles you ever did see.

They'd watched, with jaws slack, as Father had pulled out his old atlas, folded down the page, and smoothed his palm across the place called New Holland. "Look." He showed them, trailing a finger down its western coast. "When we're there, we will be able to forget about all that has happened."

The beach in front of Eliza flares white and harsh. Dunes, sharp with swaying saltbush, ripple far into the distance. Below the rail, gulls skirl around a jetty that unfurls like a crocodile's crooked tail into a long gut of mangroves.

Her father gives the order and leads them steadily off the ship— her uncle Willem, her aunt Martha, followed closely by her mother and brother. Thomas is a head taller than her now, conspicuous in this heat in his short trousers and smart pressed jacket. Glancing back, she can see the hunched shoulders of stevedores. In grubby vests and moleskins to the knee, they lug what remains of the Bright-wells' belongings out of the ship.

Grasping at her mother's skirts, Eliza steps down onto the jetty. As she does, and with the speed of a knife over lard, her feet slide from beneath her and she thuds, backside first, onto the planks. The odor is obscene, but she places a flat palm on the greasy wood. There are fish scales smeared about and stringy meat going crisp in the sun. "Come, Eliza. Brush yourself off." Her mother extends a broad, comforting hand.

Eliza rubs her elbows, smooths her skirts, and lets her mother tug her to her feet. The sun has scattered coins of light across the sea; they make her eyes swim with stars. Looking up, she finds the sky obscured by the crescent of her mother's silk hat, the brim so absurdly wide she has seen men cowering from it back home. How odd she seems against this strange new place, Eliza thinks, like a dragonfly, once resplendent, marooned in a bucket of old slop water.

They continue down the jetty, her father and brother striding ahead. Sweat pools in the crooks of her elbows and at the creases behind her knees. Beside them, men watch unflinchingly as they pass, turning caulking mallets, hammers, and dirtied blades in rough hands. Her mother pays them no heed—an easy task for someone accustomed to admiration—and looks instead across the shoreline and out to the shot silk of the sea.

"You see, my girl, it's beautiful." She smiles and kneels to the height of her daughter. Eliza hears the rush of liquid before it happens. Sees the movement at the corner of her eye but turns away a heartbeat too late. With a sigh it splashes across them—thick with chunks and foul smelling. It slides with grim slowness down Eliza's face. They turn together toward a man who has frozen in position, sun-grizzled as a raisin and with only a few gray teeth. He holds a barrelful of fish guts under an arm, and a cracked palm raised in surrender.

"My apologies," he gasps, although a smile plays about his lips. "You ladies got right in the way. I beg your pardon." He stands aside to let them pass. "Please."

Her mother gives a huff as she jerks her daughter sharply onward. Smearing the guts from her cheeks, Eliza turns to see the man remove his hat. She watches as he hawks a knot of phlegm from his throat, depositing it at his feet with a gluey string of spittle. Her mother quickens to an appalled trot, still pulling at Eliza's arm.

The words barely reach her before they are snatched by the breeze. Four words she'll always remember.

"Welcome to Bannin Bay," they say.

CHAPTER 1

Ten years later
Bannin Bay, Western Australia, 1896

S he will simply leave the cockroach to die. That's what she'll do.
Stranded on its back in the coddling wet-season heat, its legs
will slow, then twitch, then cease to move entirely.

Outside, the rising sun lays soft fingers on the land. Above the
bay, gathering seabirds soar and the dirt blushes pink in the gauzy
light of dawn. Eliza's eyes flick to the clock on the dresser, its four
moons shimmering behind dusty beveled glass. Her fingers dance as
she runs the numbers in her head.

Sixty-one.

That's how many days she has slept alone in this bungalow. And
with every night, the loneliness has built like compacted soot. On
her own, as she so often is, she has made companions of the noises:
the impatient ticking of corrugated iron, the faint *click click click* of a

roach's legs on polished jarrah wood. Today, though–a day so humid it's there to be tasted–today her home will come alive once more.

She pulls on boots and smooths down her skirts, pictures Bannin Bay beginning to stir–the shutters in town cast wide open, merchants with sagging shoulders sweeping the pathways to their shops. The wind will sing down muddy laneways, carrying with it tales of death at sea. People will greet one another with mutters of shell tallies and whispers of the coming storms that mottle the sky like rotting teeth. At the foreshore, the early luggers will slump on their sides in the blue-black mud. Later, the remaining fleets will return from months spent pearling. Her father and brother will be with them. Eliza will no longer be alone.

She tugs her hair into a bow and wipes a smear from her neck. The morning sun, sharper with every minute, bleeds through the window lattice and casts bold patterns onto the furniture. A glance over her shoulder confirms the insect is still alive. Ten years now and she's still not accustomed to the roaches. She's not sure she ever will be. She steps toward the creature and considers it, shiny and upended, legs like fractured twigs. *This is a place where dead things hover*, she thinks. The town is full of them: gas-bloated crocodiles in the traps by the Kingfish, the corpses of drowned pearl divers sunk into the sand above the tide line.

She fixes the buttons at her neck and slips out of the bungalow. The dirt paths are as familiar to her now as the streets of London once were. But in the place of thick smog and gutter muck, tangerine dust billows skyward as she walks. Galahs scream furiously in the blossoms and overripe mangoes gloat like plump queens in the trees.

It takes only a few yards; she comes to an abrupt stop in the dirt. She turns, looks to the bungalow, set above the ground on gray stone stilts. Her shoulders sink. With heavy breaths she trudges back up the steps and through the door. She crosses the boards and bends, skirts sweeping weeks-old turpentine polish. Taking a forefinger, she reaches under the insect and, with the gentlest of flicks, uprights it.

Its body seems to shiver slightly, then it probes the air with its thin antennae. It is already on the move as Eliza steps back out into the heat.

A pearling lugger can find itself at sea for several long months, its crew returning to shore preserved in thick layers of salt-like dried herrings. Alone on their small wooden boats, facing riptides and swirling currents, it is no surprise bonds are formed out at sea that no incident nor man could ever break. As the divers toil, lead-weighted boots keep them fixed to the ocean floor, along with heavy chest plates and a copper corset worn over the shoulders. Eliza has read newspaper reports detailing men knocked off their boats by the boom, left to sink to their deaths under the weight of all that metal. "The tender must take care to pull his diver up slowly," her father would say. "Not to do so could leave him agonizingly crippled." Men were pulled up dead; of course they were. Crushed out of recognition, stomachs forced into their chest cavities. Others met death with bloated faces, tongues black and swollen, frantic eyes popped clean from their sockets.

The *White Starling* has been out for nearly nine weeks now, its men plucking shell from the seabed and stashing it in the hold with the dried fish and curry powder. Eliza has witnessed many times the men's return from sea: pinched, hollow-eyed apparitions drifting listlessly from their ships, their visible bones just like a collection of piano keys, ready to be played.

She makes her way toward the jetty, drawing enervated nods from the townsfolk as she passes. Their low-browed bungalows shelter under swaying palms and silvery gums. They have all been painted beige or underbelly green, but it's not enough to stop the crawling stain of pindan dirt.

"You off to see them in?" Mrs. Riesly peers out from under a cooling cloth. Eliza strains to hear the words above the quarrel of corellas on the roof. "Back today, are they?" The old widow heaves her weight off the veranda chair. Eliza nods, smiles thinly, leaving eyes squinting eagerly after her.

Bushes buzz with the frenzy of insects as Eliza passes quickly by. Ahead, red soil gives way to pale, gilded sand. In the distance, storm-battered shacks brood under stark eucalyptus trees. The contrast still makes her swallow: the bungalows with their lush half-acre plots and the sea of crushed iron beyond them, rippling in the stultifying heat.

"Didn't fancy putting a brush through that hair?" Min calls from a nearby doorway. *She must be working.* Eliza smiles, goes to her. "Today's the day, correct?" her friend asks. Min's hair is pinned up in a neat chignon, secured with mother-of-pearl grips that shimmer like snail trails in the sun. Eliza shifts when a muffled cough sails out from the depths of the hut.

"Should be." She nods tightly, her heart twitching at the thought of seeing her father soon. "This one's felt long. But I'm fine, really. I'm fine." She keeps her voice clipped; she always does. A tiny, diamond-dove lands on a branch above the hut. They watch it briefly arrange its wing feathers until it stoops and turns a red-ringed eye upon them.

"Well, they're all hard, I should expect," says Min eventually. "Especially now you're on your nelly." She chews distractedly on the side of her lip. Her features are sharp, as if whittled to points.

"You are testing my patience, girl," a brusque voice yells from the darkness. Eliza flinches and can't mask her expression quickly enough.

"Oh, missy, need I remind you that not all of us have fathers with their own fleets?" Min tucks a loose hair behind her ear. Eliza feels a stab of guilt, then notices the jewels fastened to Min's small earlobes–a gift from an admirer, perhaps. More likely a token of apology.

It wasn't always this way. When they were children, drawn together in this town that seemed to teeter at the edge of the earth, they would talk excitedly of adventures at sea–sharing murmured dreams of exploring exotic lands. Min would speak plainly of the romances she would enjoy, the fine sailor she would marry and the children they would raise up to be happy and feed till plump. She would coo at the babies paraded by the society women of Bannin. But when she neared, the women would suck their cheeks in and bat her off like a blowfly. As Eliza and Min grew older, Min became more beautiful and Eliza more plain. Her friend would tease her, "You'll never get anywhere in this town if you show no interest in men."

"I do have an interest in men," Eliza would reply coolly. "I've merely no interest in a husband."

"An interest in the contents of a man's library does not constitute an interest in men," Min would scold.

"Oi!" The angered voice claws its way back out of the hut. "I'm not paying you to have a bastard conversation."

Min glances behind her, loosens the shawl at her shoulders.

"Better go." She kisses Eliza quietly and retreats into the gloom.

W hen she comes to it, the jetty is hot with activity, jellied under the glare of the lurid sun. The men hauling baskets off the luggers look like ants ferrying leaves to their queen, their chatter drifting toward her on the warm breeze. The stench of the place is engulfing–ripe sweat, soft creek mud, and rotting oyster flesh. It smells, she realizes with a long deep inhalation, of life and death both at once.

Some of the boats are moored already; soon they will be dug into trenches to protect them from the blows. In the mud, the cajeput ribs of a lugger are being tipped on their side. When the tide comes in fully, the water will wash over the boat, spilling disoriented rats out into the open and sending cockroaches streaking across the beach.

She casts her eye out to the retreating water but sees no sign of her father's ship. She is always surprised by the urgency of the tide in Bannin Bay. How it gushes, fast and high around the mangroves, then—in just the blink of an eyelid—draws back in on itself. The pearlers and their crews live and die by the moon's pull here; spring tides, neap tides. An endless loop of boats coming in, boats going out.

The heat is torturous; she pulls her collar from around her neck and rolls her sleeves to the elbow. Her once-pale forearms have been tanned to light brown. Her mother's old acquaintances would not approve. After years in Bannin Bay, Eliza knows that a woman is expected to be one of two things: a white-glove wearer or a common harlot. She is neither, and her refusal to give in to the first had infuriated the society women of the bay. When she sees them in the streets now, they pass looking like something you might find atop a cake—taffeta day dresses, veiled hats and gloves, clutches of pearl blister brooches clamped to their bosoms. They do not spare a glance for her.

She settles on a loose plank and tucks her skirts beneath her legs, pressing her fingers into the burned skin of her scalp. The pain of it sends a brief thrill through her blood. Nearby, pelicans preen and a lone osprey patrols the dunes. She scrapes the hair from her forehead and fixes her eyes on the ocean. Sails are beginning to break the horizon, glistening like slick bones in the haze.

"They've probably all perished." A phlegmy voice rasps behind her, followed by a wheezy crow's cackle. She turns the top half of her body until she's nose to nose with a large wooden leg. This close she can see it has been picked at and pockmarked by the jaws of burrowing worms. "Charles has never been much of a sailor." Her uncle grins. He has sunken cheeks and the type of skin that appears unfortunately waxy. He wears a white suit darkened to brown by dirt and sucks shakily on a short-stemmed tobacco pipe. The skin of his hands is livid with sandfly bites.

"Willem." She rises to be met by his sour grog breath. She ignores it. "Just thought I'd represent the welcoming party. Are you well?" She hopes her feigned pleasantness is halfway convincing. She is quite sure her uncle's timing is intentional; he can often be found lurking once the schooners have signaled the return of the fleets. He lusts so clearly after shell he himself will no longer haul in, side-eyeing the pearlers wearing smart pith helmets, wetting his lips at the whiteness of their shining shoes.

"Tell your father to come see me when he gets in, if you will," orders Willem. "We've certain matters to discuss." Eliza does not turn to watch him go.

The afternoon passes in a drawn-out blaze, the sun a clean penny high in the sky. She occupies her mind with images of her father's lugger, rolling low in the water, sails belly out, coasting on chalky turquoise seas. She pictures Shuzo Saionji, the boat's lead diver, descending slowly to the seabed at murky first light. She can almost taste the reek of drying pearl meat hanging from every beam of the ship, the sharp-sweet sweat of the rest of the crew—barefoot tenders, shell openers, and cooks who trail slack fishing lines off the gunwale. Finally, she sees the familiar face of Balarri, the scores of age carved deep into his sun-battered skin.

As her ears ring in the heat, more luggers limp their way to the jetty. They bring with them a creeping sensation that begins its slow, caustic movement through her body. She watches as spent crews stagger off the boats, reaching for rum and comfort after so long among the tarpaulins and the planks. From one vessel, two scrawny capuchin monkeys detach themselves from the mast and scamper onto the jetty. They're dressed in finely embroidered waistcoats and fez hats. Eliza barely blinks. Rakish pearlers stroll by like the men she's seen in her father's history books, with raised knees, smoking rifles, and fluttering flags. She knows their in-port uniform so well she could draw the felt hats, white shirts, pajamas, and silk neckerchiefs on cue.

The sun is crawling down the rear of the dunes now, illuminating the teasel heads of parched spinifex grass. But still there is no sign of the *Starling*. The fact hooks itself into Eliza. She tries to ignore its barb. She has played this waiting game before; soon the boat will be here, then all will be in order. That's how it goes. She swallows a sour taste and moves her eyes to the working men. She is aware that none would be interested in her plain physicality: her gray eyes, her boyish body, a nose set out of joint by a brother's fist. So she feels at liberty to watch them, taking their familiarity for a balm. But as she moves her gaze across broad shoulders and sweaty napes of necks, an itchy sensation arrives. First across her chest then up to the backs of her ears. As her eyes skim over to the horizon, she realizes, with a start, that she is being observed. A man with a wide-brimmed hat tipped far back on his head, a thin face, and an angular chin, is smiling peculiarly in her direction. The feeling it evokes is not entirely pleasant. She turns pointedly the other way.

More hours slide past and the dread thickens to something solid. The other luggers have all been strung up and stripped. The light is fading and there are just a few workers left tapping away. She is about to surrender, to make her fearful way back to the bungalow alone, when a pinhead appears on the horizon. It brings her to her feet and pushes her head to a tilt. If she squints, she can just make out the tiny silhouette of a lugger. Her throat tightens. She squeezes her eyes near shut. She can see the distinctive paintwork now too. The *Starling* has always been entirely washed in white, a ghost ship tossed on marbled blue-green seas.

As it comes in, there are men busying about its deck, but she can sense something is wrong. She scans the lugger, a coil of terror in her stomach. There: the flag is not where it should be. Instead, it sits low, forlorn at half-mast. Eliza gulps dryly. The blood ticks in her ears. She has seen flags like this before.

The deckhands leap off to haul in the mooring line, and Eliza's toes clench as she waits for her brother and father to emerge. It's Shuzo, the diver, who shows first, jaw tight, eyes chillingly wide. She calls out to him, but he avoids her gaze.

"I'm so sorry, Eliza." His voice is a trickle of water, the medals at his breast winking in the low sun. He slips past and is quickly inhaled by the town. She rushes forward as her brother scrambles into sight. His shirt is dirtied, trousers salt stained and tattered. She wonders why he has not changed into his whites like Shuzo. Usually lean like a cattle dog, Thomas is thinner than she has ever seen, his hat jammed down so tight over his eyes it casts his whole unshaven face in shadow. Something dark moves through Eliza from her feet to her throat. She pushes through the crowd, calling his name until their eyes eventually meet. His look hollows her out like a gourd. Inside of her, nerves crackle against skin. The earth seems to stop dead on its axis.

"Where is he?" She is not sure how her mouth forms the words. He blinks once. Eyes like stones. "Gone."

CHAPTER 2

1886

Y ou'll be just fine here." The man's words were syrupy and long. Eliza could not tear her eyes from his white leather shoes, polished so vigorously they had thinned to show the shapes of his toes.

The retreating steamer was now nothing but smoke on the horizon, and Eliza was alarmed at the hot air that clung to the insides of her throat. She thought of the fumes that belched from the factory pipes back home. Her chest caved slightly. How she longed for the familiar grayness of it all.

"Now, I do not wish to alarm you, but there can be some discordance among the folks here in the bay, I must warn you of that." Septimus Stanson wiped the dust from his trousers and produced a silk fan that he flapped at his face. "We are, after all, something of a motley collection, quite an anomaly on this country's soil: Europeans, Malays, Manilamen, Koepangers, countless Japanese, of course."

Globs of moisture clung perilously to the creases in his neck and quivered with every ridiculous flutter of the fan. "We Europeans are wildly outnumbered–by about a hundred to one during lay-up, I'd say–but we still hold power in the colony, naturally, and the Pearlers' Association is a most welcoming place for newly arrived Britishers." Eliza had looked to the thin man and his wife beside him. How much younger she seemed, how strangely beautiful she was in her bone-yellow dress.

"As president of the association, I have the pleasure of welcoming all new members." He glanced at her father and at Willem. "I should hope you fellows will join me for a drop of squareface and a cigar this evening. As for you"–Eliza had felt her mother flinch–"I shall see to it that Iris introduces you to the Ladies' Circle. It really is the best way for you to meet the other wives in the bay." She could not decipher her mother's expression as they looked around them at this unprepossessing place. Was this really where they were going to make their fortune? Eliza had glanced at her father. He could not meet her eye.

It was the heat of the place that was most oppressive. Trapped, as they were, under such a pitiless sun. In those first few weeks Eliza's skin swam with sweat. She'd wake to find her nightclothes soaked entirely through. When she washed them, they'd emerge tinged with the orange of old scabs. Soon enough, things started to rot. Mildew sprawled like nicked blood vessels, and mold hunkered in dark corners. Eventually the moths and silverfish descended. Before long, all that reminded her of home was ruined. Out of the house, angry March flies would bite through her blouses, leaving welts the size of eggs. The bushes would spit all manner of birds, and ticks would tumble from the grasses to bury their heads in soft skin. They would swell with her blood until Thomas showed her how to burn them off, one by one, with matches.

She'd never seen anything quite like Bannin Bay, having always imagined the rest of the world to be much the same as London. But here—the rocks, the water, the air, they were all so unashamedly bright. Did the trees not know to be green and soft? Instead, they were formless, sloughing bark like old bandages. She was caught off guard when the rain arrived—hurling itself urgently against the walls, with thunder so loud it set the teeth rattling in the jaw. The kitchen seethed with unknown creatures. Bold, unblinking geckos, the crisp bodies of old roaches. In her bedroom, spiders worked on webs; in the morning she'd wake to see crickets caught breathless in their grasp.

She'd met the girl, Laura-Min, down at the foreshore one day. She'd looked so much, Eliza thought, like a sparrow picking her way through the waste.

"Hello, birdy," Eliza had called shyly, and the girl had glanced up and grinned.

Min was the daughter of a Scottish nurse and a Chinese businessman come from a stint in the goldfields. When his wife had died, Xie Hong Yen had made his way to Bannin with his young daughter on his hip. At every town they reached, he'd told her, "No. The next one will be better." And so they continued to this place where the earth appeared to stop. He'd found work as an interpreter for the association, but when he, too, died six years later, he took Min's safety along with his life. As a prospector's daughter, Min was smart, proud, and probing, but her mixed blood confined her to the laborers' cottages on the outskirts of town.

In those early days Bannin swaggered like an animal: bony and bristling with a miscellany of men—Britishers, Germans, Americans, and Dutchmen; frontiersmen, whalers, colonists, and convicts, all drawn to the town like maggots to meat. Many had come to seek their fortune in pearl shell. Others had simply drifted by way of Sydney or the Swan River Colony. Some came via cattle stations and opal fields, parts of the country that sprawled like seas but didn't appear on the maps in England. How many, she'd always wondered, were simply forced to leave, like her family?

Down at the foreshore, men made temporary dwellings using tin and burlap–a squat of humpies and fly-infested depots, worked at by salted, sinewy hands. It didn't take long for her father and uncle to establish a small fleet, searching for shell beds, soaks, and watering points on far-off islands. It was strange and, at times, a little frightening, but what surprised Eliza most in those hazy, early years was how much men coveted and what they were willing to risk for pearl shell, for the treasures found within. A pearl has a glow like a fire or a lamp; she learned that early. It is a siren song in the shape of a stone, sending men to lengths they never dreamed they'd go.

When those ships returned to shore, Eliza would fling questions at the crews.

"From where does a fig parrot get its scarlet cheeks?" she'd ask.

"If you were to prod a man o' war with a stick, would it hurt it?"

Willem would scoff, but her father would answer with detail, scratching diagrams with a stick in the sand. Sometimes, back then, he would even set her tasks. Mysteries to solve while he was away at sea. She'd find a key under her pillow and with it an order to find a locked chest and treasure within. Or he'd pose a question–*Where do dragonflies sleep?*–and she'd spend her days seeking them out, pushing her head into the geraniums to find them clinging on like old dried leaves. She remembers clearly one day waking to a hand-drawn map at the end of her bed. She spent a week following the instructions, pacing out distances in the garden, searching for spices in the kitchen as her mother looked on. In the end she had unlocked the clues and found what was hidden for only her: a tiny charm in the shape of a mermaid stashed in a hidden drawer of her father's writing desk. She had rubbed it between her fingers and placed the cold thing in her mouth. She wanted to swallow the love she felt for it, keep that memory of her father inside her forever.

At other times she'd help him collect specimens for his papers. He was fascinated by the flora and fauna of this new land, and there was nowhere she wouldn't go to find something they had not yet charted in their notes: into the crags of low, red cliffs to haul out fresh freckled eggs, to hidden bays to seek out ship-sized squid washed ashore in storms. Perhaps one day she would make a discovery of her own and be lauded in the way a man would. For now, she'd lost count of the ways in which her quests had resulted in bruises or blood. But those scars were merely marks of how far she was willing to go for her father.

CHAPTER 3

1896

N o, there was no blood. We searched the whole ship." Thomas's eyes are cast downward.

The remaining crew file off the lugger and flow around them toward the town, shirts caked in oyster guts, skin beaten to leather by the sun.

She feels as if her heart has been dislodged. The pulse of it hammers at her throat.

"How did you not see what happened? When did he go missing?" She pulls hard at her brother's arm. He shrugs her off and flicks the brim of his hat sharply upward.

"No one saw what happened, Eliza," he hisses. "That's the point. He just . . . disappeared yesterday." A gull swoops to pick off chunks of fish at their feet. Thomas kicks at it to continue forward, neck bowed.

"Did you speak to the crew?" She follows him. Her voice is high with alarm. "Someone must have seen something. He can't have just vanished. You don't think one of them . . ."

He lets out a loud breath. "Of course I spoke to them, Eliza. How incompetent do you think me? I questioned all of them, scoured the deck, put a blasted dinghy in the water. We searched for *hours*, even rounded the nearest island. Then we set a course straight back to Bannin. This is a matter for the constables now."

She has been pushed off a cliff. Her lungs can't find enough air. "W–we must talk to them again," she stammers. "They wouldn't have done this. Something else must have happened, Thomas. They might have seen *something*." She casts her eyes frantically around the jetty. "Where's Balarri?"

"Father sent him back early on the schooner; he's not here." Thomas's pace has quickened.

"The others then; let's get them together." The urgency feels like heat; her tongue is clumsy and thick. "Thomas!"

They reach the Kingfish, the chatter of men ready for lay-up filling the air like bees. Broken glass litters the dirt and men slump dull-eyed around the veranda rail. The crew will be inside, seeking calm for their nerves at the bottom of their pannikins. They could easily go and speak to them now, ask them again what they saw.

"I've already questioned them." Thomas doesn't even glance up at the hotel. "It would be a waste of time and frankly disrespectful given what they've been through. It makes more sense for me to ready the stones. I'll need to go on to Cossack with the *Starling* at first light." He looks up at the lowering clouds. "Or sooner, if I'm to beat the weather."

His words are a flat palm to her chest. She stops in the dirt. "But. You've just got here. You can't go while Father is . . ."

His eyes flare. "If I don't go, there'll be no fleet at all and we–you and I–will be left with *nothing*." He lowers his voice. "We have debts to settle. I have to go. I can't trust anyone here anymore."

"What do you mean, debts?" There is a noise in her ears like a faraway bell.

"Meetings with the buyers to uphold," says Thomas. "If they fall apart, *everything* falls apart." His voice draws lazy glances from the drunks. "The other pearlers will swoop if we don't keep the fleet afloat–there's no mercy here; that's quite apparent. Plus, you know how word travels." He bats away the flies and leans in closer. "Someone in Cossack might know something about the crew." He checks to see if they are being watched. "Many of them take lodgings there during the Wet. Perhaps one of them had been planning . . . something. There are lay-up camps on the way. I'll pull into them, ask around. This is the shrewdest thing to do, I promise."

"You cannot leave. Don't be so ridiculous, Thomas. Please." The panic threatens to bubble up from her throat.

"Get ahold of yourself, Eliza!" His voice comes out with barbs. "This is what Father would expect me to do and this is the best thing for us to do right now, you know that." His tone is sharp but there's a hitch in his voice. He must be panicking too. "There are others here far better placed to find out what has happened. I've sent someone along to alert Parker. In the meantime, it's my responsibility to save the fleet; I won't have my family losing anything else." His eyes dart up to hers. "Come with me back to the bungalow now; we'll ready my provisions. Tomorrow you can speak to the crew if you still desire it. After a night's sleep they may remember other details, anyway."

The thought of waiting is abominable, and sleep impossible–especially while her father is out there, somewhere. She thinks of all those men buried at sea, men who'd succumbed to the divers' paralysis, men whose throats had been slit in late-night scuffles. She wants to flee, to knock on every door in this town. But she drops her head and follows her brother through the dusty streets.

That night she seeks out every drop of whisky in the bungalow to force her body into a stupor approaching sleep. When slumber arrives it is in a half form, feverish and marked with smears. She dreams of her father. "Now, Eliza," he calls, the edges of him soft like cigar smoke. "Find me three different types of bugs in this bush." She can feel the childish sense of excitement even through sleep, imagines the waxy leaves as she rubs them between her fingertips. "Find me a jewel beetle and we'll take it back to the magnifying glass. Let us see how its body shimmers like the sea." She dreams of the steamship too. Her father had called it their Great Adventure, a slow swoop of a sail to Australia from England. She had never seen anything quite like that ship. The dining saloon with its arabesque pillars and birds painted in white and gold on the porcelain. How she'd wait at the bottom of the grand staircase to watch folk descend in their finery every evening. Her father and Willem spent their days discussing life in Bannin Bay. At night she had clambered with them up to the top deck to see the Southern Cross and Argo sailing across the vast expanse of starry sky.

"If I was lost out on the ocean, would you come to find me?" she had asked her father.

"I'd stop at nothing." He leaned on an elbow and looked her square in the eye. "But you'd have to send me a bottle first."

"A bottle?"

"A message in a bottle." He had puffed his cheeks and mimed a bobbing motion to make her chuckle. "You know," he said, "many years ago Queen Elizabeth created a very important position. The Uncorker of Ocean Bottles, it was called." Eliza had grinned into the darkness. "Sailors and spies put messages in bottles and floated them on the ocean until they were washed up or found by passing boats. Only one person in the whole country was allowed to open these bottles, owing to the dark secrets they contained: the Uncorker of Ocean Bottles."

"Well, what if someone else opened them?"

He drew his finger slowly across his neck and stuck out his tongue.

She comes to with a jolt, limbs immediately twitching with impatience. Her head throbs from the whisky. She looks to the shutters; the sun is peering with one eye over the horizon. She swings her legs out of the bed. It is time to talk to the crew.

As she readies herself, the heat finds its inevitable way in through the slats. By the time she is dressed, it presses all around her like bathwater. The bungalow is strangely quiet; perhaps Thomas has not yet awoken. But as she steps through the rooms, it becomes clear that he is not here at all. He must have left under darkness, she realizes; perhaps he feared the light would bring the storms along with it. Her shoulders sag.

When she goes to leave, something stops her. It glimmers, snagging her eye and drawing it to the dresser. She goes to it—it's her father's gold fountain pen. *Odd*, she thinks, *he always keeps it with him*. But as she reaches for it, there is a loud rap at the door. She freezes, frowns; who could it be this early? She is not expecting a caller. She pulls it open to find the old widow standing there. With one hand resting on the doorjamb, her chest pumps away like a newborn bird. At the widow's side is the cane she carries to bear the weight of her arthritic bones.

"Mrs. Riesly," Eliza says. The town likes to talk of the old widow in bartered whispers. Her peculiar behavior invites it; she can often be found out walking late on nights when the moon sets the ghost gums aglow. There will be not a sound but the click of the cane on wasted wooden steps, its brass handle in the shape of a horse's head shining keenly in the moonlight.

"Are you quite all right?" Eliza asks.

"It's that Balarri," Mrs. Riesly pants. "I've just heard he's been taken in at the jail for your father's murder."

CHAPTER 4

On the outskirts of town, there stands a tree—a boab, an elephantine thing. Over time Eliza has watched it grow, running her hands over its chipped silver bark, catching its white flowers in her palms as they fall. Now she peers up into its boughs and tries to regain her breath. The branches seem to warp as they strain to reach the violent sun. She has heard whispers that they used to hang people from this tree—skin divers who had jumped ship to escape from bad luggers, bush folk who'd been hauled in for spearing cattle. The thought sows a seed of discomfort and she takes a step backward. As she does, a feathery head peers slowly round the trunk. Then a scaled foot claws its way into sight. With a blur of bright white, a cockatoo comes bursting from behind the tree. It circles Eliza with the shriek of something garrotted and lands on her shoulder, long nails piercing through cotton.

"Rumors creep on lazy feet," it squawks, and hops to gnaw at her hair ribbon. She tucks in her chin to see the creature properly, although she already knows what it is and whom it belongs to.

"Sorry about that, precious." The bosun Reynold Grant steps forward. "Confucius has a thing for the ladies, don't you, old man?" Grant's broom-handle mustache obscures his wide, easy grin. His lined skin is tough; quick eyes fringed with deep-set wrinkles. His worker's hands are rough and callused; they reach forward to coax the bird away. The cockatoo is a well-known presence around Bannin. Chatty, verging on abusive when the men have fed it rum, it's often to be spotted above the town, flying out over the laborers' cottages. If it flew in the other direction, it would pass over the camps intended to contain the natives. Even farther and it would reach the pastoralists' stations built on the land they had stolen from those they had contained. Either way, many suspect the bird is sent out to fact find on the sly. Grant's knowledge of secrets certainly is formidable; he knows which wives have which lovers, which pearlers have which whores. In fact, his insight is so pronounced that some believe him a practitioner of black magic and sorcery. Eliza wishes she possessed witchcraft enough to turn herself into the bird, to perch on the rooftops and hold an ear out for the whispers. *What would they say of her father?* she wonders. *What is it they must know?*

"What brings you round here, fair Eliza?" Grant sucks on his clay pipe as the bird settles back on his shoulder.

"They think Balarri is responsible for my father's disappearance." She casts her eye toward the lane that would take her to the jailhouse. "He's been taken in by Parker."

Grant shakes his head. "Not possible. I heard your father went missing last day out at sea?"

She nods.

"I saw Balarri at the camp before the *Starling* came in. He wasn't on that ship. Couldn't have been him, no way about it."

Her pulse quickens. She *knew* it. Thomas had said he'd come in early on the schooner, hadn't he? She nods her quick thanks to the bosun and sets off directly toward the jail. If Balarri has been taken in, it means whoever is really to blame is still out there. It means they could still have her father. She hurries into the shadowy embrace of the lanes.

The jailhouse is a mass of sun-scorched iron. It used to be nothing more than a cowshed, prisoners chained up alongside the horses as crows peered in through the thatch. Now it has a more menacing air of permanence, the constables puffed up in sashes and thick blue twill. The cells, she knows, are only ever really occupied by men like Balarri, save for the occasional rowdy squatter picked up when the Roebourne force trot into town. A European is not often punished for his transgressions in Bannin Bay, particularly if those transgressions result in the spilling of native blood. Laws enacted in faraway Perth are as good as ineffective around these parts, and as any justice of the peace within three hundred miles is involved in the pearling industry, it is not in his interest to pass prosecutions against those who facilitate it.

The building's sole prisoner today is more commonly referred to by the colonists as Billy. He had been one of the strongest divers in town at a point. But by the time he met Eliza's father, his bones were old and he didn't go down with the hard-hat crews. Instead, he cleaned shell on the *Starling* sometimes, sold firewood in town. That's how it appeared to others, anyway.

In the earliest days Eliza had been drawn like a hawk moth to those boats. She would brush up against them strung stiffly to the jetty, poke her nose in, even, to see what goods were stashed inside. It was a still, dark night when she stepped aboard one to find a strange man slumbering below deck. She had startled and he had woken, alarmed, leaping up to wildly swing his fists. He yelled furiously at this unwelcome spirit, which took the shape of a young, pale, scruffy child. As his arms wheeled about, the spirit grabbed a tin plate and launched it clearly at his skull. It struck, then clattered to the floor with the rolling sound of a cymbal. The two figures froze then, eyeing each other through the gloom. When Balarri saw what was really in front of him, he let out an ornery huff. It seemed to Eliza as if the sound the man made had filled the entire boat.

Balarri had already established then what would make him indispensable to her father and, in turn, what would ensure his mobility on the streets of Bannin Bay. He'd lead the pearler to the things he'd write about in his books. Their arrangement was not widely spoken about, but treasures of that kind came easily to Balarri's fingers. He could sift out shells from creek beds, shells just as beautiful as the drop pearls the Russians pursued, and reveal the places you could visit after a storm to see green rocks embedded in the tree trunks. He kept most of his knowledge secret—he made quite sure of that—but at the right price a colonist could be led to believe he was scratching the surface of it.

With the pearler came his daughter, and when Charles knew he could rely on Balarri for specimens, he asked if Balarri would allow Eliza to search with him. Balarri had not agreed to it without a trade: he would occupy the girl, and her father would provide him with an increased wage. He did not know yet what he would do with the coins—a man like him was not often paid money for anything, and there were many places in Bannin at which he was not allowed to spend it—but he knew the power of these shining things, given the hold they had over every other man in the bay.

Eliza could tell he wrestled with the indignity of escorting her, but hadn't he said you had to rub up against all sorts to get by in a place like Bannin Bay? For hours she would follow him to find a single turtle washed onto the mud flats, to the places where the algae in the water glowed bright blue when agitated with a finger. Even as a child she was strong, and she knew because of this, she was useful to him. She could easily climb the roost sites for eggs, fold her narrow limbs into hidden crevices. He had a fear of small spaces, a mortal horror at being confined, but it was not hard for her to slide herself into the mouth of a slender cave. There were some places that were entirely off-limits, of course, and they were not to remove any specimens. Balarri would not allow it. So Eliza brought along with her a sketchbook and worked to capture faithfully in pencil strokes what they had uncovered.

The outings began as functional and over time became frequent. He seemed only passingly rankled by her propensity to ask questions, considering he was not in the habit of asking a great many questions himself. She'd interrogate him about his favorite dinners— he seemed to derive the most unbridled joy from eating—wattle seed, billy goat plum, long soup, liver. She'd ask why he preferred a gentleman's waistcoat with his short trousers and shirt, and how old he was, truthfully. He'd bat her away with a different answer each time. "Twenty-five," he'd say one day. "Two hundred and fifty," the next. She would envy his easy accomplishments, how he could trap mullet at the low tide with only stones and mangrove branches. The fish would flail and gulp in the shallows until he raised his spear high and pierced one right through the belly flesh. He'd hold it to the sunlight, and they'd marvel at how its bloodied scales sparkled like gemstones.

She rounds the jail and is confronted by a fuss of bodies and dust. Men are cursing, limbs quickened with panic. At the foot of the veranda steps, a native tracker sits straight backed on his gelding. A uniformed sergeant is hurriedly stuffing the saddle pack. As he glances up from beneath his hat, Eliza sees his eye is bloodied and swollen.

"What do you want, Brightwell?"

It's Archibald Parker. A rabid cat possesses more civility than this officer. Here is a God-fearing man whose vice is power, who leads his prisoners out in neck fetters to shovel shell grit under the sun.

She'd seen it before, the horror of it, a chain gang that clunked and shuffled, white dust billowing around the men so that their bodies gleamed like ghosts.

She steps forward. "You know what I want. He shouldn't have been jailed."

This close, Parker has that parched skin of every frontiersman—lips white and rough with dead, dry flakes. On a thin chain around his neck an old pendant has fallen open; a small, grainy photograph of a woman peeks out from inside.

"You as well?" Parker fastens the bag. "I've already had half the bloody native camp round here this morning. Telling me how to do my damn job." A blowfly lands on his eyelid; he does not flinch. "As I told them, you're too late." The fly creeps down to his nose. "He's gone. Scarpered. Not for long, mind."

Her eyes snag on the revolver at the mounted tracker's hip. She knows the officers are recruited from the jail for their skills in hunting, their knowledge of the land. A coldness tiptoes down her spine as she thinks of Balarri out there. Without a horse, he won't put much distance between them.

"There's no need to find him," she says. "He is not responsible for what happened."

Parker moves around the gelding and she follows.

"He came in early with the schooner; Grant saw him at the camp."

The sergeant gives an incurious blink. The fly lazily detaches itself and drifts away.

"He wasn't even on the ship when my father went missing." His lack of response rattles her. "There is a witness who can vouch that he was here at the very time." The frustration scalds now. "Is it not your job to protect all souls in this town, sir?"

"Grant?" Parker does not stop his preparations. "Piss to that. A Black witness is as good as no witness to me. Specially one involved in witchcraft." He pauses to scour the phlegm from his throat, gobs it into a handkerchief, then bends to wipe his boot with the sputum.

"Regardless, once I've recaptured the native, he'll be tried for assaulting a police sergeant. Punished to the fullest extent of the law." He looks up, as if surprised to see her still standing there. "You're wasting your time, Brightwell. Be on your way."

Her mouth moves noiselessly. Her head swims. Not only is Balarri in danger; if Parker puts all his weight into this misguided manhunt, there will be no one left here to search for her father.

"Well, I shall prove he didn't do it, then."

The sergeant stops, smirks. "And how do you intend to do that?" She notices then how his greasy beard brushes the buttons on his jacket.

"I know he has done nothing." She is buying time, not sure yet how to answer his question. "He wouldn't. This is a waste of resources when you should be finding out the truth of what's happened to my father. There's no reason to believe he isn't still alive somewhere."

Parker erupts into a rattling guffaw then. It sends sodden tobacco flecks across her blouse. "If you believe that, you're more of a fool than any in this damned town."

She tries to smother images of her father's lifeless body at the bottom of the ocean. Until someone shows her otherwise, she will believe he is alive. She *has* to believe he is alive.

Parker smacks the horse's rump and the animal rears into action. The tracker barely blinks as it brays into the dust.

The sergeant moves toward his mare. She must stop him. Thoughts come to her in shards. Hot. Fast. Then scatter.

"I *will* prove it," she says, her defiance growing as the sergeant inspects his rifle. "I'll find out what happened to my father. I'll . . . I'll bring him back here. Then you'll have to call off your search. It will prove that no murder has taken place."

Parker sighs, bored. "By all means, Brightwell, sniff about this town like some sort of unleashed cur. Find me some bugger wanting to confess." He snorts. "Even better, bring your father right here to this veranda, as you suggest. You might have to set his corpse on poles to get him to stand up straight, mind."

Eliza's jaw stiffens. The sergeant has not yet finished.

"Bring him breathing, then *of course,* Miss Brightwell, I'll call off the search." His tone is treacly sour. "Matter of fact, while you're at it, bring me back a golden goose? Make it a plump one. I'm sick to the back teeth of possum gristle."

His leer is a poison, but Eliza's mind is set. If the sergeant won't help, then she must find out what happened to her father, and she must do it as quickly as she can. Her fingers twitch, then clench into fists. The men gallop away in a cloud of thick red dust.

CHAPTER 5

Breathless, she rattles open the door to her father's study. Soft light streams in, illuminating motes that twirl in its beam. Briefly, she is taken aback. The place smells so entirely of him. The earthy lingering of salt on his skin, the incense he burned to ward off the roaches.

She scans the room quickly. Her father always used his gold pen to write in his diary. If the pen is still in the bungalow, then perhaps his diary is still here too.

One side of the room is stacked with wide jarrah shelves, laden with glass jars, sextants, and finely painted globes. Below, there snake rows of battered books. She bends to run a hand over their cool spines: *Sea Sponges of the Southern Hemisphere*, *The White Whale and the Willy-Willy*. She stands again and inspects a bowerbird painting on the wall. The curious creature has been immortalized with its striking pink crest. Behind it is a bower decorated with rocks, seeds, and shells—all the trinkets it has hoarded to impress its mate. She peers into the jars below it. Eyes peek out gormlessly through murky liquid. In one, a puffer fish is stupendously engorged, its spiky skin blown up to a ball, lips pursed in an unmet kiss. In another, a small octopus sits flaccid and drooped.

It sends her memory to Sixty Mile Beach one hot day, when the land glowed amber underfoot. They had been climbing rocks after a receding tide. The shoreline had been swallowed up and spat back out again. In a rock pool she had reached down for a beautiful stone covered in blue markings. *He would so love to put it on his shelves*, she thought, and she'd gift it to him like treasure. As her fingers brushed it, the blue spots began to shimmer. She hesitated, just the space between two breaths, but it was long enough for her father to see and haul her away. "No." His voice was harsh and high-pitched. The rock opened its eyes to reveal rectangular pupils. "It's a blue-ringed octopus. You must never touch it." They had peered into the tide pool as if it had teeth. "A bite can kill a man in just a few seconds," he said. "It's not always the biggest things that are the deadliest."

At the end of one shelf she finds two silver frames. In the first is a grainy photograph of a beautiful woman, looking into the camera with a level gaze. Her black hair is hidden under a large blue hat, and jewels hang from her ears. On the woman's lap is a young Eliza, glancing self-consciously just off camera. The next frame displays a picture of a young child with snow-white hair, startled at the glare of the photographer's flash. He has been caught mid blink, eyebrows raised, his small hands making fists at the side of his body. The breath snags in Eliza's throat. She takes the frame and places it facedown on the shelf.

At the far end of the room, a desk is piled high with papers. Annotated drawings spill across intricate illustrations of ships, each one sliced in half to display its inner workings like a doll's house. Above the desk is a huge wooden board, plastered with hand-drawn diagrams. Her father's inventions. Or "experiments," as he liked to call them, failed blueprints for the "floating tricycle," the "iron wings," and the "man-transporting balloon."

Below, she can see the papers they have most recently worked on together, each alive with his painterly illustrations–deft brush-strokes bringing to life the dancing tentacles of anemones, the deep corrugated folds of a humpback's ventral pleats. She scans the desk until her eyes rest on a thick sheaf of papers, sticking out from in between two books. She pulls at them, and a collection of newspaper articles slides out, each neatly scored and flattened. She holds the first to the light.

An open letter from Mr. David Carley to the Secretary of State direct, Perth, Western Australia, Jan. 11, 1886.

The writer of this letter arrived at Cossack and Roebourne in the year 1872.

May it Please Your Lordship to read this letter from the individual who was an eyewitness to the statements herein made. The writer also reported to Captain Smith, Chief of the Police Constabulary, and to the present Attorney General (Mr. Hensman), of the cruelties inflicted on the natives; the continual acts of kidnapping and slavery, which is the common practice of the country, and the writer has stated such to the authorities time after time.

The North-West Coast of Western Australia is steeped to its neck with rapine, slavery, and murder. And though it be commonly remarked that where the British flag be unfurled slavery cannot exist, the writer of this letter can and will prove differently; for in no country in the known world have such murderous deeds been committed and natives made greater slaves of.

These natives are engaged as pearl divers, and all they get for their work is a little flour twice a day: yet these poor wretches are kidnapped, bought, and sold; and this is all done under the eyes of the Magistrates; and also the police, who are bribed for conniving with the same. The law for the punishment of slavery is a dead letter in West Australia.

The Government has for many years employed men on the police force who have been convicted in the Supreme Court, Perth, for killing white as well as black men, and still kept in the force for years afterward. In 1884 <u>Archibald Parker</u> was convicted in the Supreme Court, Perth, for beating in the brains of a man, 70 years of age, at Rottnest; he received three months' imprisonment: shortly afterward the Government made him Sergeant of Police, and then sent him to Roebourne, where the writer has many times seen his fearful cruelties inflicted on the natives at Roebourne and Cossack.

He is still in the police force.

Eliza's eyes cling to the name, Parker, and the deep score of the pen marks beneath it. She pictures the sergeant's pallid face, the look of someone who believes he's had something taken from him. She remembers one day in the Dry, several years ago now, when Bannin sweltered in the heat and two uniformed men rode slowly into town. They were announced by the hollow cork-pop of pistol fire, and as they neared, she could see them raising their Snider–Enfields and firing into the shadows. Each shot led to a yelp, or a howl of agony, and a dog or a cat would drag itself out into the open, to die under the glare of the sun. Eliza's eyes could not believe the horror, and she watched as the horses came to a stop in front of a body: a drunk, laid flat out on the dirt, the white skin of his stomach exposed and sun-blistered.

"Out the way," one of the officers ordered from his position high up on the saddle. It would be far easier, Eliza thought, for him to pull the beast to the side to pass smoothly by. The man murmured and twitched, his head lolling so his cheek smacked the dirt. A thread of saliva inched down from his gums and left a dark stain on the dust.

"Get up, or I'll move you myself." A long moment passed. The officer expelled a shunt of air through his nose, swung his legs across the saddle, and dismounted, rifle in hand. As he stalked toward the body, she could see a grin splitting his face like a smear of paint. His coarse beard reached to his chest and bushy brows framed small, deep-set eyes. His colleague, hairless in comparison, hopped down too and they hungrily circled the drunk. The clean-shaven officer stepped forward and jabbed his boot into the man's stomach, then bent down, grasped his shoulders, and wrestled the top half of his body into a sitting position, propped up in the dirt. The drunk's eyeballs swiveled wildly in his head; from his throat came a plangent groaning sound.

"You are taking up a perfectly good piece of dirt." The bearded officer spoke with icy coolness. Without warning, and before Eliza had time to look away, he raised the barrel of his rifle above his shoulder and brought it across the man's face with monumental speed. When it connected with flesh, there came a sickening smack. Then silence. Blood rained in a slow burst of crimson and scattered in spots on the ground. The officers erupted into laughter and Eliza's guts tightened with dread. The man was on his back now, limp, neck jammy with blood. The sergeant hadn't had his fill. With a dry, high-pitched snigger, he stood wide-legged over the body and unfastened his belt. He threw his head back as warm piss rained down, steam rising off sunburned skin like wisps of smoke.

She runs her tongue over her teeth as if she can still feel the dust there. The sergeant and her father have never seen eye to eye. Her father believed Parker a monster, and Parker believed her father a weak man. Could it be that the sergeant knows her father is aware of his past crime? Could this be why he will not pursue the truth of his case, why he is so willing to ignore the chance to find him alive?

She *needs* to find the diary; perhaps it will reveal more.

She considers the scene in front of her, scours every inch of her mind for any forgotten clue. She reaches further, clawing back to the times she'd been in this room as her father worked. How she'd watch him hunched over his drawings or as he fastidiously copied numbers into his ledger book. Then the thought slams into her: the mermaid charm he had hidden for her. It was in the disguised drawer of this very desk. She steps forward and unthinkingly sweeps the papers and books onto the floor. With two hands, she grasps the front edge of the desk, and with a tug, lifts the top of the thing clean open. Inside, the drawer is lined with plush green velvet. In the middle sits a leather book, embossed with gold letters: *The Diary of Charles J. G. Brightwell, Master Pearler.*

Her jaw drops open. She has seen the book many times, but only ever in her father's hands. If he does not have it with him now, there must be a reason. Dread gives a knock at her rib cage. She picks the book up, runs her hands over its cover, and carefully opens it, thumbing slowly through the pages, passing detailed diagrams of shell beds and stars, passages about life at sea, of storms and sharks. She moves her hand and the book gapes open further. She hears the whisper of something slip from its pages and sees a flash of white hit the floor. She bends to pick it up: a folded sheet of ledger paper. She turns it over in her fingers. On the back, in her father's familiar spider scrawl, set out just the way he would leave clues for her, there is a message.

Zhou A
Three Stones
Off Sheba

She frowns. She doesn't recognize the words, but the paper in her hand feels suddenly weightier. Below the writing is a tiny symbol scratched out in ink, like a sickle or a crescent moon. She runs her fingers over it. What could it mean? The room leans in a slightly different direction. Sheba, surely that has to be Sheba Lane. Her mind goes to the busy street. Is this an address? But more important, was she meant to find it? She reaches for the chair and sits. Although her thoughts are more alive than ever, her limbs are leaden. Deep inside her are the scratchy beginnings of something. She is confused. Exhilarated. But she knows one thing for sure. If she wants to find out what happened to her father, she must start with Zhou A.

CHAPTER 6

The foreshore camps shine like spit in the heat. The shoreline is strewn with flotsam—wrecks of old luggers, broken teapots, and dusty, shattered bottles. The camps are set apart from Chinatown by a fringe of shrubby sand dunes. Around them, mangrove swamps extend their fingers into creeks fat with catfish. Eliza recalls childhood days when luggers with their four-cornered sails would line up here at low tide, how she would step from deck to deck through a thicket of masts, each boat bowing as she landed, never once getting her feet wet.

She picks her way hurriedly through it all, her mind set only on her destination, on the person she is sure can help decipher her father's note. As she walks, the familiar ringing in her ears threatens to distract her from her task. It is her father's greatest irritation. "You've got your ears shut, Eliza," he'd scold. The whine grows louder with every step she takes. She shakes her head to try and dislodge it, an old habit, as if the sound might tumble out and slither off into the bushes.

She passes rows of upturned clinker dinghies and men in singlets slumped around a ramshackle hut. With glazed eyes and tobacco fingers, they send smoke spiraling into the air. Each inclines his head as she passes, raises a single trembling finger in salute. She can taste their cigarette-breath on her tongue, she realizes. Forced, as always, to swallow it down.

On the sand, she eyes the bones of what must once have been a dugong, two sinewy cats pawing at the sun-blasted flesh. Scraggy fish are strung up everywhere, eyes pecked out by the gulls. The slow breeze carries cypress shavings and the odor of rancid pearl meat from the pogey pots. It is always like this when the Wet's on the way. The once-lethargic streets start to shift and rumble, and the town's population swells into the thousands. The metallic clang of hammers tolls through the streets and the cramped foreshore camps come alive with forging, caulking, chipping, and tarring. Men, agitated as bull ants, swagger between gambling halls and visits to their favorite whores. Gusty laughter thickens the air with liquor. Eliza thinks, with a curl of dread, of what is coming for Min.

As she weaves closer to the shoreline, her eyes snag on something in the shallows. Glutinous jellyfish bells hang just below the surface. She bends to inspect them as a shadow falls across the water. In a second, her body drains of its heat. She stands, turns, eyelids squeezed shut, but she knows who she'll be faced with before she opens them. The figure in front of her is less of a man and more of a small mountain. Saurian eyes wallow in a large, wide face. Whiskered cheeks bypass a neck to meet powerful sloping shoulders.

"Miss Brightwell, what a treat."

She glowers. The breeze on the back of her neck announces that the buttons on her collar have worked themselves open. "Such a pity to hear the news of your father, you poor soul." He pins her to the spot with his unflinching gaze. She tugs her sleeves down over her wrists. She cannot stop thinking of the buttons.

"But as I have always said, men like Billy have an insatiable bloodlust," he says, "and a thirst for grog they'll stop at nothing to quench. *Especially* if not kept in order." He reaches down to pat the dog whimpering at his thighs. Its muscles are knotted like rope, its jaws moist with frog-spawn slobber. "He can smell your femininity." He yanks at the dog's chain. "Does it to all women; he's just not used to them. Shut your legs and he'll soon settle."

Eliza blinks in disgust. She should have known she'd encounter Syd Hardcastle at the camps; he's a common sight, prowling the foreshore with his mastiff, like some biblical picture of wrath. The pearling masters come from many backgrounds—settlers and pastoralists, businessmen, hardworking merchant seamen—most of them white Europeans or Asians using dummy paperwork for their luggers. But there are plenty of bad eggs too; those out to exploit a lucrative trade for profit, even if that means abusing their power and those unfortunate enough to serve it. Syd Hardcastle is the very rottenest of souls. Her eyes cling to the stockwhip he keeps jammed into his waistband. His is the only ship in the bay that still uses the labor of native skin divers. His whip is well used; she's heard it discussed often enough.

"Balarri is not responsible for my father's—" She pulls up short, unsure of which word to use. Disappearance? She can't quite bring herself to give voice to the other option. "In fact, I might ask when *you* last saw him." She slowly straightens her spine. As she does, her eyes are drawn to a nearby tree. A gray bird with a black head has impaled a small lizard on a thorn. The green body hangs there limp as the bird savages its flesh. As she watches, Hardcastle moves his hand to take Eliza's chin between his thumb and forefinger. Her eyes snap back to him. He leers so close to her that every detail of his face is a blur. Her ears fill with noise. The sea and the mud and the clouds all rush in on her.

"I haven't seen Charles for weeks," he says. His breath is a clump of rotting vegetables. The side of his mouth twitches upward. She cannot look away.

"Might you tell me where I could find the Kingfish Hotel?"

The voice behind them splits the air. Hardcastle drops his hand and she turns to see a man stopped halfway down a set of steps. In slender arms he holds a damp basket filled with shell. His hat, pushed back high off his forehead, reveals thin features and a neat mustache. Her mind flickers in recognition. It's the man she caught watching her at the jetty.

"Two streets back. You know that, stickybeak." Hardcastle's flesh trembles as he bellows.

The man nods, continues his descent down the steps, then pauses.

"Miss, I was so very sorry to hear what happened to your father." He dips his head. "By all accounts he is a very accomplished man." There's a hardness to his voice. Something foreign.

"I rather think you mean *was*, boy." Hardcastle clenches his jaw. "Now bugger off."

"Do you know him?" Eliza calls after the man, who is hurrying now toward one of the boat sheds. The door gapes and the blast of a tomahawk rings out. She opens her mouth to speak again, but he has disappeared into the shadows.

CHAPTER 7

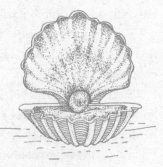

The Bannin Mission is a particularly unholy-looking place–
a smattering of bush timber huts fastened to the earth with
tumbledown chains. A church, if it can be aggrandized with such a
name, sags on spindly, rotten stumps, the ground surrounding it as
harsh as old, cured hide. Native plants have been clumsily uprooted
to make way for what might one day resemble an English vegetable
garden. There's a rudimentary school building that looks remarkably
like the jailhouse in town, and on the veranda, a pair of white trousers and a shirt bloat in the wind. Eliza looks closer, squints; if she
did not know better she might believe them ghosts.

"Dear Eliza." Father Ernest McVeigh trots out, arms wide as if
moving on wayward cattle. His beard is salted with dust and his robe
trails in the dirt. He grasps her forearms, fixes her in the eye.

"I am *so* sorry to hear about your father, Eliza. Terrible, terrible business, especially with what happened to your mother and, well . . ." His voice fades before he continues. "Charles was here just before the fleets sailed out. We had quite the discussion about the crew. He was helping, of course, to fund the cottages I'm building. The men all want to keep their crews close, but still. Ach, it's a cruel thing that Balarri has found himself jailed."

She tells him hurriedly of the man's escape and Parker's intention to track him down. His eyebrows leap upward. "You'd better come in."

Eliza knows many in Bannin consider the priest worthy of nothing but ridicule. They scoff at the very thought of an old Scot herding the Aborigines into church, attempting to teach them the Psalms, to dress their confusing nakedness in European clothing. He is "a fantasist," the pearlers holler from their groaning lounge chairs. A loon who keeps company with heathens. But she'd always found nothing but kindness in the man. Those he sought to teach humored him too, mostly, although he was here, ostensibly, to save them from themselves. But here was a man who wanted not to take, wanted nothing of their land, their waterholes, or their women. Instead, he intended to give to them: shelter, supplies, food, faith. Whether they wanted it or not.

He leads her into the fly-bitten church, dim as cold mist out of the blinding sun. She is struck by how neat it appears inside. Driftwood pews run through its center. A simple lectern holds a calfskin Bible caked in mold. In a dark corner, a set of cricket stumps leans against the wall, an oxblood ball gathering dust at their feet.

"Come. Let us have a wee seat." They settle at the front of the room and a watery light slants in through the window bars. Eliza finds something soothing in the man's hushed tones. The priest is the only soul to have shown any *real* concern about her father. The rest of the town—her brother too, so stubbornly trading in Cossack—have been continuing as normal, while her life has been hurled against a wall and shattered.

"And how is your brother coping?" McVeigh asks.

"He's gone on to Cossack to see to business affairs."

McVeigh pauses, steeples his fingers. "It's not unnatural, I suppose, to remove oneself from a tragic situation," he muses. "And we do know how he struggles."

She tries to blink away the memories of Thomas dragged near lifeless from the dens on Sheba Lane. The times she has woken to find him flat-back on the veranda, vomit caked into the folds of his neck, circling mosquitoes droning with delight.

She tugs her attention back to the room. There is little time to waste so she launches directly into her plea.

"I believe there's more to my father's disappearance than we are being told." She says it, then bites her mouth shut. Will he ridicule her like Parker did? The priest's slack face tightens but he says nothing, so she continues. "I don't believe he is dead. I don't know why, or rather I can't quite explain why yet, but if I can find out what happened, if I can find *him*, Parker might call off his search for Balarri too."

McVeigh pauses, his face blank. She is aware of how she must appear to this man, how desperate she appears to most of Bannin Bay.

"I know you'll think me foolish, but things don't make sense. You don't just disappear from a ship, do you?" She is leaning so close, drawn so much to human contact, she can feel the warmth of his body beside her. "Thomas says there were no pearls missing. No signs of any struggle. No blood." McVeigh shifts. "Plus, I found something. In his diary." Reaching into her pocket, she pulls out the ledger paper, unfolds it, and hands it to him.

"What's this?" he asks. "An address?" As he reads there is a noise from the back of the room. Eliza turns to see a child, about twelve years of age, quietly arranging books on a shelf.

"Ah, yes. This is Quill," says McVeigh, pointing a finger at the child who freezes as if caught raiding a larder. "Forgive the nickname, but he's sharp as anything, this lad." McVeigh rises and crosses the room, still pointing. Quill has a thin chest, wide brown eyes, and a small crucifix pendant on a piece of string around his neck. "Quill is one of the most diligent young chaps I have met in the bay. He was a beggar and a deckhand, would you believe, scratching out a living on the ships before I apprenticed him into the mission here. Now he helps with the repairs, digs the garden, even has a hand in some of the teaching." McVeigh nods proudly. "His mother was from the camp, that much we know, but I'm afraid we've no idea of the father, such are the circumstances round here. European, certainly, though." Quill looks to the floor. "He's a *marvelous* reader," McVeigh enthuses, "I don't know any other deckhands who can read, do you, Eliza? What a revelation. He's adept with lugger pidgin, of course, and can follow some of the other local dialects to a degree too, given his time on the boats." The apprentice glances up at her. "He's, er, alphabetizing the Latin books, isn't that right, Quill?" McVeigh finally crosses his arms. With a dip of the head, Quill places down the books and goes to leave. With the motion, something falls from the child's waistband, hitting the floor with a dusty thud. Eliza rises and crosses the boards to pick it up. It's a book, faded and dog-eared. She turns it over to read the spine. *Saltwater Cowboys: Adventures on the High Seas.* Quill has paused at the threshold and watches her curiously. She flashes a quick smile and hands the book quietly back, then returns to the missionary, who looks up from the paper.

"This address, I'm not sure I like the look of it, you know."

"You're familiar with it, then? Do you know what the crescent symbol signifies?"

"No, no, but we can assume it's not something particularly savory. Sheba Lane is not a safe place for a young lady like you. You should not be going to this address alone; I sincerely hope that's not what you're intending."

"Well, I was hoping I wouldn't have to go alone."

McVeigh begins to shake his head before she's even finished.

"Please, I need help with this." Her voice is strained. "I have to find out what happened. I know someone out there knows *something*." She pauses. Sighs in frustration. "I need a man to help me gain access to certain places." The words are necessary, but they make her itchy with indignation.

"Eliza, this is not really in my purview. It wouldn't look good."

"Well, then I suppose I shall have to go on my own." She straightens her skirts, steps away from him.

McVeigh groans. "All right, all right, I know it."

She turns to see his eyebrows knitted in concern. "I know the house it refers to," he concedes reluctantly. "It's rather infamous if you know the ins and outs of the town."

Her eyes widen.

"You've heard of the tongs?" He looks up at her. Takes her silence as encouragement to continue. "They're groups. Made up of men. Bad men. Rotten sorts, really. They do bad business. Snides and such. Gambling. Soliciting." He shakes his head. "These fellows, they call themselves the Brotherhood of the Waning Moon." He waves the paper. "Hence the symbol." He traces it roughly with a finger. "It's a calling card of sorts. A sickle-shaped wound they'll leave on a body. They're not good people to get involved with. I really shouldn't be telling you this."

She *had* heard tales of these secret societies, how they enforced their decrees, leaving bulging eyeballs and shattered windpipes behind them. Her head starts to swim.

"I've no idea why your father would have this address in his diary."

The thought of it makes her queasy. Her father, involved in trading snide pearls? Or worse, having a hand in the brothels? He has always been such a soft sort of man, but maybe a part of his heart had hardened over from simply being in Bannin Bay.

"How do I get there?"

"Eliza."

Whatever he might have done, she must find him. "You know I'm going to find out eventually, so you might as well tell me."

The priest sighs.

"I will tell you if you promise you will find someone suitable to escort you, Eliza. Someone who knows this town. A gentleman. Not some miscreant you find on the street. Someone to keep you safe."

"Of course." She hopes her expression appears convincing.

"In Chinatown, turn right at the Star, cross to the next road, and look for the place with all the fish. That'll get you near enough."

"The fish." She nods.

"You can't miss it, but, Eliza, promise me, you must find someone to go with you!"

She is already out of the door.

CHAPTER 8

The crow has observed the man in the bush for two whole days now. It arrived as he slept in the shade of a stately bloodwood, then it took a perch and hunched like an old sage above his head. As the man awoke, the bird let out a throaty hackle, followed by an ah-ah-ah that bled so easily across the plains.

The man foraged, then ate, and the crow had bent to watch him with its stark, white eye. Then, as he set off through the trees, it had drifted with tattered wings from branch to branch behind him.

There have been no signs yet of those who must pursue the man. But he has kept to the densest parts of pindan country, dodging the stretches of bare, blackened land cracked open by the wildfires. He seems to favor most the pockets of crippled woodland, where conkerberries and dry gums reach weak limbs toward the sky.

The landscape is thirsty, and scrolls of bark crunch loudly under the man's feet. When the rains come, these pans will flood and erupt with swarms of rowdy insects. But, for now, he must be grateful for what shade they do afford.

When the trees spit him out, the crow settles back onto a branch. The man raises an arm to shield his eyes. As he blinks, something shimmers on the far horizon, warped by heat. The crow sees it too, cocks its head. Plumes of dust stream skyward, kicked up by horses whipped to a gallop. Calm, the man turns and makes his way through the scrubland. They are coming for him now. The man must move as quickly as he can.

CHAPTER 9

From the top of the highest dune, the bay is a smudge under the midday sun. Eliza raises a palm to crinkling eyes and sees Chinatown hunkered in the near distance. As she descends, men from the lugger camps pass, shouldering poles laden with meat from the butchers. At the jetty, wild with pelicans and gulls, pearling officers in white suits count up their baskets of shell. A patient nag waits nearby with its cart stacked high with boxes. The surrounding mudflats are littered with coils of rope, spidery anchor chains, and white sails stretching like opened butterfly wings.

Why could McVeigh not have agreed to accompany her? It is grossly unfair that men can go places—and ask questions—that she, as a woman, cannot. She could ask one of the crew, perhaps, although that might draw more attention than is wise. Her chest clenches in frustration. If only Thomas were here to help.

At the traps she passes a small crowd, their eyes locked onto something hefty in the shallows. Peering closer, she can discern the scaled body of a crocodile. It has been hauled out and placed on show, its huge snout propped wide open. A small child with a tadpole belly clambers onto its back and hops with exhilaration. A flash from a camera box startles her and her mind stutters to her own family outings here, when she'd crawled on her hands and knees in search of tiny things to pocket. The sand would be strewn with cowries and periwinkles. Her father would make a show of laying out a picnic and Thomas would be wading about the shallows. If she lets her mind reach far enough, where faint objects appear and disappear like spirits, she can see another person there. The image is overexposed, but if she concentrates, she can see it well enough. A boy no higher than her knee. Chubby elbows encased in a cotton tunic. A curl of white hair showing itself beneath his bonnet.

"Hello there, miss." A voice nudges Eliza from her stupor. "Ah. I apologize," it stammers. "It was not my intention to scare you."

She brushes an invisible crumb from her blouse. "You did not scare me."

It's him: the man who interrupted Hardcastle down at the foreshore. The one she caught watching her at the jetty too. He is tall, about her height, and, by the looks of it, a few years older than her twenty. He stands with a small basket tucked under his arm and a battered hat pushed high on his head. The top few buttons of his shirt, visible above a scruffy brown waistcoat, are undone and a red neckerchief is tied loosely at his throat.

"I knew it was you from the way you walk. I saw you coming from a mile off." He smiles.

Eliza pauses. "I'm sorry?"

"Your walk, it's like—how would you describe it? A heron. Sort of graceful, sort of unsettling. Tall."

She looks around her. "I'm not sure how to respond to that, sir." Another flash comes from the camera.

"What animal am I?" he asks.

She gapes at him.

"It's only fair."

For a while she observes the man, who nods quickly, then freezes as if requested to pose for a portrait. Is he toying with her? Cigarette papers and a pouch of tobacco peer out from his waistcoat pocket.

"Alright, I'd say you had something of that bird, the godwit about you." She crosses her arms. "Keen. Alert." She can't quite bring herself to say "odd." He does not speak, merely stays in his position, but she can see a smile about his lips. She rushes to fill the silence. "A sort of aquiline beak. Or nose, rather. As if you're searching for a worm in the mud." She rolls her eyes inwardly.

"A godwit." He mimics her clipped accent. "I'm afraid I've never heard of such a thing. I take it you are English?"

"I . . ."

"Your accent. You are from England?"

"Ah, yes. We sailed over from London."

"Well, I would be affronted but, actually, if I am a godwit, as you say, then *you* must be the worm." He shifts the basket from one arm to the other. "So, I rather think I am the victor there. Although I would have thought I might perhaps have been something a shade more masculine. An angry kangaroo. A stallion . . ."

She does not know where to look, so she lets her eyes rest on her boots. The air smells of dust and hot kerosene.

"Have a good day." She nods politely and takes a step forward. The man cuts a long, swooping stride across her path.

"Ah, waaaait," he trills. "Who are you? I mean, your name, what is it?" She takes a step back.

"I thought you knew of my father?" A flicker of suspicion ignites.

The man colors slightly, but he looks undeterred. "My name is Axel Kramer, miss. And if you're wondering about the accent, it's German. I was supposed to be doing something of a tour." He draws a vague circle with an arm. "But I've been here for the last few weeks.

Actually, I rather like it, you know. If you excuse the cockroaches. And, well, the rats."

"I see."

"I've got myself a business of sorts." He seems keen to keep her attention. He gestures to a slouching structure a hundred yards down the beach. It's hard to tell from this distance, with everything warped and blurred by the heat, but the hut, nothing more than an open-fronted rectangle of iron, is filled with large baskets and upended wooden crates. There are a few people there, sifting through the containers or reclining in the heat.

"Dry shelling," he offers, although he looks a little embarrassed. She was aware people collected shell from the shore–fanning out along the exposed coral and seabeds, filling their baskets during the few hours each day that the mudflats were exposed–but she had never known any European to do it.

"It's a bit of an unusual operation, but you can collect quite a haul from these reefs," he says. "Pearl shell and trochus mostly. The locals, they really know this land, all the secret spots, bays, tidal pools. I wouldn't be any use on my own. I can sail but, hell, I can barely swim. We share the spoils and in exchange for their knowledge, I've agreed to facilitate the sale of any pearls we uncover. Although we've not had much luck yet. I believe I may have arrived out of season. We need a big king tide, really." Eliza is aware of the sweat at the small of her back. "Anyhow, it's nice to make your acquaintance." Axel holds his right hand out in front of him, tucking his left behind and dipping in a bow.

"Eliza. Brightwell."

He shakes her hand as firmly as she would expect him to do if she were a man. "We've been here for the last ten years or so," she continues. "My father was . . . I mean, *is* a pearler. He owns the *White Starling*, or at least he did. But you know that." She frowns. The sand at her feet starts to shift.

"Miss Brightwell," says Axel. "I heard about the pearler. Your father." He shifts his eyes quickly to the horizon. "I heard they managed to jail a man."

Her chin snaps upward. "Well, that man is not responsible for what has happened." She begins to gather up her skirts. "And the longer people believe he is, the longer others go unquestioned." She has been rude, she knows, but her mind rushes to a vision, hazy with scorched edges, of her father being taken under threat of revolver. Or worse, his listless body floating facedown in the water. She looks beyond Axel to the town. He is blocking her way to Sheba Lane.

"I don't expect you to believe me," she says. "You don't know what this place is like." She goes to pass him but his hand grips her shoulder. She shrugs him off and he coughs.

"I apologize, but there are many things about me you do not know, Miss Brightwell. If you say this man cannot have killed your father, I believe you."

She scrutinizes him.

"In fact, I will help you find out what happened to him, if that might be of use to you."

"I'm perfectly fine." She tucks a knot of hair behind her ear. "It's really no bother."

"Miss, I may not have been here long, but I do know a woman in Bannin is not afforded the same privileges as a man." His look feels like a challenge. "I would say it's fair to assume you are leered at in most establishments. Perhaps ushered quickly out of the door. In others you will be measured and found worthy for nothing but your female parts." He seems alarmed and blinks himself back onto the right track. "The truth is, you will find it easier to gain access to certain places with me around."

She thinks of the promise she made McVeigh as she studies the man in front of her. She may have found him in the street, but she doesn't fancy him much of a blackguard. In fact, she wonders if *she* might be required to protect *him*. Although she is not yet sure why he is so eager to help her.

"Do you want nothing in return?" She assesses his lean shoulders, his sorrowful hat.

"No, I do want something."

She raises her eyebrows.

"You can teach me about Bannin Bay. You were right to assume I don't know much of this town, and I'll need to if I'm to establish a business footing here. Who better to be my tutor than the daughter of a master pearler?" His quick eyes search her face for a response.

She tries to picture him going fist to fist with the men at the back of the Kingfish, or slipping silently into the establishments of Sheba Lane, paper lanterns swaying slowly in the breeze. Somehow, she can't. Something about this man feels different to others she has met. But a man is what she needs, and Axel Kramer seems as convenient as any right now. She doesn't have to tell him everything she knows. She can use him for the purpose of getting her foot through certain doors, then he can return to his dry shelling and she can find her father.

"Well, I suppose you must be *somewhat* business minded." She casts her eyes back to the flimsy shack. "You seem to treat the locals fairly, which is not the case for many people here." She absorbs his keen gaze, the beaky nose, the smart mustache. She rolls each of them around in her mind. If her father can test people, why can't she? "All right, then."

His smile is fluid.

"Are you ready?"

THE DIARY OF CHARLES J. G. BRIGHTWELL, MASTER PEARLER

A note on the sharks of North-West Australia

The discerning naturalist will know that the waters surrounding the West coast of Australia are teeming with an abundance of sea life, including a profusion of fish, dolphins, dugongs, whales, turtles, and somewhere in the region of 200 species of shark.

I am approaching the end of what has been my first season as a pearler, and it has become rather apparent that Bannin Bay is a potent place for sharks. The shallower waters team with makos, black-tips and tigers, while huge gargoyle-faced hammerheads patrol the deeper seas. One patch, a little northward of Cape Villaret, is proving particularly fatal. Men I know have had their buttocks torn off by white pointers mere yards from their luggers. A terrifying, fascinating creature, the white shark has a hefty slate-gray body and a black, dead eye that chills the soul of any sailor.

One young lad on Hardcastle's Wandering Eve had his leg clean severed not two months ago. He trembled and died in a billow of blood before any poor sod could get to him and save him from the shock. That was a dark day indeed and enough for the pearlers to declare war. They came up with a plan, tossing freshly baited hooks over the gunwales, waiting to see what beasts would take a bite from the depths. When a shark was eventually caught, its thrashing body was dragged half onboard, where it was slit open so its innards and organs sluiced out in a flood of brown-red liquid. This, of course, sent the other sharks into a frenzy, and as they gorged on the surface, the men made at them with revolvers, harpoons, and blades lashed to poles; whatever they could fashion. What a horrific sight it was. At any one time a lugger could have the bodies of a dozen sharks strung alongside it. They've driven them away, for now, but we shall see if they return when the season recommences after the Wet.

CHAPTER 10

The smell is enough to make the eyes water. Frying onion, turmeric, chili belacan, and ginger, mingled with the rising musk of sandalwood and the reek of several hundred men. The buildings that make up the low-slung town lean into one another like drunks at nightfall, each set on stumps to protect them from the spring tide floods. Luggers have spewed their crews ashore and the speed of the place is frenetic. The streets are a blur of people and cats, which stalk the shadowy lanes for vermin, gifting kills onto wooden porches.

Eliza knows a little of what goes on here. Spices, gold, and aphrodisiac powders are sold. Herbal remedies are touted—for warts and wizened livers, boils and burns. Squash shops are open late for all comers. Chinese tailors battle for space with butchers. Brothels slouch hard against billiard saloons. Rooming houses, greengrocers, tobacconists, and boatbuilders, pawnbrokers, tombstone carvers, laundries, and grog shops all hunker crookedly together.

She has never seen so many men in one place before. Japanese and South Sea Islanders; Manilamen and Cingalese; Javanese, Dayaks, Koepangers, Brazilians. All strata of society, from physicians and entrepreneurs to laborers and beggars. When the pearling season is in full swing, there are barely any men left in town, apart from the publicans and the shopkeepers, and those work-shy pearlers more content on dry verandas than out at sea. So Eliza is accustomed, for a few months of the year, to existing in a space filled mostly with women. Women who dig, women who care for the sick, women who run council meetings and organize repairs to buildings. When the men return, however, those women are expected to simply slot back into place, like tins into the depths of an old storage cupboard.

There's an unusual heat that radiates from these men, their babel talk resin-thick in the air. They step out of the way as she and Axel pass by; some of them mutter, withdraw, heads bowed. The occasional sulky rattles past, drawn by an inevitably bad-tempered nag. Men bent in half with the paralysis limp with shoulder poles strung across their twisted backs, hawking fish, mud crabs, dugongs, and turtle flesh. Mournful gramophone music spills into the air, set to an accompaniment of wailing cats and the gentle *plink* of abacus beads. On a balcony, a smiling man plays a slow tune on the ukulele.

At one shop, the Cingalese pearl doctor advertises his services. His job is a meticulous one: to remove the visible blemishes on the stones. With the tiniest of tools, he will pull apart the many layers of skin clinging to one another like rose petals. Sometimes a rotten bit of flesh can be cut out and the pearl preserved. At other times the decay goes right through to the core, just like in a person.

They come to a busy crossroads. There are no street signs, save for a few battered pieces of tin nailed to the trunk of an ironbark tree.

"Excuse me, sir." Axel stops a man strolling past; he wears a stiff shirt, and a roll-up cigarette hangs from his small mouth. "Pardon the inconvenience, but we're looking for the Star . . ."

The man glances briefly at Axel and across to Eliza. He shakes his head, then scuttles off quick as a mole cricket.

Axel, buttoned up and sweating, pulls his hat from his head and wipes his brow. "What now, then, Miss Brightwell?"

She does not look at him, instead raking her eyes up and down the rickety shopfronts. He calls her name again, then once more, louder.

"Eliza?"

She turns to him eventually and he raises his eyebrows. She recognizes the expression.

"I'm sorry." She shakes her head quickly. "My ears, they ring sometimes." Axel draws level with her, frowns. "It's like everything closes in, as if I've been buried underground." She squints her eyes. "Aha!"

Before he can move, she is already striding toward a building. Low slung and saloon wide, its skeletal veranda swarms with men. A band of bony horses out front are muzzled with nosebags. Nearby, a white eucalyptus tree struggles through the muck. Leaning against it, on a square of painted sheet metal, is a five-cornered star.

"One road along, McVeigh said." Eliza nods.

THE DIARY OF CHARLES J. G. BRIGHTWELL, MASTER PEARLER

A tragedy

I shall not dress it up with silver, today was another sorry day. After just two years in Bannin, the family has been hit by tragedy. Willem finally lost his leg, after a battle with necrosis that almost shook the life from him entirely. It started a few weeks back: the man was ravaged by a stinger in just two feet of water, right off the jetty. Must have been a box jelly, because no sooner had he shrieked from the sting—and what a howl of agony it was—his eyes began to roll and he became quite short of breath. We got him to shore and Blithe assessed him in the surgery. He needed rest, the doctor said, and so Willem laid up for the next fourteen days. But soon enough the wound began to seep and then the calf itself began to rot. Oh, the unholy stench of the thing! I couldn't go near him without a handkerchief to my nose. Martha struggled to see him in such a state so kept mostly away, but the leg surely festered, turning black and hard, the flesh glistening like fried fish skin until just a touch of the fingertips could pull the meat off the bone. Blithe sawed it off just above the knee in the end, and my brother sweated and fevered until the infection finally fled his body. We'll find him an artificial limb but I'm afraid around these parts it might have to be wood. It means our plans of running the fleets together, two brother pearlers out at sea with their hardworking men, is one that shall have to be suspended. I told dear Willem he could still be a partner from shore, until he has recuperated enough to come out on the ships. Until then I shall give him a portion of what we bring in; it's only fair, given the circumstances. But he looked grave, and turned away from me, the candlelight casting shadows across his drawn face.

Post scriptum: a note on box jellyfish (transcribed from my original naturalist's notes and relayed herewith for context). Surely one of the most terrifying creatures in the ocean, the box jellyfish has claimed more divers than I like to remember. These carnivorous, pale blue creatures are distinguishable by their cube-shaped medusae and their exceedingly long tentacles (they can reach up to 10 feet—see illustration). They are highly developed, with the ability to actively move through the water, rather than drift, and their powerful venom has developed in such a way as to instantly stun or kill their prey, so any struggle to escape will not damage their tentacles. I can say with no uncertainty that I would rather come upon a shark or a sea snake than I would a box jellyfish. Which is why I pity poor Willem and our lost arrangement so. The man has his faults, but this he simply does not deserve.

CHAPTER 11

The missionary was right about the fish. They are strung up all about the walls, eyes following Eliza as she steps from left to right. In trays below they are laid out like marbled slabs, each one covered in a perfect cobblework of scales. At the center of it all sits a man on an old stool. By all appearances he is desiccating with age. He wears trousers twinkling with scales and a thin singlet that reveals a mass of sagging skin.

"Sir, excuse me," says Eliza.

Slow as smoke, the man moves his face toward her. His pupils, she notices with a start, are milky gray.

"Do you happen to know–"

"We'd like a fish, please!" Axel interjects with an absurd wave of the arms. He throws Eliza a strange look. The man does not flinch. "A big fish. One of your finest . . . snappers?"

Axel holds his breath as the man turns slowly toward him. There is no sound but the faint bark of quarreling men from the Star. Eventually, the man stands. He turns and walks to the fish and begins to feel them, running his hands over nacreous skin. Then, his fingers come to rest on a creature with a frozen, horrified expression. He grasps it and shifts it to the crooks of his arms. He walks slowly to present it to Axel.

"A penny," the man croaks.

"Oh my. Well, yes. Reasonable. Of course." Axel rummages in his pocket to produce the coin. "Good day to you, sir." He takes the fish and tucks it under his arm. It glares accusingly at Eliza. The man begins his slow pilgrimage back to his seat.

"Why on earth have you bought a fish?" she hisses as they walk away.

"Well, it would look suspicious if we turned up and went straight round the back." The snapper trembles under his arm.

They find the entrance down an alleyway that runs alongside the fishmonger's shop. The path is dark and cool, strewn with tiny animal bones swarming with ants. The house itself is double-storied, and has nothing particularly remarkable about it. The veranda is littered with discarded bottles and graying laundry. Next to the doorway three large rocks have been balanced in a stack.

"Three stones," Eliza whispers, and marches toward the door.

"Wait! Are you really sure this is a good idea?" Axel grabs her shoulder, glancing furtively back down the alleyway. "We don't know who is in this house, or what business they operate," he whispers. "Perhaps we should just . . . pause for a moment, and think?" He places the fish carefully onto the floor and wipes his hands on his knees.

Eliza takes a deep breath and turns to him. "Let me ask you this, Axel. Where is your father?"

He pauses. Frowns. "Oh, I don't know. I should think Hamburg

at this time of year; he does a lot of business there. Buying and se–"
His voice evaporates like steam.

"My father and my brother are all I have in this place," she says.
"And my father"–she falters–"*is* a good man. I believe he is a good
man. Whatever has gone on. He does not deserve to be forgotten, or
cast aside. If *I* were out there somewhere, whether my heart was beating or not, I know he would do absolutely everything he could to find
me." Her eyes fall to the ground. "I will do the same for him, and if
you do not want to help me, you are very welcome to go back to your
beach. You owe me nothing; that's quite fair. But I am going to knock
on this do–" Before she can finish, he has stepped past her and up
onto the porch. "No, hang on!" She turns and rushes to pass him. "I'll
do it." She raises a hand to knock, then freezes. There's a tiny crescent
moon carved into the wooden frame. The door, she sees, is partly ajar,
the cool air from the house corkscrewing into the heat. She lays her
hand against the wood and pushes. It opens with a long creak.

The room is mostly dark, severed by fine swords of sunlight. It
is bare except for a large wooden table that runs almost the whole
length of its right wall. Beside it sits a small stool. Past that, another
doorway, cracked open to spill light from a room beyond. Through
the gap, Eliza can just about make out a large set of shelves. They
hold demijohns filled with stagnant liquids. There is a small sign
affixed to the door, with a name, it must be, but she cannot quite
make it out. She feels Axel's arm at the small of her back, nudging
her forward.

"Hello?" she calls into the darkness. The house rings with silence.
"Anybody there?"

When no answer comes, they move to survey the long table,
covered with cloth. Eliza steps forward and gingerly pulls back the
corner. The breath catches in her throat. She replaces the fabric and
collects herself. She knows full well what she is about to uncover.
Steadying her nerves, she slowly pulls the cloth back as far as she
can, revealing a shimmering sea of pearls glinting up at them. Neither

speaks, dazzled by the sheer number of the things laid out on the table. A strange sort of glow comes from the stones, like the fog that would hover above the Thames back home. There must be hundreds of them in front of her, shifting from eel green to dragonfly blue to soft whispery pink. Some of the stones are baroques, small and misshapen, but the largest must be almost the size of her eyeball. She carefully picks it up and turns it so it dances under the dim light. It seems to contain a whole weather system inside it–lilac storm clouds and frothy white cumulus, the flinty gray of the ocean before the sun first hits. She swallows. For all the shells brought up by the luggers, Eliza knows the chances of finding a pearl are perhaps one in ten thousand. Such a stroke of luck on a pearling craft can make its owner hundreds, even thousands, of pounds in a day. But a pearl like this, she knows, can set up a man for life. She cannot begin to imagine the wealth a collection like this would bring.

"Must be snides," she whispers grimly to Axel, as she tucks the pearl back under the cotton. Fear makes her voice hollow. "Stolen by the shell openers, traded on the black market. People kill for these things." It is an open secret that members of the crew sometimes steal the pearls, creeping up onto deck at night to slip a chock of wood into shells gaping open in the darkness. This stops the oysters from closing, and in a few hurried seconds the thieves will dangle a hook of wire into the flesh, feeling for any pearl that might be hiding within. It leaves no trace at all and the shells appear untouched in the morning.

"God knows how they got hold of all these, how much blood must have been spilled."

"Surely not," whispers Axel, but he cannot summon much conviction. "There must be some expla–" The door squeaks behind them, and the fresh click of a revolver echoes through the silence. They freeze; Eliza notices the quickening in Axel's breath.

"I guess we should raise our hands," she whispers, and the two of them turn, slowly, toward the gun.

CHAPTER 12

They had been in Bannin for almost two years when Eliza noticed a change in her mother. Instead of her usual crackling vivacity, she became withdrawn and frail—a candle that had been snuffed. Whenever Eliza looked at her, instead of sharp blue eyes, she'd see pale skin and a greasy caul of sweat. During the day, when her mother would usually stride into town or have guests for tea, she would retire to her bed and not emerge for hours. Eliza was under strict instructions not to wake her but would hover outside her room listening to the rise and fall of her breath. Her aunt Martha would come sometimes, as the friarbirds watched on and their *cheewip* chatters descended into scoldings. She'd bring freshly plucked lilies or bread for breakfast. And although they did not always agree, she would sit at her mother's bedside and they'd speak in low whispers for hours.

"We'll be praying for you, at the Circle," Eliza heard her aunt once say. *The fruit of the womb is his reward.* Eliza knew the Ladies' Circle to be a collection of Bannin's most pious and proper women, including the doctor's wife, the postmaster's wife, and Iris Stanson herself, wife of President Septimus Stanson. The women would meet in town every Thursday, their gatherings often running late into the night. They had much to cover and would discuss the indignities blighting Bannin Bay—sodomy, lust, adultery, interracial copulation, the impropriety of the gambling houses and brothels. Her mother never enrolled, a failing for which, Martha very often warned, God might never forgive her.

At night Eliza would stir as the shuffle of slippers drifted through the house. She'd strain her ears for the click of the latch as her mother stepped into the cold air. It was always a while before she returned. In the morning Eliza would ask Thomas what he thought their mother might be doing leaving the house so late at night. Was she in trouble with someone in town? Did their father, away at sea, know what was happening? "We must tell him!"

Thomas had simply rolled his eyes. "You stupid bugger," he muttered, leaving her alone with her worry.

One night Eliza followed her mother, then watched through a crack in the doorway as she paced the garden, gilded by the moon. Her eyes widened when she saw her mother bend and pluck a pebble from the grass, wipe it with her nightdress, then pop it in her mouth to suck it.

Eliza was confused. Then scared. Thomas seemed so flippant; why did he not care their mother was ill? Perhaps she had caught something from one of the other wives in town. Been sent entirely mad. She pictured her wasting away, confined to a tent on the mudflats like a diver rife with disease.

It soon became clear, of course, that her mother was in no danger of diminishing. In fact, she started to swell. First her breasts, then her fingers and feet, all sharp things rounded out. Concave turned convex. Soon, a gigantic belly protruded in front of her. Skin tight and shiny like the meat they ate for dinner.

The fire had been restoked and her mother began to regain her energy. The nighttime trips became fewer until they didn't happen at all. There was no click of the latch in the night. Her cheeks flushed, she smiled, she laughed, until one day, eyes wet with pride, she told Eliza she was soon to have a baby brother or sister. She paused, her face eager with anticipation. "Well?"

Eliza was silent for a while. "That's remarkable, Mother," she responded eventually, the poison creep of jealousy hot in her chest.

CHAPTER 13

1896

Two things are very clear. There is a gun pointed toward them and at the end of that gun is a child. He can be only eight or nine, dressed in a loose singlet and grubby shorts. His bare feet are caked in dirt. His head is closely shaven, so that his eyes look large in his skull. He shouts something in a language neither Eliza nor Axel understand. They risk a brief glance at each other, hands still raised.

"We mean no trouble," says Axel quickly. "We're just looking for her father." He gestures toward Eliza with a tip of his head, but his foreign tongue angers the child, who explodes with a high-pitched volley of words, shifting the revolver back and forth between them. Eliza's eyes cling to the slender barrel, the boy's small fingers clenched around the grip. She has never been in a room with a gun before; she is surprised at the intimacy of it.

"Maybe we should get on our knees?" whispers Axel. "Show

willing?" They both bend slowly until they are kneeling in front of the boy, who shows no sign of dropping the Webley. As they peer up at him, a figure materializes in the doorway, a body silhouetted against the fierce sun. Eliza blinks. He is holding the fish.

"What the fuck is going on?"

The man speaks quickly in accented English. He steps over the threshold and surveys the two strangers on their knees. He murmurs a string of cusses under his breath and the boy sighs and lowers the weapon. The man dismisses him with a wave of the hand and places the fish on the floor. The child tosses the gun onto the stool and skulks out into the heat.

The man, now pacing back and forth in front of them, has a Bowie knife tucked into the waistband of his trousers. Eliza can see that it glints whenever he passes through the light just so.

"I am going to give you five seconds to tell me what you are doing in this house or I'll slit your throats." The threat is as easy as a sigh. He reaches for the bone handle and draws the blade slowly from his belt.

"We mean nothing untoward," Axel stammers. "We did not know there were stones here. That's not why we came. You have my word."

"Your word?" The man's face dissolves into a sly grin. "Thank you so much, sir, for giving me your *word*." Spittle flies from his mouth. His eyes flare with anger. "You knew they were here and that is why you came. To steal from us." Eliza's eyes slip sideways to Axel's face, which is pale with terror. She hears him gulp noisily.

"Sir. I have money," she says calmly. "I can give you money if you just let us go." The man pauses, considers, allowing the knife to dangle loosely from his hand. He is being careless with it. He cannot see them as a threat. Eliza's eyes flit to the gun on the stool.

"Show me."

She slowly moves her feet. "I'm going to stand up now." She rises, palms out, and reaches into the front of her blouse. The man twitches. With a shift she pulls a handful of bank notes from her bodice. He eyes the money cautiously, before beckoning her forward. She hesitates, takes a step, but just as he reaches out she sweeps her arm behind her back.

"Sir, I will give this money to you in exchange for any information you can give me about my father." From behind her, Axel makes a strained gurgling sound. "I know he's been here. That is why we've come. We are not interested in your pearls or any other business run out of this place." She gestures around the room. "If you are willing to inspect, you will see the stones remain untouched. We had plenty of time to take them but we did not. Why you would leave them unattended I do not know." Axel's panicked groan grows louder. "We will tell no one they are here. We want none of that. We just want information about my father."

His eyebrows quiver and the muscles of his cheek flex. With the knife still outstretched, he gestures behind them. "Move backward," he barks. "Back!" They shuffle as far as they can to the back of the room until they are almost flat against the wall. The man returns the knife to his belt and goes to the stool to pick up the revolver. Then he moves to the table and examines the pearls. As he does, Eliza glances quickly behind her at the sign on the door. *Zhou*, it says. She knew it would.

After a long while, and when the man seems satisfied, he moves the cloth back over the stones.

"Turn out your pockets, give me the notes, and I won't kill you."

Axel, still on his knees, does as he is told. Eliza hands the money over reluctantly, but her eyes are fixed on the gun loose in the man's fingers.

"Now I need reassurance that you haven't hidden any of my stones elsewhere." The man moves forward until his face is just inches from hers. This close, she can smell the grit set into his wrinkles, see the large black pores studded across his nose.

"Seeing as you were so clever as to tuck your money away in there, I'll need to search it for my pearls too." He leers down at her chest. This is his first mistake; it signals to her that he is distracted. His second, his cool hold on the gun, is a mark that he has foolishly underestimated them. Swiftly, she brings her arm down hard onto the man's wrist. He cries out as the weapon falls with a clatter to the floor. For a moment they eyeball each other, frozen, and she is surprised to see, out the corner of her vision, Axel react so quickly. Before she can do anything he has swiped the revolver from the boards. Now back up on his feet, he levels it directly at the man. Eliza darts to join Axel's side. The whole exchange of position can only have taken seconds, but the shift of power is so thick in the air you could slice it up and eat it.

"You wouldn't know how to use it," the man chides.

"Sir," Eliza ignores the shake of the revolver in Axel's grip. The man waves the unsheathed knife at them now, but they all know which weapon is fiercer. "Believe us when we say we have taken none of your snides. Now, I would be grateful if you would answer my questions." The man does not react. She continues.

"My father." She is surprised by her calmness. "Charles Brightwell is his name. He's captain of the *White Starling* lugger. I believe he had business with you. Now he is missing."

The man glowers at them. "You think I killed some white pearler? You think I'm that foolish?"

"That is not what we're saying." Axel's voice is thin. "My friend here is very upset by her father's disappearance. As I'm sure you will understand, being a family man yourself." Eliza glares at him. The man looks blankly back at both of them.

"We have this." Eliza pulls the piece of paper from her pocket. "It's the address to this house. My father had it in his possession. There's a name there too. Zhou A." The man glances reluctantly at the scrawled writing. "My father is of average height and build, perhaps a bit taller than yourself," says Eliza. "He has dark hair, a heavy mustache, and spectacles. You might have noticed his ring. Two sea snakes. He always wears it on his right index finger."

The man's gaze swoops from Eliza to Axel but his expression does not change. He looks, if anything, bored by the inconvenience.

"There has been no such man round here," he eventually says dryly. "Men with fancy jewelry do not come to these parts. They are not welcome. Just as we are not welcome over there." He nods out of the doorway. "You whites are only interested in our doctors or our brothels. You want to rid yourselves of your diseases or take what you want from our women. So unless your father is one of *those* men, no, he has not been here."

She notices a thick vein close to the surface of his neck, wonders what it would be like to press the tip of a knife into it.

"It would serve you well not to talk about her father like that." Axel has stepped forward and holds the gun more bullishly now. Eliza spots the briefest murmur of fear pass over the man's face.

"All right, all right." He tucks the knife back into his trousers, raising his fingers reluctantly from his waist in surrender. "We did have a man here," he concedes. "Said he was from the *White Starling.*" Her breathing halts. How spectacularly mediocre–to get a man to tell the truth you merely had to threaten to spill his blood. "But this man, he was Japanese. Fancy-looking guy. Shiny suit." Eliza's mind flicks to Shuzo, the diver's medals at his breast.

"What business did he have here?"

The man looks irritated. "I've given you what you asked for."

Eliza holds his glare for a while, then signals to Axel. The man steps aside to let them pass.

Once outside, she takes the gun from Axel, moves its weight from hand to hand. It is unnerving, beautiful. She is surprised at the way it makes her heart beat so fast.

CHAPTER 14

The shriek of an unseen animal erupts as Parker's patrol makes its steady way through the scrub. Out in front, the mounted tracker slouches on his chestnut gelding; Parker's eyes cling to the place where his thin shoulder blades meet, sweat speckling through threadbare cotton. Above, the sun beats down from its brassy sky. The flies are bothersome—drawn to every inch of skin left uncovered. They cluster at the back of Parker's neck, his hands, the bare lines of pink behind his ears. Other winged things arrive too. Things that bite and sting. Things with long, hanging legs and hard, shielded bodies. From under his hat he spots them hovering, then a shot of fire wires its caustic way into his veins. He slaps the things dead easily, flicks their corpses into the dirt. He won't be bullied away from his task by damn insects.

When they reach a wooded copse, long shadows stain the red dirt a *bold black. The men pause in the shade to mutter. Parker wants to know the route; wants assurance they're covering all ground. When they continue onward, the landscape opens up again into something vast. The orange brightness burns at Parker's eyes. But he blinks away the agitation. He'll do this for days if he has to. Whatever it takes to find the man.*

CHAPTER 15

Y ou lost, ma'am?" The man peering across the veranda has a mouth untroubled by teeth. He reclines in the bones of a cane armchair that rocks as if propelled by his own slow heartbeat. On his neck, a tiny anchor tattoo speaks of a past life. He has a dead wallaby in his lap, its skin stripped back to reveal a shiny, blue stomach.

"I'm not lost, sir, but I am searching for something. Or rather, someone." Eliza glances at his neat front garden. Tidy rows of hydrangeas are attended by slow, fat bees. Around them, bird-of-paradise plants turn fantastical heads toward the sun.

Axel had panicked about the gun last night. Wanted to toss it into the mangroves, be entirely rid of it. But she had urged him to keep it. He will need it; the Brotherhood are more likely to come after him on the foreshore than they are to venture to the bunga-lows. She had not allowed herself the indulgence of sleep and now her limbs are heavy and hot, but she must find out what her father's diver was doing at Three Stones House, what it might have to do with his disappearance.

"Shuzo Saionji. Do you know where he lives? I believe he's rather well thought of in this part of town." She knows the season's best divers are treated like kings when they return from sea. But the man does not react as she had hoped. He remains still, eyebrow raised.

"He's the lead diver for the *White Starling*. Very successful, if you follow the numbers." The man is expressionless. "He's a sharp-looking chap." With this she gestures to her own loose-sleeved blouse. Once white, it now has a strange peachy hue to it. "Wears a blazer. Medals." The man's face softens. Eventually, he nods.

"Ah, Shu," he says, leaning forward in his chair so the wallaby's ripe organs splatter onto the decking. "That's a man who likes to keep himself to himself. There's a load of them down at the water today. I'd start there if I were you."

He directs her down a street flanked with glossy rosewoods. She breathes in their scent, slows to feel her body stroked by their shade. Her mind yawns and a memory spills out—a vision of being alone in an English forest. Thomas had led her to its center and left her there one day, said it would do her good to find her way back home alone. She can only have been four or five, and the trees had loomed like witches as she waited for her brother to return. Every rustle of the leaves was an unwanted spirit, every gust of wind the ghost of an old woman gliding by. Overwhelmed with the task, she'd simply curled into a ball and waited among the woodlice until her mother had found her. Thomas had fought against his reprimand; he was only trying to teach her to be strong. She needed it. Later that night their mother had taken a belt to his behind.

She hears the commotion at the beach from some distance away: raised voices; a sequence of explosions, each followed by a rush of falling water. As she nears, a crowd of men come into sight, gathered around a lugger stripped of its sails and tipped over in the shallows. Many of the men are shirtless, trousers tugged roughly to the knee. They carry bowls and platters in their arms; some have bags strung about their shoulders. They all seem to be waiting for something.

She has always known Shuzo to be quiet, private as an oyster, really, so it makes sense that he is standing at a distance from the crowd. The tide, she can see, is quickly rising, filling the boat until water cascades from every opening. Eliza squints, steps forward: rats are fleeing desperately from the lugger, hurling themselves into the shallows, joining the bodies of drowned cockroaches. Men with hand brooms beat more insects from the rigging; they fall like fat drops of rain onto the surface. With the curve of an arm someone from the crowd tosses in another cartridge. As it explodes, the water erupts with a roar and the men leap backward. Then, silence, until one by one ghosts appear on the surface. Eliza blinks; they are the bodies of the mullets that had gathered to feast on the roaches. With a scramble, the men tear into the water, a froth of elbows and shins as they grapple for the fish. Eliza watches as Shuzo follows slowly behind, waiting patiently until a large mullet floats toward him on the tide.

She is surprised to see him here: a lead diver is usually compensated enough to afford fresh fish from the traps; he doesn't need to scavenge. He dips to collect the mullet and places it neatly in his bowl, then he turns to walk back up the beach, freezing when he sees Eliza waiting for him.

Handsome, certainly, he is more broadly set than she had remembered. His black-tar hair is parted meticulously to one side. A pair of wire-framed spectacles perch gently on his nose. He wears a high-necked drill suit with gold sovereign buttons, and his turned-up trousers reveal olive shins.

"I expect you know that I've come here to ask about my father." There's nothing to be gained by skirting around the issue.

He looks uncomfortable, if not surprised.

"I found something among his possessions. An address for Three Stones House." The diver looks quickly over his shoulder, steps closer to her. "I went there," she continues. Shuzo's eyes widen with alarm, an effect only magnified by his spectacles.

"That is not a suitable place for a woman, Miss Brightwell. They did not hurt you, did they?" His words come out in clots.

"They did not, although not for want of trying."

He bristles.

"But I had to go. The constables. Parker." His name tastes foul on her lips. "They are not taking his disappearance seriously. Balarri did nothing, and if he's caught he'll surely be hanged now too." Shuzo nods slowly, eyes low, as if scared to meet her intensity. After a pause she launches into the other words she has prepared. Not trusting herself enough to slow down. "I ran into a man at Three Stones. He told me *you* had been there." His eyes dart up to hers. "Why would that be?" she asks. "And why would my father have that address in his diary?"

Shuzo is quiet for a while, and Eliza realizes he is holding his breath. When he eventually releases it and talks, his voice is pinched with regret.

"Your father is one of a few decent pearlers in this town." He shifts the bowl to his other arm. "And, yes, I am the reason he has that address, I'll admit that." For a moment there is no sound but the whine of mosquitoes above the mudflats. "But I cannot tell you why. I'm sorry. It would put someone in danger, someone very close to me."

She feels her chest clench. "No." She shakes her head. "I need to know." She tries to meet his eye. Her voice is urgent. "It could be linked to his disappearance. I need your help, Shuzo. Please."

The diver looks flustered, and blinks in distress. "I assure you it is not linked."

"If money will change your mind, I can make some arrangements . . ."

He looks up at her, brow creased in brief distaste. "That will not be necessary."

The heat is inching up her neck now. "Well, how can you be so sure this has nothing to do with my father's disappearance? How can *I* be sure if you will not tell me? I know what happens in places like that. I saw their snides; they did not hesitate to hold a gun to my head."

Shuzo looks appalled. He gulps thickly. "Your father never set foot in Three Stones House." He says it quickly. "He just knew we were in trouble and–"

"What do you mean, *we*?" None of this is making sense, none of it is helping her to find her father.

"I cannot say. Miss Brightwell, please. Just trust me."

She sighs through her nose and her fingers go to the space between her brows.

"Charles helped me by giving me that address," Shuzo eventually offers. "That is as far as his involvement with it goes. That's all you need to know. Your father was a good man, really. I don't know what has happened to him. I wish I did, truly. But I know it is not tied to Three Stones. I am quite sure of that."

She studies his face for any sign of deception. He looks away and her hands tighten into fists. How can he be so sure there is no link? As she watches him, the muscles in his jaw twitch. It's as if he wants to say more, but something is holding him back. They are silent for a while as men stagger past under the weight of their stunned mullets.

"Is there *anything* else you can tell me?" she asks when they've gone. "Anything about the night he went missing?"

He bites his lip; the tendons in his neck spasm.

"I need any information. Anything at all."

"You'll think me foolish." He shakes his head reluctantly.

"I shan't, I assure you." There is screaming inside her head.

He drops his shoulders. Looks up at her through his spectacles. "I'm sure you know we sailors, divers, anyone who spends time at sea, we have superstitions."

She nods slowly, thinking of the charms she's seen the crew wear round their necks—a twisted piece of hair, a length of rice paper, the tiny mermaid her father had stashed for her in his drawer.

"Many of the crew believe in sea ghosts, demons, apparitions. Some might kiss the deck before we sail, carve symbols into the mast posts, even."

"Right . . ."

"Well, the night your father went missing, I saw something I cannot explain."

She swallows.

Shuzo looks furtively along the beach. "I was sleeping in the cabin; it was the middle of the night. The whole day had been dead still, useless for finding shell. But a strong wind had set up that evening and it woke me from my bunk." A bird squawks overhead, but Eliza is fixated on his words. "I got up, climbed the ladder to lift the hatch open, just an inch. Then I saw, there were two lights on the water. They were . . . glowing like the eyes of a demon. They didn't look like any lugger I'd ever seen before." He shivers at the memory. "I froze. Didn't know what to do. I thought it was something coming to take the ship. Something bad." He blinks quickly. "I closed the hatch quick and rubbed my charm for protection. For all of us." He tugs it out of his collar to show her. "I squeezed my eyes shut and just hoped. When I lifted the hatch and looked back out there, the lights were gone."

THE DIARY OF CHARLES J. G. BRIGHTWELL, MASTER PEARLER

The price of pearls

After several years in Bannin, it has become clear to me that the trade in stolen pearls is a thriving industry. Shady buyers saunter round the pool rooms and dives, picking up snides from the "fences"–that being the name for the thieves hired to purloin the gems. They sell them on for sometimes a thousand percent profit. Quite astonishing, really. It's no surprise some men say no great fortunes are made by those who pearl legitimately.

Willem told me the other day about a man killed just yards from the Kingfish for his trophy snide. It was a huge stone, I hear, a 40–50 grain stringer; no flaws. A mesmerizing blue kissed through with pink. Certainly desirable enough to fetch into the thousands from the Russians. The man had arranged to meet two publicans down on the mudflats to trade. But these men were not interested in a business transaction. He was felled by multiple blows from a slingshot and his body was found the next morning knocking against the jetty piles–scalp split open by barnacles.

It's not just men with sticky fingers, however. I recall one occasion some years ago, when the heat had whipped the whole town into a stupor. A sum of £1,000 in notes, property of Ratchet, a fellow pearling master, vanished while in keeping at the Kingfish. The whole town was questioned, camps and cottages were ransacked, but without success (as is so often the case). Then early one morning, Grant's bird Confucius was spotted on a roof in town with a roll of notes clasped in its claws. No amount of coaxing could entice the stubborn animal to part with it–so that was that: £1,000, last seen in the fists of a bloody cockatoo! I should think that's the one and only time in this town a bird has ever been questioned by the police.

Feathered thieves aside, although the trade is healthy, the identity of those who deal in snides is a closed book. The truth is, and although I am reluctant to put the thought to paper, I do fear sometimes that Thomas is becoming far too involved with those sorts of men. I saw him conversing with the barber Lilywhite the other day. Show me one sod who doesn't know of Lily's foul deeds; he'd surely pull every nail from your fingers and sell them for a profit if he could. Thomas assures me he is not involved in the dark trade, but considers it wise to know precisely what is happening in this town. I suppose I can understand it. He says it's good for business, by any means. He will not be bested by any man. Now that, I can certainly believe. The boy has always been proud. But of late I can't help noticing his many whispered conversations with those whose characters I cannot be as sure of. He spends much time at Hardcastle's camps. Often with the young deckhand with the strange eye. Winters, I think it is. The poor chap appears to follow Thomas around like a lovesick puppy. It would not be the first case of my son toying with someone's affections in order to get to what he wants. He is quite aware of the hold he has over people. He tells me it's nothing more than two young men trading tales of lugger life. Comparing shell tallies and whatnot. And the lad can't be more than 15, scarcely old enough to grow a mustache. But I do worry perhaps there might be darker commodities being traded here too.

Post scriptum: a brief note on cockroaches. While on the subject of unsavory things, I feel it necessary to make known my thoughts on the roaches. I know I should be as fascinated by them as the other specimens I study, but to be quite frank, I loathe them. Oh, I loathe them, I loathe them! At sea, while my men and I suffocate in the heat and burn from the glare of the sun, we must also contend with roaches pestering us day and night. The smaller species (around half an inch long, I have noted), swarm all around us during mealtimes, even landing in the food, while the larger (two inches, as measured with a ruler) fly clumsily about the cabins in the quiet of the night. They bite at all exposed parts of the body—toenails, wounds, they'll even pull the hair from your head! There is no relief; they are unendurable and absolutely impossible to exterminate while at sea.

CHAPTER 16

A xel Kramer, you say?" Min rests one arm on the doorjamb and sucks on a neat cigarette. She blows the smoke out in a perfect ring, raises her hand, and spears the circle through with a finger. "I've not seen him nor heard of him. Which probably means he's a fine sort. That, or he's a molly. Not that I'd be one to judge, of course." She pulls a strand of tobacco from her tongue. "But he should steer clear of Parker, if that's the case. He'll have him skinned."

Eliza raises an eyebrow.

"So, tell me again about this *demon*." Min moves to sit next to Eliza, pouring tea from the steaming pot.

"It really doesn't make sense." Eliza shakes her head. "I know no demon is responsible for my father's disappearance. But Shuzo *did* see something that night. Out on the water."

"Did anyone else see anything?" Min shifts her legs up onto the cushion.

"He says the crew saw nothing. They were all asleep, exhausted after so long at sea. At first light they awoke and he was just . . . gone." Eliza takes the cigarette from Min's fingers and draws on it shakily. The taste makes her splutter but she needs something to steady her nerves. "I'm still not sure I can discount the men at Three Stones. I don't know why Shuzo was so shifty about it."

"So, he said *we*, right?" Min takes the cigarette back. Eliza nods. "And he didn't want to tell you because it would put someone close to him in danger."

"Correct."

Min clenches her jaw as she thinks; it makes her chin look even sharper. "I do know there's a doctor who's aligned with the Brotherhood," she says. "He works off Sheba, although I'd be surprised if he had any actual qualifications to speak of."

Eliza frowns, her mind flashing quickly to the room at the back of Three Stones House; its medical potions, that acrid smell. Zhou. "Yes," she whispers. It rushes in and swamps her ears. *You whites are only interested in our doctors or our brothels.*

"I know girls who've had to use him on occasion," Min continues. "Sought out his procedures to see to any trouble they've found themselves in, if you get my meaning."

Thoughts dart through Eliza's head quick as dragonflies. What use could Shuzo have for such a doctor, and why is he so sure it is not linked to her father's disappearance? She is trying to smother the sound of the clock on the mantel, the pressure it brings, how it speaks of time that is running out. How it makes her think of who else is out there, alone. But the *tick, tick, tick* calls to mind the thirsty squeak of a bicycle wheel. She remembers how she had run into Balarri one hot day, cycling on a rickety contraption through the lanes. He was with the Japanese photographer from town. On the back of the bicycle, a huge papier-mâché shark's head was secured with rope. She had watched, blinking in disbelief, as the men untied it and set the stiff creature onto the dirt. Its jaws had been sculpted into a wide-open position, fringed with sharp, serrated teeth. The photographer quickly arranged his equipment, bending to peer through the cloth as Balarri straightened his hat, tugged his side-whiskers, and tossed an old shoe onto the ground for coins.

"Come have your portrait taken with the swallowed man!" The photographer began to pace and whip up the meager crowds. Balarri balanced one hand on the shark's head, then stepped unblinkingly into its jaws. Some stopped to gawp at the bizarre spectacle. Others brushed past in disgust, ushered children away.

"The white shark swallowed him up to the neck before he fought it off with his bare hands. Come! See his strength. See his *gruesome* scar."

Eliza had looked at Balarri's chest and there, just below the collarbone, was a twisted snarl of flesh. It ran like a rope from shoulder to shoulder. She stepped forward, blinked up at him, handed him a coin.

Min's muttering brings her back to the room. Eliza jiggles her head to clear the fog. They run over the diver's words again. They *must* be missing something. Someone must know what happened on that boat beyond this ridiculous talk of sea ghosts.

She sighs, turns to Min. "*You* don't believe in spirits and ghosts, do you? Things out there, on the ocean . . ."

Min raises her eyebrows, purses her lips, sends the air out slowly through her nose. "Well, there are many in this town who do; that much I know." She places her cup down. "For all the men who believe in mutiny and murder, there are just as many who'd put your father's disappearance down to bad omens and sea ghosts. There'll be talk of it; it will cause fear among the sailors. I wouldn't be surprised if some of them refuse to step foot on the *Starling* again. I'm sorry."

Eliza sags. Crushed under the weight of a future without the *Starling*, without her father.

"I reckon there is something we can do, though." Min nods firmly. Eliza's head whips up.

"There's someone I think we should pay a visit to. She knows all there is of devils and demons. More important, though, she keeps the company of many men in this town, from the lowliest deckhand to the most conceited master pearler. If there's talk of what happened to your father, she'll have heard it."

Eliza swallows. "Yes. Thank you. I'll try anything. Just—as quick as we can."

"We'll go tonight, then." Min pushes away the tea and lights another cigarette. "Bring the chap, Axel," she says in an exhale of smoke. "He could prove useful."

A fetid animal stink hangs in the lanes. It assaults the nostrils, sucks the moisture clean from the eyes. "Good grief." Axel pulls out a handkerchief and puts it to his nose. Eliza blinks away the odor and steps forward.

The town's crooked streets are becalmed tonight—no movement but for the men out slaking their thirst for insalubrious pursuits. Eliza and Min usher Axel through the doorway, clinging to the shadows behind him as the door swings shut.

Inside, the shop is filled with gloom and the suspended breath of things once living. They allow their eyes to adjust to the darkness and as they do, a mass of shapes comes slowly into focus. Hanging from the ceiling rafters are all manner of birds. Albatross, pigeons, petrels and kookaburras, coucals, wagtails, pipits, and parrots. All of them with their necks twisted unnaturally, feathers limp. Eliza holds her breath. From somewhere in the room's darkest corner comes the slow-simple patter of blood on boards.

Axel hands a coin to the gentleman at the counter and gestures toward the back of the shop.

"I'll . . . just be browsing for a short while. Thank you."

The man barely glances up, pockets the coin, and returns to the pamphlet he is reading by candlelight.

They tiptoe their way to the back of the room, eyeing more strange curiosities lining the walls in unpolished cases. Large pelicans are displayed behind dusty glass, wings spread, gular skins sagging like discarded laundry. In one casket is a pile of scaly, wizened objects. Moving closer, Eliza can see it is a jumble of dried animals' feet; gray, brown, and gallstone yellow. Advancing farther, they see a pool of light spilling from beneath a thick velvet curtain. Eliza glances behind her at the shopkeeper, who is now plucking a pile of lifeless cockatoos without so much as a sniff in their direction. If she strains her ears she can hear the faint clink of glass from beyond the fabric. Min nods and Axel steps forward, slowly pulling the curtain aside.

The room revealed is lit by a hundred glowing candles. It is awash with red, walls draped in carmine silks and velvets. The air is choked with incense; it makes Eliza's head spin. In front of them is a mahogany counter from which a stout woman eyes them expectantly. She is dressed in men's trousers, shirt, and braces. She clutches a near-empty carafe of Madeira in broad hands.

"Evening, Min," she says. "Looking radiant as ever." She takes a large swig from the carafe, then thumps it onto the counter.

"Madame," Min demurs, and Eliza half-expects her friend to curtsy.

A crow of laughter comes from somewhere out back followed by the smooth swipe-swoosh of Lucifers being struck. The woman looks Axel up and down as if assessing something dead at the side of the road. "What do you have for me here, then? Looks like a tightly wound sort."

"I can assure you he has his vices like any man," says Min, flashing Axel a doubtful glance. He nods stiffly in return.

"We were hoping he might have a word with Clementine," says Min. She looks up at the woman through lowered charcoal eyelashes. "And that perhaps we might talk to her too?"

The woman leans back in her chair, boots resting on the leather countertop. Her eyes volley between Min and Eliza. Eliza has never seen a woman dressed like this before. What freedom those trousers must afford. She cannot quite take her eyes off them.

"She's busy right this moment, but if you've patience, then be my guests." She gestures with a sweep of the arm to a long bench at the side of the room. "Seeing as there's three of you, you'll be paying thrice over. That's the only way I'll allow it."

They wait as muffled bestial groans drift toward them from the hidden rooms. Axel looks alarmed when a woman in a translucent gown appears and folds herself into Madame's lap. As Madame tips the carafe to the woman's lips, crimson beads escape from the glass and inch down the soft white skin of her throat.

The scurrying departure of a rotund, red-faced man signals Clementine's eventual availability. Eliza welcomes it: there's only so much incense one can suffer. Madame takes Axel's coins and waves them through with an inebriated flourish.

"Third door on the right," she calls after them.

The corridor is low lit and stale. Jarrah floorboards lead to a warren of rooms. More groans of copulation come from behind one door. From another, an almighty crash, followed by a cluck of female laughter.

When they reach the third door, they pause. Smoke filters out through the cracks in the frame, fleeing to form ribbons around their knees.

Axel raps quickly with his knuckles and puts an ear to the iron.

"*Entrez, mon chéri.*" A singsong voice sails out from within. He pushes open the door and steps into the room.

"*Oh là, là,* what an 'ansome man you are . . ."

Eliza and Min step in behind him.

"Oh!" The woman reclined on the bed, partially obscured by the blue smoke from her thin cigar, sits suddenly upright. Her lips are bows of shining vermilion. She has a long fluffy feather tucked behind her left ear. She shifts into a cross-legged position and quickly ties her gown. "Everything all right, Min? What's all this?" She has dropped the French accent, in its place an Irish lilt.

"Sorry to ambush you." Min kisses her quickly, then takes a seat on the bed. Eliza and Axel hover awkwardly above a divan at its foot. "We need your help."

Eliza had never really considered what one might find at a brothel. Perhaps she had anticipated somewhere filled with harlots and whiskered men quaffing squareface. She *thinks* she had expected dancing. Shows. Seductions, maybe. But this is nothing more than a murmur of place. Still as a secret from the outside looking in. She wonders just who may have passed through its doors unnoticed.

Min pats the space next to her on the bed and Eliza sits. "My name is Eliza Brightwell," she says to Clementine. "My father, Charles Brightwell, disappeared from the *White Starling* five days ago. There was no blood left behind, no signs of a struggle. The crew maintain they saw nothing untoward and none of them harbored my father any ill will. I'm quite sure of that." She clears her throat. "He was a good captain. I know they are few and far between, but he was. He treated his divers fairly and ensured the safety of his crews." Clementine's eyes are fixed on hers and Eliza notices how dark they are. "I have a friend who is being blamed and whose life is in grave danger now. If I don't find out what happened, I fear we will lose him too."

Clementine breathes in deeply, considering the words. She pauses, then moves to extinguish her cigar on the sideboard.

"If he's willing to work in that industry, he's already darker than you know." Her smile is tight. "He'll have secrets, I guarantee it." Eliza sees the woman glance briefly at Min. "Even the saintliest buggers have something to hide. Filthy business, pearling."

"My father's not like that." Eliza's voice falters. "He really is a good man. I truly believe he is." She tails off, thinking of the times he had brushed away her questions, pulled doors closed behind him, masked a silence with a fixed smile.

"That's not all of it, though, is it, Eliza?" Min looks at her encouragingly.

Eliza nods and swallows, fighting the absurdity of what she is about to say.

"The lead diver on the ship, Shuzo Saionji, someone whom I know to be extremely trustworthy. He says he saw something the night my father disappeared." Clementine tilts her head and waits. "He . . . he described them as demon's eyes." Eliza stammers, flustered. "Two glowing globes on the water. Only there for a moment before they disappeared."

"We wondered if you might do a reading," Min asks. "See if there was anything untoward about that night? Perhaps you might . . . pick up a message from Captain Brightwell." Eliza is sure she sees Min widen her eyes quickly, then smile. Her own face reddens. She has no time for spirits. But with no other clues, and with two men still in danger, where else does she have to turn?

"Aye." Clementine rises from the bed. "I'll get the teeth out."

THE DIARY OF CHARLES J. G. BRIGHTWELL, MASTER PEARLER

A naturalist's note: the spiders of Australia

Many spiders in Australia are venomous but only two can cause death—the funnel web (native to Sydney and surrounding parts of eastern Australia) and the redback, of which I have seen plenty around Bannin Bay.

The redback's venom is highly neurotoxic, that is to say it attacks the body's central nervous system, causing intense pain, difficulty in breathing, violent convulsions, and eventually death. They are closely related to the infamous black widow—found in the Americas and worldwide—in fact they are almost identical, except for the startling red dorsal stripe after which the spider is named.

Their mating behavior is MOST peculiar in that they display what is known as sexual cannibalism. During mating, not only does the female entirely devour the male, but the male actually assists her in this process by flipping his body toward her so he is closer to her mouthparts. While gruesome, this prolongs the mating period, affording the chance to fertilize a greater number of eggs.

Redbacks have a preference for living near people (a packing shed is a prime habitat for a nesting redback) and as well as insects and flies, they have the ability to capture in their webs other spiders and even small reptiles and mammals. I once came across a redback spider which had trapped a small gray mouse in her web. The rodent shrieked and twitched as it flailed against the silk. The spider simply waited at a distance for it to die. It took more than a day for it to stop shrieking, but mere hours for it to be eaten.

CHAPTER 17

Clementine is clutching a small ornate tin. It is painted in delicate chinoiserie patterns and makes a rhythmic hiss as she moves.

"Come." She gathers them around a low table, clearing it first of bottles, vials, and pouches, and smoothing a hand over its rough surface.

"I need you to put your hands on the tabletop, miss." She directs Eliza to kneel and takes hold of her palms, placing them flat on the unpolished wood. Eliza feels the scratches under her fingers. Her breathing quickens; she glances around her: the smoke is clearing from the room, revealing tattered edges, old stained fabric, and the creeping scent of mold.

They watch intently as Clementine upends the tin, shaking the contents onto the table. They all lean in. They are sharks' teeth, hundreds of them, starkly white and sharp. Clementine rises and begins to pace slowly around them, bending occasionally to see the teeth from different angles. As she moves, she leaves behind a ghostly trace of her perfume. It is sweet and sickly; the taste of it clings to Eliza's tongue.

"I'm getting visions of a man in round spectacles."

Eliza briefly stops breathing. But no, there are plenty of pearlers in this bay, many of whom wear round spectacles. It's most likely a lucky guess.

"Kind eyes," Clementine continues ponderously. "Hands rough from work and smudged with ink."

Eliza's mouth is dry now. She thinks of her father's diary, its dog-eared edges, its pages crammed with inky illustrations. Still, this means nothing.

"Some kind of distinctive ring, wrapped twice around his finger. Hmm." Clementine straightens suddenly and Eliza recoils from the act in shock. The woman's hands go to her hips. "Strange."

"What is it?" Axel asks. Eliza slides her hands off the table.

"I don't see harm, I just see . . ."

"What?" Eliza's voice is a whisper. The room is still.

"I just see birds," Clementine says. "Hundreds and hundreds of birds."

Eliza's shoulders drop. She could point out that in order to get to this room they had to pass plenty of long-dead birds.

"So much white, though," Clementine continues, frowning. "A sort of blinding whiteness. It hurts to look at." She turns away, fingers pressing at her temples.

"What could it mean?" asks Min.

Eliza's thoughts run like spilled liquid. Does she really believe in all this? Demon's eyes out at sea, messages laid bare in old sharks' teeth? Surely not. Her father had always taught her there was a logical answer to everything. Problems were solved with biology and science. Not by expensive conversations in back-end brothels.

"Is there anything else you can tell us?" she asks.

"That's all the reading says." Clementine shrugs.

Axel bends to help Eliza from the floor. "But is there anything else you can tell us about the sailors? Anything that might have been mentioned by those who have . . . paid you a visit? There must have been talk. Do you know anything else that might possibly help with the truth of my father's disappearance?"

Clementine looks coyly to the floor. "I couldn't possibly—"

"We will reward you amply for your cooperation, won't we?" Min elbows Axel but he turns out his empty pockets. He gave all his money to Madame. Min sighs and reaches for her own coin purse. Eliza chastises herself for not bringing her own. She'll repay Min later. "We really need to know if you've heard anything," says Min.

Clementine raises an eyebrow.

"Well, there was something somewhat out of sorts I heard." She opens her hand to receive Min's coins, her words quickening with every penny dropped into her palm. "It can be no coincidence that Hardcastle lost a member of his crew that very same day, can it?"

Eliza's mouth drops open. "I did not know he had," she whispers. She casts her mind back to her confrontation with the man at the foreshore. His thick fingers on her chin, his smug assurance that he knew nothing of her father's disappearance.

"It's not exactly something you bellow from the rooftops," says Clementine. "You'll find no crew for your next sail if all in town believe your lugger to be cursed." She goes to light another cigar. "He's been keeping it quiet but he had a chap go missing too." She blows out a plume of smoke. "Told me as much while he was naked as a babe." Eliza grimaces and shakes away the image. "Unlike your father, however"—Clementine takes a long draw—"people pay scant attention when a deckhand doesn't return from sea. No children to mourn him. No wife to sob into her nightgown. Ordinary men just disappear, forgotten."

"And do you know the identity of this missing deckhand?" Axel asks.

"Didn't think to ask. Didn't signify, really."

"It does now." He nods.

Outside, the shell-grit paths have been silvered by the moon. Axel is quick to address his impropriety. "Laura-Min, please accept my apologies. I will reimburse you for the coins as soon as I can." He pats his empty pockets again. "A woman like you shouldn't have to use what little you have under those circumstances."

She turns to him, waiting for him to go on.

"I want you to know a woman is *much* more than what she has been forced to do to survive."

Min smiles dryly. "That's beautiful, Axel. Really it is. But what I am is perfectly solvent." He blinks. "I'm just not allowed to own the things my funds should rightly get me."

His mouth gapes wordlessly.

"Don't look so surprised. In a town full of men, someone like me can easily get their hands on coins. We just needed you here to facilitate our entry. It's only men allowed behind these doors. Well, mostly . . ." They turn to look back at the sorry birds in the shopfront window. "Unless you're working, and I don't think Eliza really fancies that."

They say their farewells and a plan is hatched; they will ask around for the missing man where they can, trail Hardcastle if they have to, find a way to uncover the identity of his lost crewman. This is their strongest lead yet; it could throw up more clues about her father.

Eliza refuses an escort, so Axel accompanies Min toward the cottages. She walks alone to the sound of shell shards crunching underfoot, but it is interrupted by the rattle of a lock and the clunk of heavy doors. Down a side street, a group of women are gathered at a low-slung building. She recognizes the slender Iris Stanson and the dowdy shape of her aunt Martha immediately. Martha wiggles the padlock in her hands as she pulls the doors to a close. Eliza sighs, relieved–it must be a meeting of the Circle, coming to a late end, although she is surprised to see those sorts of women out after dark unchaperoned. Perhaps they have been discussing her father's disappearance. Her heart gives a hopeful little kick. Her aunt glances up and Eliza shrinks backward into the shadows. She does not want to have to explain to her why she is out on the streets at night alone. She waits until she can hear the chatter of the women subsiding. Only when they are gone does she continue through the darkness.

CHAPTER 18

The sun is sharp the next morning, spearing down from a blinding sky. As Eliza hurries, it glints off the water and a string of pelicans lands with a slow, drawn-out hiss. Once again, she had fought sleep. How can she rest when her father is still out there? She thinks of the night's noises. The steady rush of the cicadas, the ticking of corrugated iron. If she were to sleep, they would certainly find their way into her dreams. It was never so in England, and it is as if she has forgotten the silent nothingness of those nights–when their house simply waited, static and patient until dawn, when the sun gave a wink and the birds set up their trilling.

A cry from a nearby fishmonger brings her back to the moment. She is on the hunt for Hardcastle, and for any information about just who went missing from his ship. All around her, people hasten about the town, going back and forth with their humdrum business.

The streets are at their busiest now the fleets are all in, crammed with pearl dealers, fisheries inspectors, shipping agents, and countless clerks. Sulkies swing by in a fog of oiled wheels and hot dung, drays piled high with baskets of pearl shell shining like new milk teeth in the sun. Their whiteness nips at Eliza's memory and brings with it a vision of a small pale body, a boy with hair as fair as flour. She shakes it away and speeds through the crowds, her eyes alert for the corded bulk of the mastiff.

It would tally that Hardcastle had a hand in her father's disappearance. There are many who stand to profit from a prominent pearler's exit, but with his bottom-rotten luggers and tormented, beaten crews, Hardcastle is teetering on the edge of financial ruin. The chandlers will no doubt be on his tail, and with huge bank loans hovering over him, it's no surprise he would want a competitor such as her father out of the game.

She continues through the town until something queer catches her eye. It's in the window of the photographer's studio. A picture sits out of place among the rest on show. It is displayed in a frame alongside portraits of families in starched Sunday best, the women with smooth hairstyles and neat bows at their throats, the men with heavy imperial mustaches and round-collared jackets. This particular photograph shows a crowd of people, all gathered to watch as a child stands on the armored body of a crocodile. She recalls the moment, the flash of the camera box, and stoops to see the picture in more detail. There, in the background, she can make out the two figures she expected to see. She and Axel stand in conversation, but it is only from this perspective that she can see how unlike the others around them they appear. Her hand goes unthinkingly to her hair as she notices how neglected the picture reveals it to be. She observes how her skirts are not smooth like the rest in the picture, how the exposed skin of her forearms is tanned to a darker shade than the other women. Shame flickers over her. There is something there marking Axel as out of place too. She cannot quite put her finger on it, something in the way he holds himself, perhaps. Not the posture of a rake or the bullish colonist. Something freer, an unselfconsciousness she only remembers experiencing as a child.

All of a sudden, white feathers swoop low over Eliza's head. She looks up, her eyes trailing the cockatoo as it glides above the townsfolk. It draws her vision toward a man in the near distance, and when she sees him her lungs suck in a sharp, hot breath. Hardcastle shakes as he bellows at a monger touting something sad with scales. The mastiff is beside him, snapping at the air for flies. She watches as the man grows redder and more furious by the second, towering over the poor merchant, who shrinks into himself like a shirt being folded. When the bird reaches them, it hovers with beating wings above Hardcastle's head. Eliza rushes forward, pushing past bodies, straining to discern its cries.

"Goodbye, Alfred. Goodbye, Alfred." The bird's strangled words hang heavy in the air.

Hardcastle boils with rage, swiping at the cockatoo. *Alfred*, Eliza thinks. Could that be the name of the missing crewmember?

"Shut your fucking beak, you fucking bastard bird." His imposing form quivers as the sweat drips from his chin. With no great urgency, the bosun emerges from the crowd and wrangles the agitated bird back onto his shoulder. Hardcastle, his whole head florid with temper, hisses, and the dog slopes over with a jaw full of fishbones. Together, they muscle off into the crowd.

Eliza steps forward to follow, but in a beat her body is hauled backward. The hand clasped around her wrist is cold and clammy: she'd know those smoke-stained fingers anywhere. She looks up to find her uncle grinning.

"You surprised me," she says, and attempts a forced smile.

"Sorry, dear, but you looked rather as if you were about to bolt." Willem slaps a mosquito on his neck. Behind him, a tiny bronze cuckoo flitters upward from an old branch. At his side, Martha stands as if her time is being wasted.

"Who are you pursuing?" he asks, peering over her shoulder.

Eliza shakes his hand off gently.

"Can I help you with something, Willem?"

He frowns briefly and she feels a stab of guilt.

"I'm sorry." She glances tentatively at Martha. If her aunt saw her out on the lanes last night, she doesn't betray it. "I was just in a bit of a hurry." As Willem leans in closer, she catches the fug of liquor on his breath. Her uncle–previously as abstemious as his God-fearing wife–had developed the taste for grog when he lost his leg. Because although the surgeon sawed that limb off and although there is nothing but wood beyond that stump of meat and bone, he seems to feel it as if there were still dying flesh there. So, every day he faces pain as his mind imagines a limb long rotted away. In order to live with it, he drinks and he drinks–and Eliza has to remind herself you cannot always see the thing that hurts you.

"I was hoping you would tell me where I could find young Master Thomas," Willem says. "I have business matters to run by him." She watches Willem wide-eyed as the words unfurl. Now she regrets not being sharper. "Given the circumstances, I'm sure there are conversations to be had about safeguarding you both and the fleet."

She steps back from him as if she has been bitten. This man is her uncle, her father's brother, yet he is willing to forget her father's disappearance just like that? And not only is he eager to forget, he intends to profit from it too.

"Funny that you are so interested in the fleet," she snaps, watching as Willem's confused eyebrows twitch into life. "One might question why you are so quick to ask after the ships when your brother has just gone missing . . ."

He shakes his head, seems startled by the accusation, but she sees his face shift from surprise, to anger, to intent. He pauses, as if weighing up whether to speak. He's beaten to it by his wife.

"We might ask similar questions of Thomas, you know," says

Martha in a voice that is surprisingly sharp for a woman of such staid appearance.

"Is it any coincidence that as soon as your father disappeared, Thomas left town?"

Willem's leg sounds a soft thud upon the earth. "Now come on, let us not get carried away." He spreads his arms to split the two women. "Eliza, I've been asking around about your father. There are lay-up camps all around these bays–Percy Sedgewick's at Boolgin Creek, Cape Bossut, Beagle Bay. I even rowed over myself to the trepangers at Cowrie Point. That wasn't easy, let me tell you. None of them had heard anything helpful about Charles. As for the fleets, I simply thought it best to handle matters before things get run into the ground. I want to ensure you are taken care of. Heaven forbid you and Thomas would be left with nothing."

She feels a wave of regret.

"Has your brother given a decent account of what happened on the ship?" Martha interjects so quickly Eliza has no real time to respond to her uncle's explanation, to apologize. She wonders instead if this is what the Circle have *really* been discussing. If they have been using their meetings to build their case against Thomas. "Has he been taken in for questioning like Billy?"

The two women stay very still, glares wielded as weapons.

"Shows how little you know of your own family," hisses Eliza. "Thomas is trading at Cossack. Someone has to, to keep the fleet afloat, to help us get through this. You should surely understand that if it's what you are so intent on too. And at least *he* is doing something to help the situation. My brother cannot afford to sit around drinking himself into the dirt like others in this town." With this, she spins on her heel, but her exit is blocked by a cage of scruffy chickens teetering on the back of a bicycle. She fidgets from foot to foot as it passes, then she storms onward, her chest heaving with vexation.

She casts her eyes about for Hardcastle and the dog, but sees nothing distinguishable among the monotony of the crowds. It's not possible. Is it? That Thomas has withheld information? That he might somehow know more than he has told her? The half thoughts stumble out. She thinks of his drawn face before he left, how his shoulders had been so tightly hunched. Her brother's anger has foiled him so many times, he surely knows well enough by now to remove himself from situations that might end badly. She has seen the fights, has collected him, bleary-eyed, from the cells, has been there when he has tried to rid himself of his cloying need for opium. She has watched as he has cried out into the darkness, yelling of monkeys, snakes, and parakeets, how they clawed his face, bit at his hands. She had always held a cloth to his skin as he fitted and groaned from the withdrawal. But one time, as she had soothed him, he'd flailed out so violently his fist had met her nose. It brought blood and shattered bone with it, and as she held one hand to her face to stop the warmth pouring out of her, she used the other to stroke her brother's sodden hair.

Can it really be true Thomas knows nothing of what happened on the ship that night? Perhaps she should go to Cossack herself, haul him out, demand he tell her every minute detail. Was there really no blood? Was anyone acting strangely? Why have you gone? Why have you gone? Why have you gone?

30 November 1896

To be presented to Master Thomas Brightwell—boarding house unknown, Cossack

Dearest Thomas. I am sorry to prevail on you while you are away on business. I hope your negotiations have been prosperous and that you have secured some fine trade while in town.

The truth is, I can wait no longer. There are questions I simply must ask you. I was not in the correct mind before you left and

there are details I desperately need to clarify. Your presence is much missed back here in Bannin Bay.

I should appreciate if you would let me know, by return, when I can expect to see you home. I am sure you have matters to finalize, but if I do not hear back within the fortnight please expect another letter.

She pauses, dips her father's pen again, then adds a final line.

I am alone and the house is one of shadows. I look very much forward to your return.

Your loving sister, Eliza.

CHAPTER 19

1887

The day the whales came there were jellyfish in the trees. The sky was dull following a raging blow, but even without sunlight, the waves glittered like fish scales.

Eliza had woken to find her parents' bed empty, sheets crumpled and discarded, the shapes of their bodies sunk deep into the cotton mattress.

She went to Thomas's room.

"We'll go and look for them," he said, pulling boots over his nightclothes, grabbing his father's hat from the stand.

Mrs. Riesly hollered after them as they trudged down the road. "You two all right?" Glancing back, they saw her body hanging half out of the window.

As they neared the beach they could sense something was different. Something in the air seemed out of place.

They crested the highest dune and were staggered by the sight that met them. All along the beach, stuck to the edge of the tide mark, were huge, black, bulbous bodies–skin stiff and distended, fins collapsed onto the sand. There must have been thirty of them, spaced out along the beach that morning. Above them gulls wheeled and dived; in the water, tail swishes signaled sharks gathered to feast.

Between the whales, two figures were flitting, scooping buckets of water in from the shallows. They were swift in their task, returning again and again to the whales. Her mother had hitched up her skirts and tied them in a knot at her hip, pale legs glowing like matchsticks through the grayness. Eliza had never seen her father so focused before and felt a strange sensation at witnessing her parents behave this way. She wanted to draw away, to leave them there, as if interrupting them would be to disturb something shared and private. Thomas disagreed. He turned to Eliza, the hat slipping down across one eyebrow. "We must go and help."

For hours they labored, with salt-chafed skin, trying to save the whales. Her father explained that if one whale was sick it would beach itself and the others in the family would do the same. They could simply not exist with one of their pod gone.

After a time they were joined by the men from the foreshore camps, who brought larger buckets and lengths of cloth for soaking. If they could keep the whales alive until the tide came back in, the animals could be shifted slowly back into the surf if they all put their might behind it.

Thomas was military in his approach to rescue, ordering the men back and forth, allocating teams of two to attend each stranded creature. The men did what he said swiftly and without question, even though, in physicality at least, he was nothing more than a boy.

In the afternoon the clouds piled into one another. Soon, the tide began to creep back in. They stood in a line and waited, watching to see when the water would come close enough to get the whales afloat. The waves crawled in to taste their toes, then swelled greedily around their ankles, and her father ran the whole length of the beach. On his return they could see his sprint begin to slow, until it was a jog, and then a walk, and then something less than that. When he reached them, his face was heavy. He shook his head.

"None of them?" asked her mother, voice wavering.

"I'm afraid not, my loves."

Eliza felt a sob lodge itself in her chest. She wanted to keep going, to push them back into the water, to see if they could soak the life back into the whales. Her father came to her and put his arm around her shoulder. "We tried, Eliza. That's the main thing. We tried to give them a chance. That's all we could do."

She had glanced toward Thomas then as the rain began to fall. His fists were clenched, his jaw tight, and on his face a look of sheer fury.

CHAPTER 20

1896

Eliza had found the dress sewn neatly into a calico bag, stashed at the bottom of a long-unopened trunk. Her mother must have done it in a bid to keep her best clothing from the mold. She holds it to her cheek, the material cool and stiff. She buries her nose in it and inhales. There: faint but hovering on the fringes is the floral sweetness of her mother's perfume.

Septimus Stanson had returned to Bannin that morning on the flat-bottomed steamer. Eliza pictures his linen-suited frame sweeping through the busy town. Eyes small and pinched, mouth neat like a guillotine, with his beautiful young wife walking demurely beside him. Min had come to the bungalow and told Eliza about that evening's dinner, hosted by the president of the Pearlers' Association. She'd be working, as women were often paid to do at these functions—pouring drinks, blowing on dice, seeing to the whims of every man in the room. But as a pearler's daughter, Eliza would be welcomed as a guest. Her uncle Willem and aunt Martha would be in attendance too. And while she could think of fewer occasions she'd relish less, the chance to be in a room with Hardcastle and the other pearlers was too good not to exploit. Where better to get the details she needs than straight from the horse's mouth?

Townsfolk watch her, eyes like skewers, as she makes her way through the streets. A woman of her stripe is expected to take a sulky to get about. But Eliza prefers, as always, to walk, battered boots peeking out from beneath her mother's green faille. In fact, she likes best striding for miles out of town, beyond McVeigh's mission house, then looking back at the bay from low red cliffs. From up there she can more easily rearrange the place, picking up folks like pieces on a chessboard and moving them into more satisfying positions.

The bungalow in front of her is as fine as any she's seen. Neat steel cables cross the roof then disappear into cement, shielding the building from the winds. Ornate white fretwork frames a huge veranda, filled with easy chairs and hammocks and woven mats from Singapore. It has been strung for the occasion with hundreds of paper lanterns, its boards polished so fiercely they shine like fresh-blown glass. The air is hot and speckled with biting insects. The gardens are bathed in circles of lamplight, and tumbling fistfuls of pea flowers flaunt their forms alongside the bougainvilleas and the jasmines.

As Eliza pulls on the French doors, voices spill into the evening. She wishes she could escape into it too, but instead tugs at the neck of her dress and enters a room crammed with people. Pearlers in tropical suits cast off curlicues of smoke from slim cigars. Silver trays burden the arms of harried servants, stacked with glasses full of gin and imported champagne. The air is thick with laughter and the tinkle of ice against polished cups. Many of the pearlers' wives—sensitive types that crumble in adverse weather conditions—have already gone south to Perth for the Wet. But there are still a few women dotted around, among them her aunt Martha, Iris Stanson, and a handful of others from the Circle. Gone are their veiled hats and high-ankled shoes. Instead, they parade in pastel gowns, strings of shining pearls at their throats. She looks down at her own dress, rubs her thumb over a stubborn crease.

"Eliza, I almost mistook you for the help!" A tight-faced woman knocks into her shoulder as she passes. "You really should not spend so much time in the sun." Eliza recognizes the woman as one of her mother's old acquaintances, although she doesn't recall her mother ever speaking warmly of her character. She is on the arm of a man who glides across the floor with a languid air of entitlement.

"She always was slightly feral," Eliza catches the woman mutter as she walks away. "Just like her mother."

She steps through the party as women laugh flutily and men pull carelessly on cravats their wives have tied for them. Some play poker or use loose coins for two-up. Beyond them, long tables are covered with thick embroidered cloth, set with crystal glasses, majolica plates, and hefty silver cutlery. Above them, a huge Union flag has been spread across the wall. On closer inspection Eliza can see its edges have been beset by mildew.

She spies Min at the back of the room. Black dress, tight over her bodice, long peacock feathers woven into her hair. She is smiling sweetly, draped over the shoulder of a gentleman so lost in liquor he can barely keep himself from sliding off his chair. She looks up and their eyes meet. Eliza gestures quickly to the door.

The lounge is quiet with just one lamp lit. Two stuffed chairs observe them from a plump Turkish rug. Min grins at Eliza. "Well, don't you look elegant."

"Very amusing. I think we both know I look about as elegant as a trout."

The walls are covered in framed photographs. Men in hunting jackets pose with glassy-eyed deer. In wide-brimmed safari hats, they nuzzle rifles next to slaughtered elephants. Eliza leans in closer to inspect pink tiger tongues lolling through long, white teeth. She turns to Min, who is fixing loose plumage.

"So, what's the plan?" Min asks. She seems distracted. Eliza supposes she can't be kept from her work for too long, not when men like Stanson have any say in it.

"Just keep Hardcastle topped up," says Eliza in a whisper. "Give him as much as you can. We need him loose if he's to let anything slip about his crewman."

Min nods, pauses, casts her eyes over her friend's face. "You know, we'll be much more successful in this if you go against everything your instincts tell you to do."

Eliza pauses, searches Min's eyes. "What on earth do you mean?"

"Well, I love you dearly but you can be quite . . . impulsive." Min crosses the room, steps one foot out of the door to check for passersby. "You're a passionate person—bless you for that—but you do often rush into things. You're led by your heart, you always want to *save* everybody and, sometimes, it can create a bit of a mess."

"I'm merely strong in my beliefs." Eliza is singed by her friend's observation. "And I do not believe I should be held back or act any differently because I am a woman."

"That's all well and good, Eliza, but you need to consider what will really get you what you want." Min moves in closer, lowering her voice. "If you truly want to know what's going on, the wisest disguise you can put on is deference. It will serve you better in Bannin Bay than determination, or passion, or guile."

Eliza blinks at the conceit.

"If there's anything men like less than an empty gin glass," Min continues, "it's a woman who challenges what little they have inside their skulls. They are stubborn buggers, these pearlers, *dangerously* proud; undermine them, press their bruises, and they'll seize up entirely or lash out like snakes." Eliza thinks of Septimus Stanson, surely the most powerful man in the bay. She remembers how one of the young pearlers had made a drunken pass at his wife. That man had been cast out of the Association without mercy. His fleet went to seed and he never fished for pearls again.

"Sit pretty, however"–Min raises an eyebrow–"and keep your mouth shut; they'll soon start talking."

Eliza turns it over in her head. Nods. Min goes to leave, casting a disapproving look at the pictures on the wall.

"And they have the gall to call *us* sand lice."

The dinner is a slow, drawn-out affair, each course laid in front of Eliza like a penance. She is seated with the women, including her mother's old acquaintances and the ladies of the Circle. Willem is embroiled in conversation with the pearlers, and Hardcastle takes his place next to Stanson at the table head. The two of them talk in low mutters, candlelight shining off alarmingly pink foreheads. She sees Stanson tap a cigarette from its box and light it. He then tends to Hardcastle's thin cigar before shaking out the match with delicate hands.

Min's words are still rolling around in her head. She can't help but think of her mother, how she had fought against her "place" as a woman. When they'd first arrived in Bannin, she had held court from their bungalow: dinner parties, tea parties, tennis, and bridge. Chess tournaments were lively, poker games tightly fought. By day she taught Latin to the children and the wives; by night she played Irish songs at her piano.

"If you want to learn how to hold your own among these men, you need to get into the mindset of a gambler," she would tell her guests. "Think one step ahead, never let your guard down, and always, *always* watch your back." This last line would get a polite laugh from the wives, who swiftly smoothed their skirts and reached for their white silk gloves. Back at their bungalows they'd tell their husbands of the shocking lack of decorum. Her mother would be whispered about. *A woman who simply doesn't know her place.* It never stopped her, however, from behaving exactly as she wanted to behave. Even her aunt Martha had surprised Eliza at times, joining Willem to regale the pearlers with their plans for their shipyard, discussing how the best divers might be coaxed to join the fleet, how they might acquire more ships from the Japanese chandlers. Eliza had always thought it odd that Martha, with her plainness and her lumpish qualities, had not found it crass to speak so openly about her desires. But a small part of her had envied her aunt's directness, her lack of regard for what was expected of her as a woman.

Eliza looks to the table. It groans with a feast of gluttony, more food than she has ever seen in a sitting. Plates of glistening hog belly, mutton chops, and slick, shining cherries, platters of buttery potatoes, and brimming carafes of madeira that leave stains on starched damask. Jellied-consommé slides thickly down her throat as the wives continue their talk of embroidery patterns. Fatty duck and rich buttered rolls sit like lumps of coal in her stomach. But she nods politely and thanks the wives for their platitudes about her father, makes conversation about the weather and the season's finest divers. On occasion, she catches Iris Stanson watching her eat. Under her gaze Eliza feels inadequate, conscious of her old, stiff dress and the dirt trapped under her fingernails. When the woman looks away Eliza moves her eyes to Hardcastle. He licks his lips and demands triple helpings. Min keeps his glass filled diligently to the brim.

When the main meal is complete, the dessert—an enormous trifle ringed with dozens of sponge fingers—is presented with a flourish. Thick slices of strawberry slide off from the top of it in the heat. *How on earth did they get hold of the cream?* Eliza wonders. When it has been eaten, and with a screech like a gutted quoll, Hardcastle pushes back his chair.

"Gentlemen." His eyeballs swivel in his head. "To the veranda."

He places a fresh cigarette in his mouth, before frowning and turning it round the other way.

A few men filter outside as the rest return to their loungers, more tempted by liquor and women than the sticky sheets of their own beds. Eliza takes a glass from a passing tray and puts it quickly to her mouth. The drink is cold and sharp; she feels its fingers around her throat. Casting her eyes around—it would not be good if she were being observed—she crosses to the back of the room and slips out into the dim hallway. Treading quietly, she crosses a long partitioned room, enclosed by fine steel mesh and full-length iron shutters. She pauses, waits to see if any footsteps follow, then slips out of the back door into the shadows of the fly-netted veranda.

The air is ripe with eucalyptus. It is dark but she tucks her body behind a post, keeping her breath still. From here, she can see the shadowy outlines of the men, the only light the tips of their cigarettes glowing like fireflies through the blackness. She can just make out the shape of the pearler Franks—all side-whiskers and drooping mustache—whose reputation for bedding women reaches much farther than the outskirts of Bannin. Next to him is Masterson, long limbed and stringy. His is a wholly dry business, conducted from his bungalow's veranda. His indentured men, however, must put their lives on the line to enable his fleet to thrive. She cannot see Hardcastle, but she can hear him at least, his sentences peppered with slow drags on his cigarette. She is nervous. Her ears ring so loudly everything comes in a minor key. What if she cannot decipher the words when they come? The pearlers have had a skinful, and dissolve, every now and then, into wheezes. She considers storming straight over to them. Demanding to be told what Hardcastle knows. But she must wait. Min was right. She cannot make a scene if he is to bring up the missing crewman. She needs to wait and see if the name Alfred will arise and confirm her suspicions.

The stars drift like ash as the men discuss the usual well-worn topics: which pearlers are hauling up after a poor season; which brothel girl has the most accommodating demeanor. It's only when she hears mention of the *Starling* that her attention quickens.

"Ah, the poor sod," mutters Franks. "He's been chucked overboard by his own men. Someone who wants a piece of that fleet, that's for sure." A Lucifer is struck and the air fills with sulfur. "He's got a temper, that Brightwell boy, I've seen them clashing heads before. Add in the predilection for opium and you've got a very troubled soul indeed."

"Aye, it's the devil's drug, that," hollers one of the men. "Would drive a man to do anything for a taste. That's where my money's at."

"Fight on ship gone wrong," barks Masterson, before drawing noisily on his drink. "I reckon some Malay sliced him and they're all keeping quiet. Don't want to wind up in the jailhouse like the old Aborigine." She strains an ear toward them; the purr of the ocean swallows the edges of their words.

"There's no evidence to suggest old Billy did it, though."

The men snort.

"You may laugh, but I'm right." Franks's conviction is thick.

"And when has that ever stopped Parker?" Masterson asks. "He's jailed natives for speaking their own bloody language before. Plus, you know he's got history with Brightwell." Murmurs of agreement. "Lock up the Aborigine and the case is closed; Brightwell goes unfound. And Parker would do anything to destroy Charles Brightwell."

She thinks of the newspaper clipping in her father's study, proof of Parker's unpunished crime. Her chest feels hot. Her hands are slick with sweat.

"What do you make of it, Hardcastle?" With this there is a long pause. Eliza holds her breath.

"We needn't waste our time worrying what happened to blasted Brightwell," Hardcastle eventually slurs.

"Why bloody not?" says Masterson. "We could all of us be killed by our own crews. Did you not hear about Tsutsui? His cook put

pulverized bamboo in his food. Horrible death that one. Slow."
Someone sneezes. "And what about Bruhl? They found him in the
end, knifed clean through his guts. Whoever killed him cut out his
tongue, and his fingers. Chopped off, they were. Stuffed so far down
his throat they found one in his stomach."

Voices swell from inside the party. Eliza hears the screech of
tables being shifted; they must be starting the dancing. The pearlers
resume their conversation at a lower volume.

"What a load of bull. Charles Brightwell was not killed by his
bastard crew." She can hear the leer in Hardcastle's voice. "They are
none of them capable of it. They don't have the balls." More clinks
as glasses are refilled and quickly gulped down. "If you went to his
shed on any evening after the sun had gone down, you'd see why
the bugger had been keeping quiet of late. What he lets his divers
do behind closed doors. He comes off all high-and-mighty, but he's
rotten in parts, that's for sure. Naaaaasty business going on there.
Disgusting. Worse than animals." She hears him pull on his cigarette
with wet lips. Another voice comes. Masterson.

"What about your missing boy?"

Eliza's eyes widen in the darkness.

"That odd-looking fellow. Glass eye, isn't it? Something not quite
right about him, sorry."

She waits for the name Alfred; it *must* be Alfred.

"Is it true some tong lodged a fork in it, that's how he lost it?"

"Shut your damned mouth!" Hardcastle's words come as a hiss.
"Don't be talking of all that here. I don't want Stanson thinking I
can't keep my bloody men alive."

"Well, it's going to come out eventually . . ."

"He's just a deckhand," Hardcastle says, flippant now. "No one'll
pay any mind to it; he'll be forgotten soon."

There are a few coughs as the men settle.

"Well, regardless, if Brightwell's out of the picture, then I for one am pleased to buggery." Franks roars with laughter. "Saionji's got the numbers this season. I wonder if he might be tempted over to the *Ethel.*" He sniggers. "My pockets would be fuller than ever!"

As the men announce their need for more liquor, Eliza pulls away from the veranda, skin cold and clammy. She storms through the party, blurry eyes following her before returning to their cards and their champagne. Everything moves quickly as men toss their heads back for more rum. Hazy women fan themselves in the delirious heat. Eliza's head swims as she pushes past, ignoring their gasped complaints.

"Everything all right, Eliza?" It's Iris Stanson, her milky brow creased in concern. Elegant hands reach forward. But Eliza cannot stop, she must get to the door. She cannot breathe.

Outside, the stars are watching eyes as she tears down the steps onto the shell-grit trail. In the distance, the sea shimmers under a fingernail moon. Something with heavy wings lifts from a nearby tree. Eliza startles then freezes as she sees a sudden movement on the path. Someone is there, looking up at the bungalow. She hears her own breath loud in the air, but as her eyes adjust to the darkness, the shape makes more sense to her. It's Axel, a spray of fresh flowers tucked into his buttonhole. He raises a hand.

"What are you doing here?" she asks, then: "I have to go." She doesn't wait for his answer.

He turns, but she has grasped her skirts and hurried away down the path.

"You look beautiful." She thinks she hears him say it. But she cannot stop.

CHAPTER 21

I n the shade, the man crouches, breath still as glass. *The crow watches on*
from a twisted gum branch; the bush will always shelter someone who
gives it all his secrets. It observes as the horses approach and the hidden
man taps out the steady beat of their hooves on the soil. Leaves shift under
his fingers. Loose dust breaks free and spirals upward with the hot wind.
Slowly the man lowers his body to the earth–his chest, belly, and thighs all
flat against the soil. With quick, silent movements he pulls deadfall over his
trousers, thorns snagging his shirt and tearing the fabric open as the men on
horseback close steadily in.

When they are just a few yards away, the pursuers come to a halt. The
white man takes a canteen into his hands and tips his head backward,
pink tongue extended. The horses snort in hot complaint and the hidden
man holds his breath in the leaves. The tracker leans away from his sad-
dle and spits a thick gob of brown sputum into the dirt. The flies claim it

immediately. The hidden man waits. The crow waits too—until eventually, with an impatient scuff of hooves, the pursuers move off into the old blood-wood trees. When they are nothing but a mutter of dust in the distance, the man slowly unfolds from his shady hiding place. He stands and with a quick eye to the sky continues, unnoticed for now.

CHAPTER 22

Her father's shed stands at the foreshore. Iron and whitewashed timber set above concrete steps. It had always looked to Eliza as if it could swallow a whole traveling zoo. She knows now, of course, it is only home to supplies and shell for grading and packing. She has not been inside its doors since she was a child, when she'd play hide-and-seek with Thomas, scurrying between dusty baskets filled to the brim. She remembers eyeing the drying divers' suits, empty as spent chrysalises, as she held her breath and tucked herself into the shadows. Thomas was exacting, stalking each aisle with merciless focus—hauling her out with tight fingers once he'd found her secret hiding spots.

Could something else be happening inside the same shed, now? Her ears swarm with Hardcastle's words from the veranda. *Nasty business going on there. What he lets his divers do.*

She strides toward it, the weight of the night on her shoulders. The cooler air has sent the townsfolk back to their houses, leaving the streets empty as wan light spills from the shanties. There's only the whistle of the breeze and the muffled clang of a few traders shutting up shop.

She rounds the front of the shed and moves toward its doors to slide them open. As she does, she notices a chain with a brass padlock at its end. Of course. Her heart sinks. What did she expect? She rattles the iron, the heat rising in her chest, threatening to escape as an agonized sob. She circles the shed. Pulls at the window bars. But she knows it's fruitless; the iron won't budge. When she reaches the door again, an idea grabs her. Swiftly, she reaches behind her head to pull a pin from her hair. It has an unraveling effect and the tangles slump across her shoulders. She bends to try and pick the lock, wiggling the pin this way and that, but it does nothing. With gritted teeth, she pounds on the iron and the opaque sound shifts a few bats from the trees. She turns and leans her back against the door, her knees giving way until she slides into the dirt. The night has firmly bedded in now, its charcoal cloak settling quietly across everything she sees. Her fingers itch. She's certain there must be clues behind this door—a letter, a forgotten weapon, a tryst between two lovers, something much, much worse.

Nasty business. Worse than animals.

She stands to begin the reluctant walk back to the bungalow, but as she pulls herself up, a half thought arrives. She shakes her head to rid herself of it, but it returns, a bluebottle circling back to meat. Her father's is not the only packing shed on this foreshore. There are others here too, four or five, owned by the other master pearlers. Hardcastle's shed is mere yards from where she stands. Smaller than her father's but there, no less. Who's to say it doesn't shelter secrets too? She glances behind her at the town and then down the long beach: nothing but dark waves pummeling the shore. The roof of

Hardcastle's shed cuts across the star-studded sky. There's no one else around. She makes her way across the sand.

She is astounded to find no lock on the door. There is no man more greed-driven than Syd Hardcastle, so it seems staggering he wouldn't keep his bounty under the strictest security. Perhaps he is as foolish as he is cruel. Perhaps *he* is using his shed for another purpose this evening. With a rattle, she pulls open the door. The shed is cool and dry, and the grit in the air clings to her teeth. It takes a moment for her eyes to adjust to the half light, but here and there are piles of dusty shell. Atop a stack of hogshead barrels, stockwhips and knives have been gathered together. She shudders to think of their use. The town is soaked with tales of the mistreatment Hardcastle levels at his men. How he orders his slowest divers to hang from the rigging all night until the sun comes up to save them, how he'd once tied a rope around a man's throat and dragged him through the water behind the lugger until he drowned.

She blinks. She can see clearer now. The floor is lined with boxes, each of them filled with neat lines of shell. She reaches inside one and brings up a large, flattish object. She turns it over in her hands, running her fingers across its rough carapace. Even in the dim light, its smooth inside glimmers like an eyeball, a swirl of pinks, grays, and blues. She pictures her father's lugger and its crew out on the water, the divers hanging from the ladder, shell bags around their necks, ready to go down. She sees the pump attendants sweating with toil, and the tenders, patient with divers' lifelines in their fingers. They'll wait, she knows, as the diver walks the sea bottom, as he uses his suit valve to increase the air flow and lift himself over the reefs. They'll wait for him to give a tug on the line, to signal where the shell beds are, to direct the lugger from the very bottom of the ocean. She moves the shell from hand to hand, wonders if any of Hardcastle's men gave his life for it.

The footsteps take her by surprise. They grow louder until a shadow appears in the doorway. She knows in half a heartbeat it's him. She can tell by the preposterous size of his shoulders and his ragged breath dragging its weight through the air. She ducks behind a large basket, gathering her skirts and folding long limbs inward, remembering those games of hide and seek, keeping her body as still as she can. Through the shadows she can see that Hardcastle is not alone. A woman cowers next to him—small with slender limbs. He has her by the base of the neck. She wears a black dress with something woven into her hair. Fear drips from her skin.

"Over there." He shoves her toward a row of crates. But she does not move. Instead, she stands glassy-eyed, swaying like a slaughterhouse animal. The woman moves her face a fraction and light falls across her features. It's Min.

"Well, if that's how you want to do this." He grabs Min's hair and with a wrench of the arm yanks her head downward. The horror in Min's scream is enough to summon bile.

"Shut your hole. Pathetic cunt. I said *over there.*" He raises a leg and kicks the back of her knees. She travels easily, crashing against the boxes and slumping to the ground. Her mouth opens and closes noiselessly. Hardcastle thunders toward her, and Eliza watches as he reaches for his stockwhip.

The shell creates a hissing sound as it skitters across the floorboards. Hardcastle's head snaps up toward the shadows, where Eliza sits poised with another in her hands. His black eyes scrutinize the boxes. While his head is turned, Min pushes herself up and runs toward the door, then out into the night's cool arms. Eliza's shoulders slacken with relief, but Hardcastle's eyes do not move from her dark corner.

"What's going on here?" he barks, making his slow way through the shell. There's no sign of the mastiff. Eliza is thankful for that. The dog could almost certainly sniff out her position, tear her to pieces, glory in the blood.

"Show yourself, poxy thief." His voice is measured as he strides toward the whips. But his hands settle on something smaller, sharper. He raises it to his face. It glints in a thin sliver of light.

"I've no problem removing your head from your body and placing it at the entrance to this shed. I've got all night. It'll be a good way to ward off the rest of you mongrels."

In the corner of her vision, Eliza sees it: a bag of shell has shifted out of position, just a few feet from where she crouches. It is overfilled, sagging clumsily to one side, threatening to spill its contents with ringing announcement onto the floorboards.

"Show yourself, coward. I'll lash your dick red raw with this whip." Now he grasps the stockwhip from his belt and brings the leather to the floor with a flick of his wrist. The crack rings out, bouncing off the walls like bullets. She recoils. The bag looks ready to topple. Slowly, inch by inch, she stretches her leg outward. If she can just prop it up with her boot, she can wait it out and stay undiscovered in the shadows. At least until Hardcastle gives up and returns to his liquor. But as she moves, her eye is drawn to something small crossing the floor. It's no bigger than her palm, but she is sure she can see its distinctive red dorsal stripe. Her blood scuttles. Those long black forelegs. She's seen them before, of course, every time hearing her father's words loud in her ears. *"Never underestimate a redback,"* he'd say. *"A bite can kill a man in minutes."*

With a flicker, the spider changes direction. Eliza flinches in response. Just a tightening of muscles, but it's enough. What happens next comes in what can only be a second. Just as her foot reaches its edge, the bag erupts, sending shell across the boards with a roar. Hardcastle's head whips toward it. He turns, and in the quickest of moments, is upon her.

THE DIARY OF CHARLES J. G. BRIGHTWELL, MASTER PEARLER

A breakthrough

I must confess I am finding it quite the challenge to write as my hands are shaking with passion. I fear I shall break the nib, I am gripping the pen so tightly! Oh, Willem and I have stumbled across something exciting. Something monumental, I might allow myself to believe.

We have been prospecting for a while now on the masses surrounding Brolga Island. While Brolga is large and home to mammals and reptiles (it must shelter several hundred wallabies if my records are accurate), there are smaller islets around it, many of which were used by the whalers years ago, but all have been abandoned now. I went there and I found something. Oh, I found lots of this certain something. You might call it a gold mine (if gold were as white as bones and stank to high heaven). It took several days, prowing the lugger through the channels, but I landed eventually on a mid-sized island, perhaps half a mile across. Even from the shore I could see it. Piles of it, everywhere, like white chalk hillocks. The substance builds up over thousands of years and in places rises to almost 100 feet high. Guano! Manure! Seabird excrement! Whatever name you want to give it. Gray and foul-smelling when laid; powder-white when it dries. White gold!

This could make our fortune: we'll mine it and sell it by the ton for farm fertilizer. I wonder if I might contact some of my old business associates in London. The Americans have been doing it for decades, of course, mining the remote deposits on the Chinchas in Peru and filling their ships to the deck beams. We must keep it a secret for now. Not even Thomas knows about it, nor Martha. But we can use this. We can use this!

Eliza Brightwell. I should have bloody known." He seizes her by the shoulders and hauls her to her feet. She is tall but she is no match for Hardcastle's form. Close enough to smell what's stuck between his teeth, she is aware of how easily he could overpower her. "I needn't ask what you're doing in my shed," he spits. "Sniffing around like you Brightwells do." She feels as if her legs might buckle but she won't give him the satisfaction.

"I'm not surprised you didn't want anyone in here." She thinks of Min, how she had quaked with terror. "I know what you really use it for now. I know exactly what type of man you are." He explodes with rage. She sees nothing but a wall of flesh as he brings his arm hard across her face. The room dissolves into a dizzying swirl of stars. Her ears bulge, as if she has been plunged underwater. She sways, numbed, eyes rolling in her head as her tongue finds the taste of warm iron on her lips. She raises her arms in clumsy defense but he grabs both her wrists. Before she can do anything to free herself, she has been turned and propelled forward until her body hits a waist-high basket of shell. She struggles with all her strength, straining against his grip, but his hands are claws. He grasps her neck and lowers her head, his whole form pushed up against her back. Alarm is a keening in her ears, but through it she can hear that he is talking.

"Women like you are what's wrong with this damn place." She feels his hot breath in her ear. "Lofty bitches who don't know when to keep their gobs shut."

She manages to turn her head slightly and sees him take his whip into his hands. With horror, arms pinioned, she can do nothing as he draws it taut across her throat, grips either side, and jerks it backward. The pain is white and hot. She tries to cry out. She cannot breathe, cannot see; the life is being choked from her. She feels as if she is falling. The pain is everywhere, throbbing like a pulse. The edges of her vision are turning amber. The hue of the English leaves in autumn. She thinks of her mother, following her off the steamer and onto red soil. Red. The color of foxes that would strut across the gardens back home. Hiding in the forest. Chasing her mother through the trees. She watches that beautiful face disappear and reappear. White teeth bright amid burning autumn foliage. Eliza can feel herself slipping away. She battles to stop the dark tunnel narrowing to nothing. She thinks of the beach at low tide. Mudflats as black as coal. Walking with Balarri to collect shells on the shoreline. She feels Hardcastle's stiffness pressing into her back. The smell of her mother's hair. Laughter like fresh flowers. Her father's mermaid charm. Precious treasure. Ned. As the velvet curtain tumbles, she feels Hardcastle reach for her skirt and pull it upward.

She is almost too gone to hear the crash behind her and the smacking sound that follows—the sound of something heavy meeting flesh. She is certain she must have died, but Hardcastle's huge weight collapses onto her. The whip slides from his grip and falls silently to the floor. With eyes wide, Eliza battles for air, ushering the redness away with each shallow breath. With all her might she shoves herself backward, pushing his body off hers until she hears it slump to the floor. Slowly she turns, gradually inching toward whatever is behind her. When she sees it, it is steeped in vermilion. An old woman, soft around the edges, a look of horror on her face. Raised high above her shoulder is a cane topped with the golden head of a horse.

CHAPTER 23

Mrs. Riesly is shaking. She lowers the cane and it clatters to the floor.

"We have to go." Eliza's voice is brittle. She steps over Hardcastle's prone body, the blood already jammy on his skull. Mrs. Riesly looks down at it, the wound a burl of meat in pink skin.

"He'll wake up soon. Won't he?" Mrs. Riesly whispers.

Eliza reaches for her arm and they stumble into the night air.

"My dear, are you all right?" The old woman's voice is urgent.

They reach the sand, the sea a gentle whisper before them. Eliza looks up through bloodshot eyes. She can see another figure now, rushing toward them. "Father?" she rasps. The words shatter the air into glossy fragments. The moonlit beach narrows. With a welcome veil of blackness, she collapses onto the sand.

Again, the redness. It is gluey at the edges. It yawns and burns and simmers. Voices come and go. Is it just one voice or a chorus? Is that a song? A face appears through the haze. *Eliza?* Warm wind pours in through the slats. She claws at her neck until it bleeds. The face comes again. The smell of hot coffee. Her mind slips into darkness. *Eliza?* Something tickles her face. White hair at her eyelids. In that half space between death and life, a little boy drifts in on the breeze.

She wakes with a start, the stink of salt pork flooding her nostrils. She is lying on a wicker couch and the room around her is unfamiliar. It is decorated neatly, with well-stocked bookshelves and vases of bright flowers positioned around the furniture. As she goes to pull herself up, Mrs. Riesly rushes in through the doorway.

"You're awake! How are you feeling?" Her voice is kind and Eliza feels a wetness on her cheeks. It burns at the back of her throat. Beside her is a bowl of water, in it a cloth soaked through with crimson. She raises a hand to her face and recoils from the touch of her own fingers. Her eyes, she can tell by only blinking, are swollen and stiff. She traces a large wound from her right eyebrow to the middle of her cheekbone. It aches. She is desperate for water.

"Mrs. Riesly, I . . ." Eliza's lips stick to her teeth. Her own words sound strangely loud in her skull. She experiments with a quiet hum at the back of her throat. Her shoulders sink. The hearing in her right ear, already patchy, has been blunted to almost nothing.

"Dear. It's Jean, you know that." She puts a small china cup in front of Eliza and settles into a chair, folding her hands in her lap. She is quiet but her face speaks its discomfort.

"I don't know what would have happened had you not found me, Mrs. . . . I mean, Jean. I don't know—" The words are salt dry and stiff. "I wasn't strong enough."

"Well, it wasn't just me," says the woman. "Your friend Axel—

a charming young man–he arrived just as we lost you and he carried you here."

Eliza feels something indiscernible in her chest.

"He said he'd be back tomorrow morning to see you safely to your bungalow where you can rest, once Doctor Blithe's been here to look at you, of course."

"What about Min?" The sudden thought sends panicked heat to Eliza's stomach. "Is she all right?" She tries to push herself off the seat but the small movement flings stars into her eyes.

"She's been here, darling; she's shaken up but she is fine. She's more worried about you."

Eliza sits back and nods reluctantly. Frustration swells inside her. She *needs* to be out there searching for her father. Not here.

"Eliza." Mrs. Riesly is rearranging her hands. "I must apologize to you." Eliza blinks. This woman just saved her. There is a pause and her face throbs into the silence. Mrs. Riesly clears her throat. "What my nephew did to you was nothing short of monstrous."

The moment snags.

"Your what?" The words rip through her throat. She grasps at the skin there and Mrs. Riesly leaps from her seat, putting the tea to Eliza's mouth.

"Sydney is a troubled man," Mrs. Riesly says. "Powerless to his vices. He's slower than most men in mind; he struggles to get his head around things and that angers him–he doesn't know what to do with those feelings. But that is no excuse for what he has done to you, of course." The woman's voice breaks and she returns the cup to the table with trembling hands.

Eliza's throat is stopped. She had no idea Mrs. Riesly had family here other than her husband, and even he was rarely glimpsed before he died. Most in town had her down as a slothful old widow–rattling around her bungalow alone, asleep on the veranda, mouth slack and open like a rock cod. Then, of course, there were the bizarre late-night walks. Although had it not been for those, Eliza would not be sitting here right now. Her ears hum with the horror of what Hardcastle might have done with her.

She scans the room: one seat with one squashed cushion, one book lying open on the side. This is a life lived alone, even if Mrs. Riesly and Syd Hardcastle are bonded by blood. When Eliza's eyes fall back on the woman, she realizes she has been watching her.

"I think he might have something to do with what's happened to my father," Eliza says tightly. "I'm sorry."

Mrs. Riesly's shoulders drop before Eliza has even finished the sentence. Her head nods slowly toward the floor. She stays like that for a short while, the air ringing with the military ticking of a mantel clock.

"I am not surprised to hear you say that," she says. She is trying to put conviction behind her voice. "I am sure I would think the same in your situation. But Sydney is not involved. I give you my word on that."

Eliza scoffs, but the sound comes out as a sob. The old woman reaches out a hand, then moves to sit alongside her on the lounger. She smells of cinnamon and salt. Eliza finds herself leaning into it.

"Your father and Sydney may have been competitors, but they were more involved in each other's business than you might have known."

Eliza frowns. Shifts. Mrs. Riesly's hands return to her lap.

"I do Sydney's books, you see. He's not so good with numbers because of the . . ." She taps her forehead. "I am aware of every coin that goes in and out of his pockets." The wicker sighs as she leans forward. "It also means I'm aware of any business arrangements he may have."

Eliza blinks up at her.

"Your father and Sydney were, let's just say, financially involved. They had their own arrangement of sorts." There is a pause. Eliza wills the woman on with her eyes.

"Well, I'm just going to have to say it, aren't I?" Is that a hint of relish in Mrs. Riesly's voice? It wouldn't be the first time a Bannin woman has worked herself up over town gossip.

"Several years ago, Sydney fathered a child."

The words bring folds to Eliza's forehead. Although she shouldn't be too surprised; it is not uncommon for the men in Bannin Bay to impregnate whomever they so choose. "The circumstances were not ideal; the mother was one of the young women from the native camp. I believe you know her father, old Billy from the *Starling*." Eliza swallows. It's like trying to gulp down an egg.

She never knew of this. Hardcastle, and Balarri's poor daughter. He hadn't spoken of her much before but this would not have been a consenting agreement. Her fingers go to the bruises at her own throat.

"A little boy was born. Alfred, we called him. We took him in and we raised him here. In this bungalow." Eliza's eyes bulge at the name. *Alfred.*

"My husband stayed with him mostly. Read to him. Kept him occupied away from prying eyes. The mother, I don't recall her name, she died eventually." Mrs. Riesly waves her hand as if batting away a mosquito. Eliza's mind is swirling. Alfred is not the missing crewman. Alfred is Syd Hardcastle's son.

"When he was about five or six, Sydney decided to sell him."

Eliza's breath stops; her mouth falls open.

"What?" she asks, disgusted.

"He knew an American gentleman had been nosing round the stations. Acquiring for the circus. Broad and Bartley's, I believe; rather famous it is too." The woman nods. Eliza feels the nausea grip her guts. "They were wanting a boomerang boy to join their Australian Cannibals exhibition." Mrs. Riesly says it plainly. "Sydney thought it a grand idea and they were offering a large sum of money. But your father intervened. Billy had told him about the boy." Eliza looks up at the woman. "They had an odd relationship, didn't they? Your father and old Billy? I always thought that such a queer thing. Well, it turns out your father couldn't stomach the thought of the child being put on show, so he convinced Sydney instead to send the boy to one of the large missions in Adelaide. He knew a clergyman there, and they had a good program for young boys. He agreed to foot the costs of transportation and paid Sydney a monthly sum to make up for what he lost out on from Broad and Bartley's. As I said, it was substantial." She raises an eyebrow as if Eliza should be impressed. "When he reached that total your father wanted to shake hands on it, but Sydney twisted his arm and he continued paying."

Eliza blinks, confused. "What do you mean, *twisted his arm?*"

Mrs. Riesly leans in even closer, as if gifting something precious. "Well, I never knew the precise details, but there was talk of some information Sydney knew about one of your father's divers. Cohabiting with someone he shouldn't be, I believe. An Aboriginal woman. He agreed to keep quiet if your father continued the payments. It's clear Mr. Brightwell doesn't want that information made public. He doesn't want the diver sent away. He'd lose his most valuable asset."

"A diver," Eliza whispers. Her mind goes to Shuzo and his dealings with the doctor. Had he been forced to Three Stones House to hide the proof of a relationship that was sneered at by the rest of the town? And what of her father: what other secrets has he kept? What else might he have done to ensure his most lucrative crewman could remain in Bannin Bay? She feels a sting of shame. The facts have a distinctly bitter taste to them.

"Anyway, Sydney was thankful for it all in the end. He'd even ask after the boy occasionally—considered writing him a letter once. I don't think your father ever knew of the boy's status. But he paid that money every month and Sydney would not have done anything to harm the transaction. He sorely needed the funds, you see."

Eliza's eyes are tight with tiredness and salt. Her thoughts have scattered like spilled marbles. Does she really believe this arrangement would stop Hardcastle wanting to dispose of her father? And if Hardcastle is not responsible, then who can be?

The two women are silent as the sound of the sea sweeps in through the windows.

"Why were you out there anyway, Jean? Why do you go out so late at night?" Eliza asks quietly after a while.

The old woman pushes her body slowly off the chair. In a breath, she's at the window. Watching birds dart about the branches. When she eventually speaks, it's to the slats.

"I could ask the same of you, dear. But I suppose we are both finding ways to cope with empty houses."

CHAPTER 24

With the sun tucked under the horizon, the surrounding bush is dim and cool. Moths bumble about in the half light and frigid stars peer tentatively in through the gloom. The crow had watched on as the man lit a fire–there have been no signs of those that pursue him for days now–and the smoke spirals into the air like skeins of gray-blue silk. The man has found ample water and food from the bush. He looks strong from up here, sharp, his ears attuned to every scratch and scrabble of the landscape. It must be a surprise, then, when the rattling sound of horses comes rolling up the path. With it, a flash of blue twill through the trees.

Parker is suffering, the scarceness of food and sleep exacting its toll. His cheekbones have been finely sharpened, giving his countenance an even more malignant quality. His uniform has become ragged, buttons dulled to gray by the blasted dirt. But however slumped his posture might appear, *you'll still find him atop his horse each day. His eyes will still rake the bush for what dares to show itself.*

With a sudden movement, the tracker raises a hand and the men halt their horses. Up above, a solitary wedgetail soars across the sky. The bush holds its breath. The tracker turns, raises a filthy finger to his lips. Parker watches as he swings down from his saddle and makes his way off the path, clearing branches and leaves with his boots as he goes. With their removal, a smoldering pile of embers is unearthed. The tracker lowers to his knees, feels the dirt around the fire with his fingertips. Once satisfied, he stands, raises an arm.

"He went this way."

CHAPTER 25

Eliza has seen men in agony before. Eardrums torn open; lungs bubbling with infection; hands savaged into suppurating lesions by sea snakes. She's seen the remains of men, stripped of their soft parts by sharks or crocodiles. She's seen men so weakened with scurvy they had to be carried ashore to die. She remembers dark nights when her father would rush home, wild-eyed through moon-shot streets. He'd install one of his divers on a makeshift bed, then tear across town for Doctor Blithe, who'd come and slowly shake his head. Into the blackness the divers would moan—joints seizing and bodies bent double, racked with cramps caused by rising too fast from the seabed. She had watched one night, through tightly strung flymesh, as one diver had wailed in the throes of paralysis. Her father was frantic, applying poultices to his limbs until the man began to fit so violently, he had to hold him down with the weight of his whole being. The men shuddered together until the morning sun clawed in through the lattice. When she awoke, everything was silent.

She had never imagined she would find herself in agony too. It's been seven days since Mrs. Riesly raised her cane in the shed, and nearly two torturous weeks since the *Starling* returned with its flag dropped to half-mast. And although Eliza, interned to her bungalow, wishes with every fiber of herself to be scouring the streets for clues, it is a struggle even to take one step. Every second she wants to howl with the need to be searching for her father. Every night she has faced the horror that he could be lost at sea alone. She has calmed herself with fabrications; tales of drowning men rescued by passing ships, of sailors swallowed by whales then spat out onto sunny shorelines. There was a story her father loved to tell best of all, about a storm at sea that had sunk a schooner with all hands but one. That sole survivor had been tossed into the water and avoided drowning only by clinging to a floating barrel. Back on shore the days ticked over and transmuted into weeks; the family believed the man drowned and began slowly to mourn him. It was almost a month later when he was sighted staggering along Sixty Mile Beach, entirely naked, scorched with sunburn, dragging a dead gannet by the neck along the sand.

Now, in the bungalow, a place laced with shadows, the mornings come with brazen birdcalls. They make Eliza's head ache–the fluid *hoik hoik hoik* of curlews, the chattering squabble of the crakes. They bring with them painful memories of her father. "Listen to that–*coo, coo*," he'd say. "You know when the shrike calls, bad things are coming."

On the third day of her confinement a kookaburra arrived. It landed with a flash of blue wing on the veranda rail, and for the whole afternoon set about its shrill calling. She had tried to shoo it away, rattled the storm shutters to dislodge it from its perch, but it merely turned its pale eyes to her and barked like a dog. It came the next day too, and she noticed how its feathers caught the light. The next day she slowly dragged her chair to the window and watched as the breeze ruffled the scalloped orange bars on its underside. When it came one final time it brought a frog in its bill. With a soft repeated *thwack*, it beat the body against the rail, then gobbled it down whole before throwing back its head and unleashing its cackle.

Axel had arrived promptly at Mrs. Riesly's, exactly when he said he would, to collect her and bring her back here. Without a word he had shouldered Eliza's weight and helped her home. When they'd reached the veranda, she had paused, not knowing how she would possibly make it up the steps. With a quick glance to check for onlookers, he had bent to reach for her legs.

"*Don't*," she had warned him, and he had smiled although his face glowed red. She had felt a stab of guilt then and offered him her elbow, leaning her weight more heavily into him than she truly needed to.

Once inside, as he helped her to the chair, she had felt the stirrings of something. When he'd bent to lay her gently onto the cushions, so close that their noses had almost touched, she had felt something warm take hold below her navel. He stayed there, eyes searching hers. She knew what he must have seen. Her knotted hair. Her filthy dress, bruised face. But he looked at her as though he found it hard to swallow. Her skin had buzzed expectantly. She could not recall the last time she was carefully touched, and was surprised to find she ached for it. She could have reached out and pulled him to her, felt his weight against her body. Instead, she closed her eyes and in the darkness, an image flickered as if illuminated by lantern light. A small child turned toward her laughing. Her eyes clicked open. Axel released her, took a step back, and coughed.

"Well," he said. "This is the place, then. A master pearler's bungalow."

Aware it was being seen by fresh eyes, she couldn't help but notice the dust eddying in the sunlight, the unmistakably stale smell of dampness and old incense. But Axel was entranced, as if it was the most magnificent thing he had seen. He stepped slowly past the piano, sweeping his hand across the rosewood, then made his way to the bookcase.

"This is quite a collection." He moved his eyes along the rows—most of them her father's, gleaming with bright gold lettering.

"Well, we are a family of readers," she'd said with a cheerless smile. Axel's eyes had flickered up and around the empty bungalow.

"And who might these two be?" He held a frame to the light. The bleached photograph was of two children, their faces smeared with mud. One child was no more than a baby, grinning gummily at the camera; the other, a solemn-looking young woman with a mess of curls. Eliza cleared her throat.

"That would be me, and my brother."

"Is that right? What a picture." He placed it back on the shelf and she could see that his hands were shaking. "Funny, though, Thomas is surely older than you are?" Eliza shifted in her chair. Axel looked at her for a beat too long.

"That is my other brother. Ned."

He had not known what to say then and so had announced his departure in flustered haste. He wished her a smooth recovery, recommending a few more days of rest and a saltwater gargle for her throat.

"Anything else I can do for you, Eliza?" he had asked before he left.

"Go to the jail," she'd pleaded. "Check on news. Any information." But when he returned he had nothing of import to relay. Parker had not yet returned from his manhunt.

Now, with Axel busy on the beaches, the air has thickened—so woolen even the flies hang suspended. Only Min has come, carrying steaming pots filled to the brim and glass bottles of bitter lemonade.

"Donations," she said. "Courtesy of Madame Riesly." But Eliza had no appetite.

Still, Min had smiled soothingly as she helped tend Eliza's wounds. They had spoken in murmurs of their parents—what Min could remember of her mother's smell. Eliza's first memories of her father. They'd talked about what might happen to people's souls when they died; then Eliza had asked Min what she missed most about her own father. "His voice," she'd said in a hollow whisper. "His hands." She described nails bitten to the quick, rough palms scuffed with prospector's scars. A burn in the shape of a five-corner star. "I don't want to ever forget them. Eliza, make sure you never forget." As they cried, the sun sent silky shafts in through the window slats.

Min had told her too that Hardcastle had left Bannin in haste for the stations; when his men went to the packing shed, they found nothing but a door left firmly bolted. They'd maintained he had left to pick up fresh crew for his ships, but she knew, everyone knew, why he had really made himself scarce.

"I hope a snake gets him in the bush and I hope his death is painful and slow," Min said one day with a quick flash of bloodlust. "Or maybe a scorpion. Or a spider. Which do you reckon's most horrible? Eliza?" Eliza had looked to her with a dutiful smile but she was distracted. "Whatever it is, he'd deserve it," Min continued. "Nasty pearler like that; just think of what he could have done to you, or to me, in that shed. Think of what he does every day to his divers. He's mad with, what's that word, *avarice*, that's it. Just like the rest of them."

Min kept talking but her words were smothered by the thoughts swarming in Eliza's mind. The ones she had tried, time and time again, to push aside. Eventually she turned to her friend.

"Do you think my father is a good person?" she asked.

Min blinked, kept her features calm.

"Can he have been a good person if he did the same every day as the rest of them? Send divers down for shell. Put men in danger.

Chase wealth so furiously as pearlers do." She glanced at the crescents of red dirt under her fingernails. "Can you do that and still be good?"

Min sighed.

"I don't know, Eliza. What can *good* even mean in a place like this?" The corellas screeched and fought outside. "Am I good? Are you good? Is it as simple as that?" She turned her face to the window. "I think I am both. I am my good bones and my bad bones. No one is all of either, whatever we do. Everyone's got something to hide."

Eliza had nodded, given a small smile, but she couldn't ignore the discomfort setting down its roots.

"I think this town maybe had a hold over my father," she said after a while. "I think it hardened him until he was not who I thought he was at all."

CHAPTER 26

She reclines against the cane, stymied and bitter. The armchair leaves deep indentations on her skin, and the bark of far-off hammer strokes fills the air. She pictures with envy the blur of activity at the foreshore–men scrubbing furiously at boats; paying deck seams with pitch; packing shell into neat wooden boxes. She thinks of the workers clearing barnacles from callused shells. Pressing tongues into their own cheeks as they slit the adductor muscle with a blade tip.

The days are growing hotter now, the air swamped with the loamy smell of mud and the bloated sense of something building. In the miserly shade of the veranda, the hours have swept slowly by, and Eliza has thought her way along the channels and across the rolling seas. She has imagined being a bird above, watching as the boats leave their anchorage, as they glide over reefs that slough their hulls like dead skin, passing mother ships and schooners, scattered fleets beyond bobbing on the surface. Around them the tendrils of mangrove swamps bleed like opened veins, and at night, when all is quiet and dark, the water coils as deep as a dreamless slumber.

She has wondered if what remains of her family will ever return to her, haunted by the shadows of those no longer here. She had managed to make the short walk to the post office, at least. At its entrance is a board reserved for the divers' notices. Death has been busy at the bottom of the ocean this season. But she had read the list of names twice and found no trace of her father among them. The boy at the desk–full of freckles and buttoned up in a waistcoat–had appraised her cuts, pursing his lips and swallowing his words. It was not uncommon to see a man in Bannin with flesh ripped out of him like a baitfish. A young woman of Eliza's standing? It did not happen.

There had been no letter for her from Thomas, the boy had announced, and her body had taken on a heavier weight. As she'd turned to leave, he had spoken again, the air whistling quietly through the gaps in his teeth. "Haven't seen you around much recently, miss." He gestured to the window. She could see, in the near distance, her own bungalow framed within its arch. "Not that I've been watching." He was flustered. "Just, can't help seeing you when it's quiet here. Everything all right?" Eliza had nodded quickly and turned her face away, in case he could see the tears in her eyes.

She has been back three times to ask if any message had been sent. Every time the boy has responded with a small, sad shake of his head. She will have to write to Thomas again, although she fears her last letter never reached him at all. The need to see her brother now is stifling. She has replayed that day, the one just before he and her father had sailed out for their last trip, how she'd prepared a late afternoon supper as the men took their place on the veranda. They had spoken in furtive tones, had they not? Or was it that they had stopped talking completely when she neared? What had certainly happened was that a magpie had struck the fly netting so violently that it fell to the dirt below. Her father had leaped up as Thomas followed slowly. The bird remained motionless, wings crooked and glassy eyes fixed open.

Now there are spaces opening up in her mind, and solemn thoughts are moving in. Her father must surely be dead, his body lost to the ocean. If he weren't, she would have heard something by now. There would have been a sighting, a message; it would have floated toward her on the tide. *The Uncorker of Ocean Bottles.* She has tried all the paths she can think of and has not been able to find answers. What now? She feels cauterized, squashed like a louse. Slowly, she rises and crosses to the window. On the shoreline she sees a small dinghy, empty and abandoned. At the corner of her memory: a flash. A boat on the tideline; a boy with white hair. Her skin begins to prickle. It starts at her toes and creeps upward until her fingertips buzz. Her feet move her body; although her mind wills them not to. She is weary but they carry her forward, slotting themselves into soft leather boots, taking her through the bungalow and out to the raw, scraped streets. It's a short walk to the cemetery yard but the sun gnaws at her skin. The glare of the water is harsh. She puts a hand up to shield herself against it.

When she gets there, the headstones—together, one big and one small—are neatly kept and clean. Their careful letters rise above the dry dirt. She looks around at the other stones in the yard, all that's left of mothers, sisters, and sons. Some are faded and unreadable, others shine like wet pebbles. There are sparse tussocks of grass on the ground, like a head that's losing its hair. Beetles trundle in meandering patterns around them. As she watches their march, she remembers the day, five years ago now, when her mother's pregnant belly could grow no bigger. That morning the needles of every barometer in the house had plummeted to nothing, the land washed in a cold light that set the boabs aglow with a strange opalescence.

When Eliza put her head out the door, she noticed only silence, for the birds had stopped their singing in the trees.

The family paced all day, waiting for the clouds to build, and that night, when Eliza and Thomas were abed, a sound of sheer agony came tearing through the house. When Eliza reached the door, she saw her father running faster than she had ever seen down the street. He hadn't had time to put on his whites and looked faintly ridiculous catapulting down the road in his bed shirt. He returned soon after with Doctor Blithe in tow, who looked about as pleased to be woken at that hour as a possum roused from its nest. The walls had shaken with her mother's wailing and the rain came too. It started soon after the doctor appeared and it spilled in a heavy deluge over Bannin. Eliza did not sleep. She sat upright in her bed, alert to every noise in the bungalow. Her mother sounded to Eliza like nothing more than an animal. A beast caught in a trap. It embarrassed her and, as the baying grew louder, as she heard the door slide open and bodies stream in and out of the house, she held her palms flat to her ears to drown out the sound of her mother's disgrace. Sometime very early in the morning, when the sky had not yet been stroked by the sun, the house fell silent, then shifted as if it were exhaling. Eliza strained her ears, waiting for the cry of the child. Instead, she heard something else. Something she had never heard before. Something so acute she had to hum to try and block out the horror. Later she would know what it was: the sound of a heart tearing in two.

Her father was making the most chilling of noises—a low keen that rose to a repeated blunt statement. "No," he remonstrated. No. No. Eliza froze. The very guts of her knew before the rest of her did. She ran to the hallway; the bedroom door was half-open and through it she could see Doctor Blithe leaning over the mattress. Her mother's face was still, her dark hair sodden. She was near translucent. Her eyes were fixed on the ceiling and the once-white sheets were stained a gaudy red. Slowly, the doctor reached down and pulled the sheet over her face. A glance at his pocket watch confirmed the time. As if ushered in by the horror, Eliza pulled the door open further. Her father was there, a tiny pink bundle in his arms, tears forging a path down his ruined face. He rocked the child and with every movement left and right he continued his whispered denials: two letters wrought with pain. As Eliza's knees gave way, the child began to scream.

With a collective screech, a mob of corellas passes overhead. It jolts her back to the present and she looks again to the graves. Her eyes cling to something at the base of her mother's stone. She blinks. There are lilies there. Freshly plucked and fragrant, just like the ones her aunt Martha brought her mother years ago. They can't be more than a day old. The queasiness creeps as her eyes linger on gluey sap. She reaches down to feel them, as if they might not be real, fingers brushing the suede-soft petals. No one ever leaves flowers here. Not for years. But here they are—bright and taunting, heads as bold as bones. Her skin bristles. She looks around for any departing figure, anyone watching from the shadows. But there is no one, just the lonely shape of an eagle making its journey across the sky.

When she steps back onto the path, there are men running at full pelt toward her. The breath stops in her throat. Shocked confusion chills her blood. The men are encased in a cloud of tangerine dust, but as it clears she can see each of their faces is warped with fury. One of them wields a broom high above his head. She looks behind her. They cannot be coming for her, surely. Should she try to run? The bungalow is not far; she might make it if she can withstand the pain. She casts her eyes around frantically for anyone else they might be pursuing.

There is no one else in the road.

Her ears roar; her feet are anchored to the dirt. The men close in. She knows she should flee but her mind is swarming. They are getting closer still. She can feel the rage emanating from them like heat. As they arrive she is enveloped in the stink of male bodies, and she squeezes her eyes closed to brace for the impact.

It does not come.

Carefully, she opens one eye, turns, and sees the men have passed by. They must have dodged her. She looks up, raises a hand against the sun. Oh. From this perspective she can see what it is they are really pursuing.

"Bastard thief," one of them shouts. "Bring that back or I'll slit your damned throat."

Above them, Grant's cockatoo swoops and hovers. She squints to see it clutching a small jar between its feet. The sun glints off the glass like a conspiratorial wink.

She watches as the bird takes up perch in a tree.

"That bleeding cockatoo has my pickle jar!" One of the men, dressed in whites, turns to hiss at no one in particular. "There's stones in there. That bird is a thief. A fence!"

Ordinarily, Eliza would find this beyond amusing, and she almost smirks at the prospect of relaying the story to Min. But something else is building in her mind. She knows this isn't the first time the bird has done this. But how does she know that? She shakes her skull to try and order the thoughts.

"Haaa haaaa." The bird's squawk is an unnatural parody of laughter. It enrages the gentleman holding the broom, who leaps and swipes at the bird most inelegantly. In response, the cockatoo turns its backside to the men and begins to wail a ribald shanty song.

The men roar in unison, but Eliza cannot focus. Her ears ring incessantly. The thoughts blunder into one another. They come in burning arcs. Explosions. *There.* She can picture the page now. She'd read about it; Grant's bird is accustomed to this trickery. But there was something else on that page she'd foolishly neglected before, wasn't there? She sees it now and it sends her running.

Soon enough she is bursting through the doors of the bungalow, ignoring the pain that sets her ribs alight. She rushes to the table, finds what she needs at its center. With shaking hands, she plows through the pages of her father's diary. She finds it, there, the passage about snides; the tale of how Grant's bird, the inveterate thief, had stolen the notes at the Kingfish some years ago. But that's not what she's after. She runs her finger directly downward until it finds her brother's name. She settles on the sentence she seeks, appalled that she had allowed herself to overlook it.

He spends much time at Hardcastle's camps. Often with the young deckhand with the strange eye. Winters, I think it is.

She slams the book shut. That's what she'd overheard the pearlers talking about at the party. The young man who'd gone missing. With the glass eye, they'd said. *Winters.* That must be the name of Hardcastle's lost crewman. And now a link to her family she simply cannot deny. The pulse beats hard at the base of her skull. She has waited long enough, held back until now by fear of Thomas, of what she might uncover. But now she is going to find her brother.

CHAPTER 27

The day is breathless. She feels its lack in her lungs as she rifles through the bungalow, pulling coins from the strongbox and picturing the gun in Axel's shack. She fastens her bag; her eyes go to the window. The Wet is on its way to them. She shifts her canvas pouch onto her shoulder.

When she arrives at the foreshore, she is sticky with sweat. He looks at her, smiles, grabs his hat. "All right then, off we go."

The road to Cossack is rutted and raw, and they beat an eager track through the dirt. Axel had hired horses, and they sit astride the two bay mares. The animals huff and stamp their feet if drawn to a stop. With back straight and stirrups long, Eliza has swapped her day dress for a pair of her father's pajama trousers. She has tucked them into boots, scooped her hair up and hidden it inside a wide-brimmed hat. Tall and broad-shouldered, she is certain that from a distance they could pass as two pearlers making their way south to trade.

If they ride steadily, it should take them three days. Their saddlebags are stuffed with whatever food they could salvage from the roaches, two bedrolls, and some canvas under which they can shelter at night if needed. She has relieved Axel of the Webley and it feels heavy at her waist. But she likes the weight of it there, likes the power it promises.

As they canter though hoary pindan wattle, the horses flick their ears to rid themselves of the attendant flies. The sun lays its warmth on their skin, whips the scent of wild pear and saltbush into the air. Around them, kurrajong trees show off their heart-shaped leaves and the jigals are heavy with big brown seedpods. They reach a trail, and it soon becomes clear it is not often used by humans. The dirt has been pocked with puddles and stamped into ridges. For a while Axel is forced regularly to dismount his mare and hack a path through the understory so they can continue unhindered. As Eliza waits nervously in her saddle, she is sure she sees twists of blue smoke curling through the trees.

The trail widens and the breeze hisses softly through speargrass. Here and there, wallabies poke their heads out of holes. Farther still, gorges rise high around them and creeks trickle meagerly from the clefts between the cliffs. Now and then she fancies she sees the shape of something large in the bushes—dark, unnerving shadows—but in a whisper they are gone.

She wonders how her brother will react to her arrival. Following their mother's death, Thomas's grief expelled itself from his body as anger. While her father attempted to reshape himself, to expand his bones to fill that maternal void for his children, Eliza would find herself tending to wounds her brother had collected from bar fights. She would know to confine herself to her room when he staggered in late from the dens. Her aunt Martha had eventually inserted herself into the situation. "That boy needs the word of Lord God for guidance," she'd say, rapping on sliding doors with her knuckles and shifting the Bible to the crook of her elbow. "*I can do all this through Him who gives me strength*," she'd announce. "Philippians 4:13." She had implored Eliza to join the Circle then. "The Lord will save you from this anguish," she promised. And, momentarily, Eliza was tempted. Anything that might assuage the gutting presence of grief. But her father had distracted her with work on the diaries, and over time she had learned to simply expect unkind words from her brother.

When the path narrows again, hoofbeats send the dust rising higher than the trees. As morning turns to afternoon, the bush stirs further beneath them. Tiny ground larks rise from the grass like butterflies. Insects screech, rats ricochet, and trees hunch haughtily as they continue on for hours. Eliza thinks briefly of bushrangers, imagines finding one swaggering astride in the center of the trail, holding a sawn-off carbine and a bulging sack of swag. Without thinking, she taps the Webley at her hip.

The rhythmic huff of the horses' breath is soothing, and in the languid afternoon heat Eliza sees Axel's shoulders drooping. She watches as he fights it but eventually his body slumps forward in the saddle, hands slowly loosening on the reins. It means he does not see the thing there, hanging from the tree, until it is too late. Before he can find his grip, the horse has stumbled and begins to panic. Unable to get its footing, it rears up on its hind legs, wide eyes rolling with terror. As Eliza reaches for him, he is thrown clear of the saddle and his body lands in the dirt with a sickening crunch. She draws her mare level and quickly dismounts, calming the horses and tying them together. She rushes to Axel, falling to her knees. There is agony etched into his face. She sees his eyes move up and over her shoulder, to the thing dangling there.

She turns and looks. Sees it for what it really is. Like a sack, turning on a rope tied to the branch of an ironwood, hangs the body of a white male. He is naked. Puffy flesh bulges around the rope under his armpits. His hands are tied behind him. His head lolls backward, blood settling like muck into deep lines. His mouth is fixed in a rictus sneer, and under his chin, his neck gapes wide. It has been slit to leak red all over his body. His eyes are open and accusing, staring straight down the trail.

Eliza helps Axel to his feet and he winces. They eye the man's body in horror.

"There are stations all around here," she says grimly. "It's lawless land." The rope creaks and turns. Carrion birds hunch on dry branches overhead. Eliza had heard stories about the stations, how over the years some folks had been complicit in unutterable acts. As well as exacting retribution on their own, some would corral the natives, keep them captive until the men from town would ride out and pick them up for their boats. The Lockyer brothers sold Aborigines to desiring pearlers for eight pounds a head, Thomas once told her. They'd round them up like cattle, burn their feet to stop them escaping, save the young girls for their own sordid uses and purposes. Eliza drops her head in front of the dead, turning man. In the dirt below his body, a word has been written. "Thief," it reads in wobbling crimson letters. She turns her face away.

It doesn't take long for the bush to empty of its heat. She had urged Axel to move down the trail, far from the slow-turning corpse, then to take some rest in the shade of a grizzled boab. He had fought against it at first—the man's distorted face seared into his mind—but the pain had worn him down until it pushed him into a doze. Eliza had forced herself to rest too; she could not allow sleep; instead, she replayed a conversation with Balarri. They were searching for urchins one day when the luggers had been staked down for the Wet. The men were spent, staggering in a solid mass toward the rooming houses. Far out at sea, toadstool clouds were building. Every now and then, lightning noiselessly illuminated their insides.

"How is it that you have no family?" she'd asked, nervous at how he might respond. He had paused, looked out to sea, and she was sure she had seen something strange pass over his face.

"I worked on them ships before I ever worked with your father," he'd said, as he knelt to inspect something lurid with purple spines. "Was forced to." He'd told her how strange men had arrived in the bay one day. How they had turned up as the sun rose, announced only by the rattle of hoofbeats and dust on the horizon. They yelled orders Balarri's people didn't understand. They had guns. They put chains around their necks. Not just men: women, children too. Some fought back, Balarri said, grabbed their spears, resisted until the end. But it was too late. Their homes were razed to the ground. Eliza's throat had tightened, her eyes fixed on his lips. She thought with unease of the pearlers. The crews they'd used to staff their ships. Her place in this town. The land her very own bungalow was built on. "I did have a family." Balarri nodded as his fingers grazed the surface of the tide pool. "My wife had a swollen belly; we were going to have another child. But that bossfella said the woman with swollen belly makes the best diver. He made her go to the water, made her dive deep for shell." His eyes had dropped to the sand then. "She went down to get it, but she never did come back up."

When Eliza comes to with a start, her hat is nowhere around. Her hair scratches in thick knots at her neck. She picks out the burrs and flicks them, one by one, into the bushes. The bark of the boab scrapes at her back and she tilts her chin upward. The tree is dripping with vines. She wonders how far its roots must spread. How long it's been here. What it has seen.

She takes the canvas from the saddlebag and fixes it between two trees to form a shelter. Then, she makes a fire. It's a sticky night; there are locusts in the bushes, and a nightjar flaps by in a blur. The fire sends embers shooting skyward; she takes out a billycan, finds a heel of old damper to eat. They'll be here for the night. She glances back at the trail through the clearing. The horses are still secured to the bloodwood. They scuff their feet; one releases a thick stream of piss onto the dirt.

From the corner of her eye, she sees Axel stir.

She jumps to her feet and grabs the slush lamp. He tries to stand but the pain stops him short. He slumps back against the tree.

"How are you feeling?" She stands over him.

"I'm all right, but my shoulder's in trouble."

"Let me take a look." She squats and puts her hands gently on his arm.

"This ought to be the other way around, don't you think?" Axel smiles weakly.

"Not liking your role as the distressed damsel?" she asks dryly.

"That's not exactly what I meant." He laughs. "I did some training at the London Hospital some years ago, so I should know one or two things about patching someone up."

She holds his shoulder in place and guides him into a standing position, then leads him at a shuffle to a log she has dragged to the fire. He sits gingerly.

"I was God-awful, of course," he continues. "Only made it there because of my father's so-called connections. We'll need to get something to hold it in place," he instructs. "I'll keep it still and see how it feels in the morning. I don't think anything's broken, thankfully."

She leaves him at the fire a while to see what she can find to hold the arm in position. As she rummages through the bag, a small green branch sways softly beside her. It shifts, rises, and moves forward with spindly legs stretched wide. "Goliath stick insect," she whispers, as it makes its slow way through the scrub.

She returns with a shirt she found among Axel's possessions. She kneels in front of him, parched starlight falling onto her face as she works.

"Eliza, will you tell me something?" His sharp features are pulled into a serious expression but he winces now and then from the pain. At length she nods.

"Will you tell me about your other brother, Ned? Did something happen to him?"

Her stomach tips. She swallows. But something about his eyes is soft. She has seen the look before and feels for it along the edges of her memory. When she grasps it fully, her body warms. It is the way her mother used to look at her.

She glances over his shoulder into the darkness of the bush. Takes in the trees, the dirt creased with historic exhalations of the land. Quietly, she anchors herself to it, takes a deep breath, and speaks.

"We were excited that day. Father had just got back from a long spell on the lugger. The whole bungalow rang with his presence, the sort of happiness that sings. I was fifteen, Ned was three; we'd been in the bay for just a few years then. It was hot—when is it not?—and we decided to go to the beach. Father made a picnic, curd sandwiches and plum pudding. I remember because he said, 'Might as well give the flies a feast.'

"Willem and Martha came with us; we did all sorts of things together then. We walked down to the beach and Mrs. Riesly waved, asked how we were. Everything was normal.

"I remember that clear, perfect blue. The sky. I shut my eyes against it and saw little lines dancing on the insides of my eyelids. I took off my boots and wiggled my toes in the sand. The sun was fierce, but Father had put Ned in a little straw hat. He looked so dear. Thomas was setting up a game of cricket. Martha and Willem were busy unpacking the picnic. They laid out a big blanket for us all to sit on. I said I'd take Ned to look for jellyfish on the tide line. He loved doing that. Would always squeal when he saw them."

Her breath catches in her throat as she hears the beating of a bat's wings above them.

"The heat was blistering as we walked, the sky filled with gulls. I held on to his little hand and it was hot and clammy. I remember how it felt. He loved to run, and at some point I let go and he trundled on ahead. I always knew where he was. I did. I could see him; his feet left tiny tracks in the sand.

"We came across a dinghy, just a little one left grounded. The tide was washing in all around it. It would only take a nudge to get it afloat. I looked about to see whose it was, but there was no one there; it was ours for the taking.

"The others were just specks in the distance but I wanted to show Ned the fish in the shallows, maybe find him an octopus on the edge of the reef. He'd love that. So I made him get in. He didn't even want to. He pushed against the boat with his hands. But I picked him up and put him in it. I told him it was all right.

"I pulled on the oars to get us out to the reef. Ned was more interested now, peering down at fish darting about. He was laughing, reaching, trying to touch their colors.

"I only took my eyes off him for a second.

"I heard a thud and a splash and he was gone. I looked around the boat but he wasn't there. I stood up. I couldn't see him. I *screamed* for him. I shouted his name over and over. I shouted until I was sure my throat would bleed. I jumped in. The water dragged at my skirts. I swam under the boat and down, looking for him, but there was just the sun spearing through the water. It hurt to keep my eyes open but I had to. Then, I saw something on the seabed. It wasn't moving, so I pulled my way to the bottom. It took a while—I hadn't realized we were out so deep; the current must have carried us. When I reached it, it was an old sail from a boat. I screamed then, under the water. I remember the bubbles shooting up to the surface.

"On my way back up, my ears just . . . exploded. Something inside them tore open but I couldn't even feel the pain. At the surface I looked desperately around me, searching for him. Then I saw it.

"In the water near to the shore. His straw hat was floating there. I kept screaming his name. My ears were screaming too. Just a wailing, high-pitched noise; it blocked out everything.

"In the distance I saw Thomas running up the beach. He must have seen us go into the water. Then, closer to me, there was something else in the shallows. I thought it was a fish at first, a dolphin. But it was him. Ned. He was there, facedown in the water. His hair, his beautiful white hair, was spread out around his head. Thomas got there before I did. Crashing through the water, dragging him out. I was shouting at him, yelling at him to make him breathe. He carried Ned to the beach and I just grabbed at his arms. Begged him to save him. I didn't know what to do.

"The others reached us then. Father took him. Laid him down. Tried to breathe the life back into him. I couldn't hear anything. Just ringing, ringing in my ears. Martha was covering her face with her hands. The noise got louder. I saw everyone shouting but I couldn't hear what they were saying. They grasped at him, beat at his chest, gave him all their breath. But he was gone."

Tears have left tracks in the dirt on her cheeks. Axel's eyes glimmer in the light of the fire as he watches her.

"Your ears," he says gently. "That's why. The ringing."

She looks away.

In the months that followed the accident, she would convince herself she'd done it intentionally. That she must have caused it. That somehow she must have *made* it happen to punish the child for taking her mother's life. The subsequent guilt was a physical presence. It erupted from her skin as rashes, sent her speech to a stutter if she ever dared to talk. She could not imagine how she deserved to eat and so her father was forced, for a time, to hold her down and feed her.

It is quieter now, the guilt. But it is there, always, the ghost of something forever in the throat.

She reaches for the shirt at her feet and takes Axel's shoulder gently in her hands. She slowly binds his arm in place, their faces so close she can see the beginnings of stubble on his chin.

"It's not your fault," he says softly. "It was an accident. Eliza, it was not your fault."

Without knowing what she is doing, she leans forward and plants a kiss on him. It is clumsy and ends up landing near his ear, and she sees him hold his breath as she pulls away. After a while he draws his face up. He is not smiling, but from the little wrinkles at the sides of his eyes she knows he is glad. Slowly, he leans forward and puts his lips to hers. She feels herself fall away and more tears spill down her face. There's no sound now but for the whisper of the wind through the trees. The grasses and the branches shift, continuing their silent dance under the glow of the moon.

CHAPTER 28

By the time they reach Cossack, the clouds have built to towering thunderheads. The hot wind wails in complaint and frail flowers have drooped their heads against the insufferable humidity. Axel's shoulder is still bound, the rudimentary sling chafing at his neck, but they have been able to ride at a fair pace, the two of them resting together in the night's darkest hours. Yesterday their bladder bags ran dry. Exhausted, they lead their horses slowly toward the town.

Cossack is tired and dispirited. Something gone to seed. Built on a long strip of sand, it's fringed by boulder-dotted hills. In the distance, dunes tremble in the heat. Before them, slick mudflats are veined and wrinkled. On the town's outskirts, ramshackle huts are fastened down with chains. A few stone buildings lend a pretense of solidity. But mostly, Eliza thinks, it looks just like Bannin Bay.

Momentarily, she is deflated. Perhaps she had pictured Thomas in his neatest attire, attending formal meetings with American buyers and the French. It was important that he came here, *necessary* that he did—in order to showcase glowing pearls on blue velvet, packing them off to the highest bidder with a firm handshake and a freshly lit cigar. But this place looks surprisingly luckless for a town that turns on the profit of pearls.

As they trot through the streets, the sun winks in through marbled slabs of cloud. They pass a wooden church, a few stone-built general stores, and a small Chinatown. They tie the horses up outside a fly-bitten boardinghouse, and the animals plunge their heads into the murky trough water. Eliza, handing the proprietor a few coins, asks him if he knows of a Thomas Brightwell who's been staying in the area. The man, in shirt and braces, a sheen of sweat on his leathery skin, simply shakes his head and shrugs, although she sees his eyes flit quickly over her shoulder. She turns to see a run-down public house, as becoming as a feral dog with an empty belly. Axel draws a drink from the pump, then offers her his canteen. She takes deep gulps of the liquid. It tastes of metal and stone.

"Where do you think we should start, then?" he asks. "He could be anywhere, I suppose."

"Well, I don't think we're going to have to look far." Eliza gestures to the pub just as a man bursts from its doors. He staggers heavily, swaying on his feet, upending a bottle and draining it with visible gulps. He hurls it to the ground in a crash of glass, then belches before stumbling into the middle of the road. He takes a few faltering steps before dissolving to the ground, where he groans and rolls onto his back, arms outstretched. They share a look before stepping over him and into the building.

It is quiet inside, airless and lowly lit. It takes a while for Eliza's eyes to adjust to the dimness. There are a few big-whiskered men sprawled on upturned barrels, clutching well-worn pannikins in desperate milk-white knuckles. Some snore loudly, slumped forward on their arms. Others mutter in shadowy corners. At one side of the room, a group of deckhands bark and pummel one another on the back. A ferret-faced man spits a wad of tobacco juice to the floor, then takes a pack of papers from his pocket and begins to lick sticky edges. Another with bony shoulders tucks his thumbs into his braces, while his head lolls backward, snapping up when the crick in his neck jolts him awake. The whole place is as filthy as an old, blackened lung. It makes the Kingfish look like a palace.

There's a young woman behind the bar. Eliza is surprised by her beauty. With red hair to her shoulders, neat pointed features, and thin lips covered in rouge, she has purple stains under her eyes and the neckline of her dress is low. At her throat sits a large, gleaming pearl. Perhaps she is someone's wife. It is more likely she is a whore.

She greets them with a fixed smile and only the briefest glance at Eliza's bruised face. She scrubs the insides of a tankard with a dirty cloth.

"You two ain't from Cossack." It's not a question. Eliza notices a fine scar on her top lip that pulls her face into a slight sneer. "What's your poison?" she asks. "Gin? Sake? Opium?" Her faded yellow dress gives away the shape of her suspender clips. She leans forward onto the bar and Eliza notices Axel's eyes go to her cleavage.

"We're looking for someone, actually," says Eliza. The woman raises a single eyebrow and returns to her cleaning. "Thomas Bright-well. Has he been round here?"

"Aye, I know the man." Eliza notices the barmaid smile to herself and blushes at the thought of her brother using the woman's ser-vices. "He's been staying in one of the lodgings. But I can't let you go back there, on account of privacy." She begins stacking the dull tin on a shelf behind the bar. Eliza bristles.

"He will want to see me. I'm family."

"I'm under orders not to send anyone back there, I'm afraid." She lifts her shoulders. "My hands are tied."

Eliza pauses, thinks for a while. "I presume you're being paid to uphold this agreement?" The woman stops her stacking and glances up at her.

"I'll double it."

The boards groan underfoot. The passageway is dark and cool, opening onto a small landing, off which are three bolted doors. The woman gestures to the farthest room, then turns to Eliza. "I never let you back here." She takes the coins and scurries down the corridor.

Eliza knocks but there is no response. Again, she raps with her knuckles and puts one ear to the door.

"Pisssssssssss off." The voice from inside stretches like glue.

"It's me."

Silence.

The visitors hold their breath until shuffling sounds and curses come from within. Then the harsh clink of bottles being kicked over. Eventually the door opens, just a crack. A pair of eyes peer through it, their whites shining.

"Hello there," Eliza whispers dryly.

Slowly, the door yawns open and Thomas is revealed. But this is not her brother, surely. The man demands a sharp intake of breath. He is gaunt and pale, dressed in formless trousers and a jaundiced shirt that hangs with cuffs unbuttoned over his wrists. Thomas has always been tall and broad and this sort of boniness diminishes him. But his wide-set eyes give his true identity away. They are the same as Eliza's—gray as pebbles and sharp as pins. The sort of eyes that in a man signify authority but in a woman are simply thought of as cold.

The air that flees from the room smells like sour milk sweetened by opium smoke. Over Thomas's shoulder, the walls are dirty, the floor a sea of uncorked liquor bottles. By the stained mattress Eliza can see a green glass laudanum bottle, half-empty.

She looks down as a cockroach, blue and oily, scuttles over her brother's bare foot.

"Thomas, what on earth . . ."

"Who'sat?"

The gust of breath is putrid.

"This is Axel." Eliza glances quickly at her friend. "He came with me. From Bannin. I couldn't travel alone, you know that."

Axel smiles tightly and dips his head.

"I thought you'd be home by now," she says to her brother.

"You got the letter, then?" Thomas squints into the light and rubs his chin.

"My letter, returned?" she asks.

His expression is vague, as if he is not really there inside his head.

"Axel, I'm going to help my brother clean up." She keeps her eyes on Thomas as she says it. "We'll meet you down at the bar."

Axel does what he is told, and Eliza takes a deep breath before entering the room. Thomas does not protest while she undresses him as a mother would. Nor when she takes a cloth to wash under his arms and remove the scabs of dried vomit from his cheeks. She finds an only partially soiled shirt and dresses him patiently. She orders him to rinse his mouth with water from her canteen and wets the tooth powder before forcing it in with a brush from the sideboard. He takes it and slowly moves it reluctantly around his gums.

"Have you heard anything of Father?" Her question is small and quiet. Thomas pauses his brushing and answers with a subtle shake of the head. Eliza feels something she was holding on to leave her grasp.

When he is in a decent-enough state, they make their way down the hall. Axel is tucked neatly into the corner of the bar, watching the outgoing tide through the window.

"I think we'll be better off on the beach," she says, leading her brother toward the door. She sees Axel notice them, but he does not follow.

She has to shoulder her brother's weight as they stumble slowly toward the ocean. Although small, she feels the weight of the laudanum bottle in her bag. She had taken it when Thomas wasn't looking. She knows men and women who've poisoned themselves with the same.

When they reach the sand, they stand there for a while, watching as the waves slowly retreat from the beach. As the water withdraws it leaves behind its detritus—upended shells and tangles of weed; five-pronged starfish and crabs the color of robins' eggs.

"Give it back." Thomas's voice is low.

Eliza stops in the sand and looks to her brother. His face is shattered by a sneer. He repeats the words.

"What do you mean?" she asks weakly.

"Don't bugger about, Eliza. Give me the bottle." The sobering effect of the air must have been almost instant. His hand goes to the soft flesh of her arm.

"N—" He scrabbles for the sack on her shoulder. She tries to hold him off, but he locks his arm around her bruised neck. The pain is blinding. Her feet push desperately against the sand, slipping. She's been in this position before, many times over the years, at the receiving end of Thomas's rage. The sea roars in her ears as she tries to loosen his grip on her throat with her fingers. Eventually, he stumbles and her lungs fill with air.

"I'll give it to you if you tell me the truth about Father."

Thomas's arms drop to his sides. He takes a step back from her. Slowly he turns his hands as if the palms might be covered in blood. "I'm sorry." He shakes his head in agitation. "I'm sorry."

She plucks the bottle from the bag and tosses it toward him. It lands with a soft thud on the sand.

"You know why I'm here." She tries to keep her voice calm. "You owe me answers. An explanation. You can start by telling me who Winters is."

Air gusts heavily through Thomas's nose, his face a picture of resentment. But eventually he sags a little, then his forehead drops into his hands.

"It was supposed to be over by now. It was supposed to all be sorted."

She cannot have heard him correctly, surely.

"I don't know where Father is." Thomas's head lifts up and his voice becomes more urgent. "I don't even know if he is alive anymore." Eliza's stomach plummets. Thomas runs a shaking hand through his hair. "It wasn't supposed to happen like this."

"He *was* alive, then?" The question is hot. It burns her mouth. "Thomas. He was alive?" She feels as if she might be sick.

"I don't know," he snaps. He seems confused. A result of the laudanum, perhaps.

She swallows her frustration. "Is Father alive?" She asks the question slowly, tries to keep her voice calm. "Thomas!" Her brother turns his face away. "You know, Willem, the others back home, they think you had something to do with what happened." She will provoke more information out of him.

"And you believe them? You believe Willem?" Thomas's jaw is clenched tight.

"I . . ."

"Of course, you do. Look, if we're going to have this conversation"–he smooths his hair back again quickly with his palms–"I need a drink. I need liquor. I cannot think straight."

The proprietor of the grog shop moves at an agonizing pace. Heavy-set with long side-whiskers, he has a face that the sun has fried like an egg. His apron is smeared with something brown and his heavy-lidded eyes avoid them as he moves. He appears to know Thomas's habits well. Without word he takes a bottle of rum and places it on the counter. Eliza scratches at her arms to give her fingers something to do. The silence is excruciating. Thomas counts out dirty coins and shifts them toward the man.

Outside, the fish-flesh sky has lowered and the air smells of mud as they walk toward the sea. Eliza feels as if she is standing at the edge of a cliff with her toes teetering over. It takes all her effort not to beat on her brother's chest. To claw at his face. To demand that he tell her everything. But she knows him. She knows she must wait for him to talk.

He waves away the sandflies and puts the bottle to his mouth. It leaves a trail of liquid on his chin. He pulls it away and shudders with the blissful intensity of the drink.

To keep herself from screaming, Eliza studies the sea. It shifts slowly in front of them, like velvet roughened and smoothed under hand. Questions take light inside her head. She wants to pluck them out and fling their heat at Thomas. Make him talk.

"I do know what they all think," he eventually says. "I am quite aware of that." The words hang in the air as he takes a noisy swig from the bottle. "Willem and everyone else. They think I want the fleet. That I somehow got rid of Father so it would all be mine."

Eliza says nothing. She has to let him lead this.

"That is not what is happening." He watches the sand as he speaks. "Well, that was not the plan, at least." He takes another gulp of liquor and Eliza's breath jerks. The air shivers and grim clouds on the horizon flicker with lightning. She is not quite sure what she expected him to say. To confess to his own father's murder? To wail and howl and beg for forgiveness? No. She knew that he would appear calm until it was too late. That was always his way. He turns to her. "But it is my fault that he had to go."

THE DIARY OF CHARLES J. G. BRIGHTWELL, MASTER PEARLER

The menace of whales

I must make a written record of what has happened today, because I fear those who did not witness the events will not believe them.

I lost a man. A good, hardworking man in the most unlikely, appalling circumstances.

I shall try my best to faithfully describe what happened below.

I have detailed in this notebook the hazard that sharks pose to a master pearler and his crew. We face threat from all sorts of marine creatures out here, from giant gropers to manta rays—so curious that they occasionally hook the great lobes on either side of their head to a diver's air line. But no doubt just as destructive are the whales that frequent these waters; mild-tempered leviathans who roll through the ocean with ease. Whales are enduringly curious of divers, strangely attracted by the bubbles that shoot upward from an air hose. At times one of them might even mistake a lugger for a fellow whale, and lumber over to the ship for a better look. Sometimes, while close, it will launch its whole body out of the water; shaking itself like a wet dog, sending suckerfish flying from its skin and onto our deck. I have had whales rubbing up against the keel to scratch away barnacles before (it is quite a task to keep a lugger upright when that happens), and I can confirm from experience that the whimpering of a lost baby whale at night, just inches from your ear, is a disquietingly eerie thing.

Whenever whales are sighted on the horizon, we'll set about banging whatever pots or tins we can find to rouse them off. Often they'll still approach and circle, but usually we've had enough time to haul our divers out to safety by the time they arrive.

Today, I gave the call to rise early. We had set in to fish just off the Cockatoos, when two large humpbacks came barreling toward The Starling. We could see their stony eyes, the nobbled barnacles on their heads. Kurayami and my second diver, Nishioka, relaxed with a cheroot on deck until the whales moved on. By late afternoon, all was clear and the two divers descended as planned to 16 fathoms. But as Nishi later recounted, he was suddenly jerked off his feet by an unseen force. Then, a powerful tug on his lifeline lifted him way up into the water. Through the Stygian gloom he caught the pale flash of a whale's underbelly, and saw, with horror, his own lifeline tangled around its right fluke. On the surface, the tender braced with the lifeline hissing through his fingers. The beast's tail thrashed and spasmed until the line eventually slipped off and Nishi was dropped, clawing and kicking, to the sea floor.

Meanwhile, the maddened whale must have turned and plunged against Kurayami's air line instead, and with every thump of that gargantuan tail, his airpipe became more and more ensnared. Eventually he was lifted clean off the seabed too. The humpback twisted and lurched—that's 45 tons of muscle and blubber tearing through the water—and tossed the helpless diver around on its mighty tail. We watched as the surface heaved in fractured waves and the sunlight glistened, just for a second, upon a huge black body. Nishi signaled frantically, shut tight his air-escape valve, and shot like a cork to the surface. But Kurayami, still snagged on the leviathan's tail, was being towed through the water with alarming velocity. What terror he must have felt, that poor, poor soul. Suddenly, we felt an almighty wrench as the airpipe reached its limit. The hose must have been torn from the helmet then; the whale bolted, and the ocean rushed in to claim Kurayami. He sank like a trunk as we desperately hauled him in. By the time we got him to us, it was too late. My good Kurayami was gone.

CHAPTER 29

The air is even denser now; thick as soup it boils and broods. Terns skim low over the water, letting out long metallic cries. From out at sea, rollers storm onto the beach and collapse into froth.

"It happened one night a couple of months back," says Thomas coldly. "On the foreshore, by the boat sheds. Someone saw us, evidently."

She frowns and tries to meet his gaze. His face is tight. He looks away from her.

"We had to meet there whenever her husband was in town. She'd always said if he ever found out he'd have both our necks slit."

Eliza shakes her head. His words swill about the air, ungraspable.

"Men wet their cocks in Bannin's brothels without so much as a raised eyebrow. Or else they take what they feel they deserve by force. But there can be *no* greater crime than interfering with the wife of the most powerful man in town." He says it with the mock authority of an officer but his voice cracks.

"Thomas, no."

"Inclined to disown me? It wouldn't surprise me. Purity, monogamy, Christianity. That's what they say at the Circle. Am I wrong?"

"Thomas, I–I don't understand. Not Parker's wife, surely?" She pictures the round, lumpish woman from the sergeant's pendant.

"Stanson," he says plainly, blinking. "Septimus Stanson; we've had to hide it from him for months."

The words fall into place, pieces of a puzzle fitting silently together in her mind. "The woman is *Iris Stanson*? Good God." Eliza's heart plummets. Septimus Stanson is not a man to be toyed with. She remembers Min's words about the pearlers: *Undermine them and they'll lash out like snakes.* She wonders how long her brother has been involved with the man's wife. She's older, certainly, but undeniably beautiful. She'd always appeared so out of place next to her small, cruel husband. Then the memory comes, of Iris Stanson watching her so intently at the dinner party. Had she been wondering then exactly how much Eliza knew?

"But how can that have anything to do with Father being gone? Where is he?"

Thomas sighs, takes a long sip of liquor, sets his jaw tight. "We were always careful. We didn't know we'd been seen until Father received a letter. It was from an anonymous sender, of course; the watermark had been torn off and they must have disguised the hand; it wasn't one we recognized." He runs his palm across his mouth. "It said they had seen Thomas Brightwell attack Iris Stanson at the packing sheds. They had the precise date and the precise time that the crime had been witnessed. Said they'd tell her husband, as well as the constables, the whole bay, unless Father abandoned his fleet and left Bannin immediately."

She cannot fight the sensation of falling.

"I was to go too. If I stayed, people would expect me to take on the fleet. They wanted both of us out; with Father gone from the shelling game there would be beds to plunder. Huge sums of money to be made, just plugging that gap."

"But . . . you didn't accost her," Eliza says. "Did you?"

"Who do you think I am, Eliza? For Christ's sake," he hisses. She nods quickly, trying to ignore the fact that he only recently had his arm around her throat.

"We've been . . . meeting for a while. I am in love with her. It's pathetic, really."

"Then she would explain that to her husband, would she not? You've done nothing wrong in the eyes of the law, they cannot jail you for adultery . . ."

Thomas sends the air though his nose at a shunt. "Your naivete is maddening, Eliza. Truly it is." He turns sharply to her. "Do you think Stanson would rather appear a cuckolded coward or a husband out for blood from the man who defiled his wife?" Something hot creeps slowly up her neck. "He has a reputation to uphold, and the ear of every officer and magistrate for miles. What Septimus Stanson says, goes." *That's right*, she thinks. *It does.* He'd had that other man cast out of the Association for merely leering at his wife.

"I'd be jailed and Father would be shunned from the Association. It would ruin the family. Everything. Every single thing we've built here, after all that's happened."

"But she would support you, surely." Eliza's words are tumbling out. "She would say that no attack took place."

"You would think that." He draws on the drink. "But it seems that's not the case. She cut things off as soon as I told her about the letter. Said she'd side with her husband if anything came out. She has a reputation to maintain too, apparently."

Eliza is surprised to feel a coil of anger take light in her stomach.

"How could you do something that puts so many people in danger, including yourself? How could you be so reckless?"

Thomas glares at her. Eyes ready to do battle. "Well, you wouldn't know, would you, Eliza, because you have never suffered the inconvenience of desire."

The words sting and she recoils slightly. Neither says anything for a while. In front of them, a hermit crab makes its slow way over tiny dunes.

"So Father just left?" She prises the silence open.

"He was in anguish," Thomas says quietly after a while. "He fought it, hard. He didn't want to leave you. But he knew that if he didn't, at least for a while, they would make true on their threat. I told him it didn't matter, that I would face the punishment even though I wasn't guilty. We argued, every night on the lugger. But you know him, Eliza. He had to protect his family and go."

Her mind goes to Parker's cruel face. The sergeant's brow so heavy it almost demands holding up. She pictures the newspaper clipping she found in her father's study. Parker would take whatever opportunity he had to get one up on Charles Brightwell; throwing his son in jail would be a fine victory.

After a long pause she asks the question that has been slowly taking form.

"Why did you lie to me then?" Thomas's eyes close. The wind buffets the shearwaters above. "You could have told me. I would have helped you. Both of you, but you chose to lie."

"You know why." His tone is sharp. "It's not exactly something I'd sing through the streets, Eliza. The fewer people that knew, the lesser the risk of word getting out. You're included in that. I'm sorry, but you are." The words singe. "And Father, he wanted to protect you from all of this mess." He shifts position as his voice becomes more urgent. "Knowing it would have made you vulnerable. You might have done something rash. Gone to the constables about the blackmail. Tried to save the day, like you always do."

She winces at the betrayal. "How could you let me think that he was dead, then? And what about Balarri? He'll be hanged if Parker finds him."

Thomas takes a long breath in. When he speaks, the weight has vanished from his words. "We had a plan." He shakes his head as if trying to dislodge something. "He was going to return to Bannin eventually."

She whips her head to him, frowns.

"If we could make it look like Father had been injured or that he'd fallen overboard while drunk, no one would be blamed; it would simply be a terrible accident, right? And he'd be out of Bannin Bay, so we would have done what they wanted." Eliza's heart is a drum, beaten out of time. "We needed someone to help get him off the ship unnoticed, to meet him with a dinghy; we couldn't use the *Starling*'s. Winters agreed to do it." His eyes drop to the sand.

"Winters," Eliza whispers. That's how Hardcastle's missing deckhand fits into all of this.

"The boy . . . looks up to me." Eliza remembers her father's diary. *The poor chap appears to follow Thomas around like a lovesick puppy.* "I shared the details of the letter with him, in the strictest confidence. He said he would help however he could. He truly wanted to help, really." She feels a flood of shame for the boy, embroiled in something that was not at all of his making.

"They had lanterns," Thomas continues. "There were no other luggers for miles, no wind forecast. It was supposed to be a good night to be out in a dinghy." Shuzo's words ring in her ears; how he had seen "two lights on the water, glowing like the eyes of a demon."

"We'd agreed they'd go straight to the Rosellas. They're a small set of islands, not too far from the Lucettes, just a few hours in the boat if they stuck in the right direction. He knew there was water there to sustain them both for a while. They could fish for barra with a line, lure crabs from the mud, build a shelter. I only needed a week–two at the most–and then I would go and retrieve them in the *Starling*."

"*A week?* You thought a week would be long enough to keep them happy? When they wanted you and Father gone for good?" Her frustration is getting the better of her. "And what on earth were you going to do here? Just wait around and give your liver a hiding?"

"Of course not." He casts her a barbed glance. "The blackmail letter bore a Cossack postmark. I suppose the fool hadn't thought well enough to disguise that. So I sailed straight here to make some inquiries, being as careful as I could, of course–there are many secrets to be snatched from the walls of these gambling halls. We'd agreed that I would try to secure a sale for one or two of the luggers under another name, if I could. We hoped that once I'd uncovered the blackmailer's identity, they would be appeased with that; it's the sort of money that could set them up for life. We had no other way to get it–Father is still struggling with debts–but if we could, no one in Bannin would ever have to know and we could return."

Eliza's mind is reeling. How could they ever have thought that this was a good idea? How foolish they'd been. "Well, what happened?" she asks urgently. "Were you able to find the blackmailer? Where is Father now?"

Thomas's head sinks. "My inquiries were met with sealed lips and locked doorways." His cheeks tense. "My efforts to arrange the sales of the luggers were unsuccessful. I was able to build up a sum of money in the gambling halls. But I was followed, late one night, and relieved of my winnings."

"But you went to get them anyway. Father and Winters, Thomas. Yes? Where are they now?"

"I went, of course I went." He is talking quickly. "But there was no trace of them. I circled all of the Rosellas, went ashore, scoured every inch of soil. They weren't there."

Eliza's mouth falls open. She leaps up from the sand, appalled. "You didn't try hard enough," she hisses. The anger makes her chest shake. "You gave up on them, like you always give up."

"What is that supposed to mean?"

"Why did you not search farther? Extend your course? What if they'd been thrown off position by the wind?"

"Eliza, don't be ridiculous. The ocean is vast—if they were thrown off course, they will have drowned. I couldn't risk it, or risk wrecking the lugger, with the weather coming in."

"The *weather*?" She pauses. The realization comes like a heavy weight dropped on the sand. It is a miracle it didn't arrive sooner.

"You didn't try because you knew that if he were actually gone then you could take the fleet. Did you do this with her, with Stanson's wife, deliberately?"

"Eliza. No. That is not true." His words are slow.

"You've always wanted it," she spits. "You always thought he was too soft." Disgust sends her back and forth across the sand. "How *could* you?"

"*ELIZA!*" He leaps up. His voice a roar now. "That is simply not true. I searched every one of those islands. It wasn't safe to go farther and would have been fruitless to do so. They are gone. I wish that wasn't the case, but there is nothing we can do about it now."

"I'm going to find him, then." She says it, plain as stone.

"Eliza."

"If you are not enough of a man to go out there and search for your father, who did all of this just to save *you*—"

"To save the family business."

"Because of a reckless mistake that *you* made." Her head feels like an ant's nest; it scritches and jitters. She tries to claw past the mess, to find a way through, to think clearly. "I have no option but to go myself."

"I will come with you, then." He sighs.

"I don't want you there. I cannot trust you."

"Eliza. Do not be so ridiculous. You cannot sail. You'll be wrecked. Just . . . searching for a corpse."

"He's. Not. Dead."

Thomas pauses. Looks to her as if she is touched in the head.

"I was told by someone in Bannin, someone who can see these things. He's not dead."

"Who told you that?"

"Someone Min knows; it doesn't matter."

"Not that whore psychic." His face is full of disgust. "You are *preposterous*, Eliza."

"She said that he is alive and that he is surrounded by birds. She saw birds everywhere." She does not care anymore if she sounds ridiculous.

"Good Lord," Thomas spits. "You're even more deluded than I thought. Look around you, Eliza," he shouts, and spreads his arms wide. "There are bloody birds everywhere. Any hackneyed old whore would have said that for coin."

"It wasn't like that."

"You are risking your life and risking the ruin of an asset by doing this."

She stops, folds her arms. "You see," she says through gritted teeth, "that's just the problem; you see life merely as a collection of assets. You see those around you as pawns—you used Winters's affections to send him out into a dangerous situation and now he's lost too." She turns to make her way back toward the town. Spirit lamps burn in shadowy porches and the murmur of men spills out from the gambling halls.

"I'm going out there," she calls back to him. "I'm going to find him."

CHAPTER 30

D rain a mangrove of its water and it will still thrum with life. When the tide pulls backward, snatching shells, stones, and crabs, when its tangled roots are left exposed, slick and glistening like organs—life continues in the wet hotness of its belly. Paw at the flesh of that mangrove, take great clods of mud in your hands, and you'll see that eventually it spits out its secrets for you.

On their arrival back in Bannin—having pushed their horses at a sprint through two days and nights—the whole town seems to be craning their necks skyward. Surely the rain will come soon, but for now it waits in low, furious clouds.

Thomas had watched as they set off at first light, as the long-necked cormorants collected in a gust at the wharf. Eliza had glanced back and the thought had arrived that if she did not return from searching for her father, or if Thomas found his way back to the bottom of more bottles, she might not see her brother again.

She had gone first to the jailhouse, rushed there in a flurry of dust and sweat. What news was there of Balarri? Might she find him in one of the cells? But when she got there the place was empty. She asked the deputy for news, for the whereabouts of Parker. He simply looked at her with dull gray eyes and gestured out to the bush beyond. "Still out there," he said. "Still stalking."

Min's cottage slouches on its stumps, tightly fastened shutters as blank as eyelids sewn shut. Around it slump broken-backed cottages that no one has paid much mind to since they were flattened by the last nor'wester. Trees graze their fingertips across the old rusting roof, and galahs–feathers blood-red from rolling in pindan soil–drag their bodies over iron to gobble up bugs. The whole place seems eerily quiet, but Eliza knocks impatiently. No answer. She tries again. There's a scuffle on the roof and the birds flee and titter, wings beating a loud chorus above her head. Slowly, something moves inside the cottage and there comes with it a long, metallic sound. Eliza steps backward to see Min, hair tangled, eyes small with sleep, propping open one of the shutters.

"What are you doing waking me up at this hour, Brightwell?" Min pushes her hair from her face and squints into the midday sun.

Eliza waves and Min ducks back inside, eventually emerging and closing the door behind her. Her skin is paler than Eliza has seen it and she pulls her shawl tight around her shoulders despite the heat. A shimmer of gold thread catches Eliza's eye. They take a seat on two wicker loungers yawning with holes.

"I looked for you," says Min. "Waited at the bungalow for hours, gave up eventually." She shields her eyes with a palm. "Where were you?" There's irritation in her voice.

"We left quickly. I'm so sorry." She tells Min about the ride to Cossack. The state in which she found Thomas, and in a low whisper–in case the wind has ears–the secrets he revealed.

Min lets out a low whistle. "Astonishing. But if Stanson's involved, you're right to be cautious."

"You cannot tell *anybody*."

"Who do you think I am, Jean Riesly?" Her smile is tight, but her eyes have softened.

It's a picture, Eliza realizes, with brushstrokes of pity.

"Your father, then." She frowns. "He just left you? Just like that?"

Eliza straightens uncomfortably.

"What are you going to do?" Min asks.

"That's why I'm here. I've come to say goodbye."

Min looks around her, as if searching the trees for an explanation.

"I'm going to go out there and find him. Find them both, my father and Winters, if I can."

Min's mouth gapes open. Eliza grasps her hands.

"He's alive, Min, I feel it in my *bones* that he's alive. Clementine said so too, didn't she? And if he is, if he has been blown off course–Shuzo said there was a strong wind that night–then he has been let down in the most appalling of ways."

Min's mouth moves but she cannot seem to summon any words.

"Balarri's still out in the bush," Eliza continues animatedly, "pursued by Parker and his tracker. If I can find my father and bring him back, he'll *have* to call off that search. I'm sure of it."

"And where exactly are you going to go?" Min's voice is incredulous. It surprises Eliza. "You could be searching for months and never find him. This is not the heroic gesture you think it is. The ocean is bigger than we can even imagine, Eliza. You could die out there; the storms will hit soon!" Eliza looks up at the clouds. A paint pot of navy, gray, and yellow has been spilled across the sky, then smeared down its length with a colossal thumb.

"I know it sounds absurd, but if we can get out to the Rosellas, we can make a base from which to search the nearest islands. There are two sets: one to the southwest, the Nevermores; one to the northwest, the De Vitts. Depending on which way the wind was blowing, they could have ended up on either. Axel and I have already marked them on the map. We just have to get there as soon as we can."

Min lets out a long sigh. "It's a bloody death wish, Eliza. You don't know how to sail a lugger. I mean, it's ridiculous–really."

"Axel can sail."

Min gives her a sidelong look. Then sags a little. After a while she pulls a cigarette out of its box. "I don't suppose anything I can say will stop you?"

Eliza shakes her head and Min leans back in her chair. They sit in silence as the sun warms their skin. After a time, Eliza notices her friend seems restless. She knows she has something else to say.

"Go on."

Min finishes the cigarette and tosses it to the ground. She lets out a frustrated huff, then speaks quickly. "If you're going to go out there, I need to tell you something."

Eliza waits for her to continue.

"I wasn't going to say anything because I didn't know you were going to do . . . *this*." She gestures to the air.

Eliza wills her to speak quicker.

"The truth is"–Min's face is strangely scrunched up–"Clementine is a grifter. She's a con artist. Those teeth are just a show for customers."

Eliza's breath catches.

"The reason she knew so much about your father is because I told her."

"But the birds." Eliza's voice is desperate. "She said she could see birds."

"Your father is always banging on about birds, Eliza. With his diaries and his notes. It's not proof that he's alive. It's anything but that."

Eliza is trying to shake her friend's words out of her head.

"I'm sorry. Really I am, I was trying to help you. I know what it's like to lose a father, I thought you might find it a comfort . . ."

Eliza stands, steadies herself. The pressure is building in her chest. She looks at Min—the corners of her friend's eyes are creased in anguish.

"Eliza, please."

"I'm still going to go."

Min's face drops.

"Eliza, come on. Get ahold of yourself."

"He still needs me; he's still out there somewhere. I'm still going to go."

CHAPTER 31

It's McVeigh who gives them the lugger. The *Starling* is still in Cossack with Thomas, stripped of its rigging and stashed in mangroves out of town.

They had told the missionary about their plans to sail out to the Rosellas and then beyond to search the other islands. McVeigh had paused. Frowned. Pulled his thumb and forefinger through his beard.

"You know I do have a lugger myself?"

The weakening sunlight had made its way in through the window, and Eliza's face broke into a smile. The boat was a gift originally, he had told them, from a wealthy pearler whose son McVeigh had traveled to and given last rites some years ago.

"She's called *Moonlight*," he said with a shrug. "I've never sailed her. She's yours."

After they'd thanked him and turned for the door, he stopped them. The sound of bird chatter filled the spaces between his sentences.

"Just so I have this clear. It's the two of you who are going to be taking this boat out?" They nodded. "You, a woman, and you, a beachcomber?"

"That's right." Eliza had tried to ignore the waver in her own voice.

"Won't you be needing a deckhand or a chef? Someone to help . . . navigate?" The two had looked at each other, belief in their own plans faltering slightly.

"May I offer my services, miss?"

The voice was quiet but confident enough. They turned to see that it had come from Quill, the apprentice, who had once again appeared at the back of the mission house without anyone noticing.

"I've learned to cook from the most skillful Chinese chefs, carpentry from the Malays too; I'm a better deckhand even than any Manilaman you'll find." The child looked pointedly at them, eyes clear and unflinching. "I've been on plenty ships before, opening shell, watching anchor, I can read the tides and the currents. Maybe I can help with some language, even. You never know who you'll meet out on the water."

Eliza had let out a laugh.

McVeigh had turned to them, eyebrows raised. "Well, I never. I should think that's a rather good idea, if you'll have him?" Eliza had paused, looked from Quill to Axel, who seemed to weigh the thought like flour.

"How much you paying?" Quill asked, bolder now.

McVeigh had blanched and apologized. "The boy doesn't need paying," he said dismissively. "He just needs meals. Shelter. Something to wear on the ship."

Eliza had looked to the apprentice and remembered the book

she had handed back the day they first met. How Quill had taken it from her and hugged it tightly. *Saltwater Cowboys: Adventures on the High Seas.*

Quill had held her gaze.

"The deckhand will be paid," she said.

CHAPTER 32

The dust storm comes from nowhere and slams into Parker like a wagon. The force of it beats the breath from his lungs and immediately he is lost in a swarm of burning amber. They had been cantering at a steady pace, no sign of anything untoward on the plains, then BOOM! He knew there was a reason he never ventured into this godforsaken landscape. He splutters and heaves, thrusting an elbow to his nose. He cannot open his eyes, and his legs buckle and clench in alarm. It sends his damn horse into a panic, and the beast rears and brays as the devil's dust whips around them. He chokes on the dryness of it, gasping for breath like a fish in a bucket. The wind has gathered up branches and stones in its fingers. They slice his skin until beads of blood inch down his face. Something larger revolves into the fray and smacks into the soft part of his skull. It sends stars chorus-lining across his vision. He cries out for the tracker, but the other man must be lost to the dust too. With a gut-shaking roar, the wind finds more strength, *plucks the hat from his head, and sends it spiraling into the swirling sky. As Parker looks up to watch it go, he feels something heavy fall from his pack. He yells out; it better not be his blasted rifle. With a grunt, he seizes the reins and gives the mare a hard kick so she sets off at an immense speed. Parker clings on until his knuckles are white. Eventually, the men emerge, breathless, from the storm.*

The instant calm is jarring, and he looks over his shoulder to see the dust devil whipping its way across the plain. He turns his head to the tracker, waiting expressionless at the side of the path, untouched by dust. He looks down at his own filthy trousers, raises his fingers to smudge warm blood into his beard. He quickly bends and pats his saddle pack. Goddammit. A flicker of dread; it's his water canteen that was lost to the wind.

CHAPTER 33

U nder the filmy light of early morning they load the boat with
provisions. It would do them no service to have all and sun-
dry watch them go. A lone lugger sailing out so late in the season?
Tongues would certainly talk.

As they work, it doesn't take long for Eliza's discomfort to show.
She can barely look at the water smacking like a flat palm at the bottom of the boat. Its force reminds her of a story her father had once
told. How a diver had become so overwhelmed by a shoal of herrings he almost drowned. The fish had emerged like a cloud while he
walked the seabed and soon engulfed him with their tiny, frantic bodies. They glued themselves to his helmet, swarmed his chest, his back.
As he tugged on his lifeline, more fish arrived–bigger ones, pursuing
their prey. When the diver came to the surface, he was consumed by a
deadly mass, his copper helmet beset by thrashing creatures.

Under the weight of a rice sack, Eliza squeezes her eyes shut and takes a breath to still her nerves. If she does not acknowledge the water's presence, she can imagine that it is not really there at all. She can forget what it is they are really about to do.

"Thirty-five-foot from stem to stern." Axel wades through the shallows with a grin. He's in his sailing clothes—loose-necked shirt and moleskin trousers. His shoulder is healed enough not to need the sling now. But it still causes him pain and she catches him, occasionally, rolling his stiff arm. The day is warm but the morning breeze makes the trees shiver. "Twelve tons, jarrah planked, laminated frames." She nods but cannot muster a smile for him. "All hacked from bush timber. Cajeput or karri, it must be. Shallow draught so the divers can easily come aboard in their suits. Designed to drift with the current. Simply marvelous artistry from the Fremantle builders."

Sandpipers leave forked prints across the surrounding mud. In the bushes, honeyeaters hop on restless feet. Eliza looks beyond them to the low-slung town, the red pindan glowing gold under the rising sun.

"We'll only clear the bar at high tide," announces Axel. "Get it wrong and we'll find ourselves stuck on a lee shore, or dashed on the shoals. Foiled before we've even started. Then we'll really look like fools!" Eliza raises an eyebrow dryly. "But we've got all the provisions in the forehold and plenty of water in the tank, so we're good once the sea allows it." Over his shoulder, Eliza sees a white-necked heron perched on a mangrove tree. Its bold yellow eye watches them unflinchingly.

When the tide eventually lifts the lugger, Axel and Quill let loose the mooring line, and as the boat slips easily through the channel, Eliza's eyes move slowly across the bay and up the beach. They take her across the dunes and over the belts of brittle spinifex grass, making their way to meet the rippling iron of the town. She thinks of Balarri out there in the landscape, stalked in the bush by two men on horseback. She pictures the bungalow, sitting patiently on its stilts and within it a polished calendar clock. With every second it makes its message known: *Hurry. Hurry. Hurry.*

Soft splashes come over the gunwale as the bow dips to cut through the turquoise water. Soon the town is only a brushstroke on the horizon; eventually it threatens to slip out of sight entirely. She must get higher; she cannot leave it behind, not quite yet. She puts a bare foot on the gunwale, grasps hold of the rigging, and hauls herself upward. Bannin is merely a hairline crack now. The wind pulls at her sleeves. Her skirts billow out behind her.

"Are you quite all right?" Axel blinks up at her, and she steps heavily down to the deck. "Come, the wind is picking up," he says.

The boat rolls gently as it cuts through the waters, making its way out to the open stretch of the sea.

Y ou'll get used to it soon enough," Axel calls across the deck as Eliza sways at the halyard. Quill is busy inspecting an old air pump through the hatch. "We'll find your sea legs yet." She is not so sure of that.

Looking out onto the water, she imagines her father and her brother out at sea, easy limbed, no doubt, and soothed by the swaying. She wishes she were as fluid on the water as the gulls. Her eyes move across to the dinghy, parbuckled to the ship. It looks so small there. So breakable. If her father can set out in one of those, she can surely do this.

After a few hours she relaxes, shuffling along to the rail to peer down into the water. Everything seems so astonishingly close, the lugger so low in the water you could tickle the fish with a finger.

Barely three feet below, jellyfish pass like transient clouds. A sleepy turtle, basking on the surface, raises its periscope head before disappearing with a ripple. When sharks arrive, they do so in a pack, their strong bodies crisp in the glassy water. They don't so much move as dance, a liquid sway from tip to tail. Beyond them, in a fleeting flash of silver, fish launch themselves from the water, returning to the surface with a smack.

In the afternoon she sits alone in the shade of the sails, lulled by the singing of the wind in the stays. She sips a cup of sweet tea and thumbs her way through her father's diary, studying every illustration, hearing his deep voice in every word. The gulls flank the boat closely, keeping welcome company. They barrel incessantly into the welter of spray, emerging with tiny fish that wriggle in their beaks. Axel is at the helm, alternately eyeing sails and compass. Quill heaves pots around the deck, preparing food for the evening's dinner. Eliza looks at the apprentice, considers for a while; she is uncomfortable knowing so little about him. She goes across the boards and settles onto a tarpaulin. Quill quickly returns her smile but does not stop the work at the pots. Eliza smiles again, then shakes her head; she has already done that. How best might she begin their conversation? She has not much experience of talking to children, although Quill seems so at ease on the boat he might be mistaken for a man.

"You enjoy your work with McVeigh?" she finally asks.

"Aye." Quill nods, taking a blade from a pocket and sawing the top off the sack. She wonders if the apprentice has any memory of being mothered. Whether Quill's mother would sing as her mother would, whether Quill too can recall her scent or softness of touch.

"Well . . . what do you like best of it?"

Quill gives her a brief, upward glance. A few grains of rice spill onto the deck.

"Cricket."

"Cricket?"

Quill nods. "Father McVeigh's a fine batsman. He's teaching me all he knows. We play it at the camp too, there's some skillful bowlers there."

Eliza had never really understood the appeal of the game; so much waiting around. But the pearlers treat cricket as a way of life during lay-up, and the whole town gets involved. All stripes of men.

"I like reading the books too," Quill continues. "There's a lot to be learned from books."

Eliza smiles inwardly at the earnestness.

"Is that how you have learned so much of languages?"

Quill scoops out the rice with slender palms, forms fists with them and slowly unclenches, allowing the grain to filter neatly into the pot. "That's right, miss, it helps, but I learned most things out on the luggers." She imagines the apprentice in conversation with the many different types of men that make up the crews. Do they resent it, the presence of a child with such a mind?

"They make out like it's English that'll get you furthest here." Quill runs a hand over a damp forehead. "That's the language of power in these parts, we're told. But it's not really." Quill shakes the pot. "It's all the other ones, the ones been spoken for ages. There's hundreds of them. Father McVeigh and I have been making a list of all the words we hear. We have to guess the spellings but he says it's important to make a record of things that'll soon be gone."

When darkness becalms the sea, they anchor the lugger for the night. Thick clouds obscure all but a few bright stars, and by the light of the lanterns they eat in companionable silence. Once the dishes have been rinsed, Quill sets out the tarpaulin and clambers onto it. Axel stands and makes his way to the aft, settling against the cabin as he opens a book. He nods at Eliza to follow. She steps carefully across the planks and sits beside him.

"Any good?" she asks. Its cover looks old and worn. He cracks the spine and the title *Purgatorio* creases in half. Quietly, he begins to read aloud.

"Night, circling opposite the sun, was moving together with the Scales that, when the length of dark defeats the day, desert night's hands; so that, above the shore that I had reached, the fair Aurora's white and scarlet cheeks were, as Aurora aged, becoming orange."

Eliza looks up to the stars, hanging low like fallen angels. Her knees kiss Axel's now and then, rocked by the movement of the water. The minutes trickle by as Quill's gentle sleep noises rise and fall in the air.

"Bet you didn't think you'd end up here," Axel says, placing the book down.

"Australia?"

"No." He smiles. "On a lugger in the middle of the ocean."

She smiles and drops her head. "No, I don't think I could have quite foreseen that."

"Why did you end up in Bannin, though?" He shifts his weight so he is facing her. "Was it your father?"

She turns to face him. "Actually, it was my uncle."

"Is that right?"

"He and my father have always been close. We weren't wealthy when we lived in England, but Father made a living in the factories. He was restless, though, desperate to make a name for himself as a businessman. He'd take what funds we did have and place them into new ventures. They were always outlandish, things no one else would touch: flying machines, protective eyewear for chickens, trapdoors for coffins should someone be buried alive." Axel raises an eyebrow. "Mother sometimes got frustrated but Father argued there was always food on the table." Eliza shifts her legs. "It changed one day;

he placed his money into an ambitious deal that went sour. He has always been a passionate man and can be . . . spontaneous with his decisions. If you were being unkind you might call it erratic. Fanciful, even. As it turned out, he'd been hoodwinked and the gentleman in question disappeared with the entirety of the investment. We didn't know it but he'd placed everything we had into that deal. Almost overnight we lost it all. I was only young; I can't recall the details. But in the end, Willem used his savings to get the whole family out here—us, him and Martha, out to Bannin Bay, to build a new life."

"I had no idea." Axel nods. "Your father certainly has turned his prospects around."

"What about your family?" she asks. "You rarely speak of them."

He looks at her but says nothing, tossing the question away with a shake of the head.

"We're out here, searching for *my* father," she urges. "You know about Ned, about Thomas, my family's path out here. What about you?"

He sighs.

"It's only fair, go on. Do you write to your parents often? I bet they love hearing about your adventures." She wills him on with a gentle nudge of her shoulder.

"Not quite." His words are clipped.

Eliza pauses, confused. "I thought you said your father was a trader? You must have had a nice life back in Germany."

He moves just a fraction away from her. It's not much, but it's enough.

"I'm not close to my family like you are," he says uncomfortably. "I've no siblings. No cousins. My parents and I, we don't speak a lot."

"Why not? It is with their wealth, I presume, that you are able to travel as you do?"

Axel exhales sharply, and looks out to sea. "If you want the truth, my father squandered any inheritance I might have had." He shifts and crosses his legs. "He drank it away. Every other penny swallowed by the gambling halls."

"I'm sorry." She eyes him cautiously. His quiet anger is unfamiliar.

"It's all right. He got what was coming for him. That's what my mother always said anyway." He shakes his head. "I'm not sure I was ever told the specifics but some venereal disease, it sent him mad after a time. They took him into an institution in the end. From what I can tell he's still alive, just about. I haven't had any news otherwise, so . . ."

"Axel."

He shakes his head sharply. "He was not a nice man. An adulterer. Rough-handed. He could be violent; he did not treat me and my mother well."

She allows his words to settle. He had lied, then, when he first told her of his family, when he'd said his father was a trader. She supposes she might have done the same in his situation. "Your mother, at least. She must wonder how you are?" she asks.

"She left when my father was taken ill. The shame was too much for her; she could not bear the whispers. I received one letter, a couple of years later, to say that she was to be remarried to a naval officer. I never heard from her again."

"How old were you when they left?"

The hollows of his cheeks have sucked up the shadows. "Perhaps I must have been fourteen or so. I've been working for myself ever since, making my way from place to place. It provides a remarkable sense of adventure and the nagging assurance that one never truly fits in anywhere. That's why, I suppose, I'm in the constant act of moving on. Perhaps someday I'll find the right spot and settle, but for now . . ." His voice peters out.

The water around them glistens like oil. Eliza nods slowly. She is not the only one with ghosts in her past.

"I'm glad we met," she says.

"Yes," says Axel, moving to close the gap between them again. "I think perhaps we were both a bit lost."

They stay that way for a while, sitting together but minds apart. Eventually, Axel sucks in a lungful of air, stands, and slaps his legs. "Now, Eliza, I have a very important question for you."

"Anything."

"I think we should have some more rum, don't you?"

CHAPTER 34

S he knows as soon as she wakes that the day will be different. The boat is still and the air stifling, closing in like hands around the throat.

She dresses quickly and scrapes her hair into a braid, climbs the four-step ladder, lifts the deck hatch and freezes. To the right of the cabin top, she can see Quill performing the morning's ablutions. To the left, shielded from sight, Axel is still asleep, hands clasped together, in his hammock. She goes to duck back below deck, to afford the apprentice some privacy, but something out of place stops her. Quill squats over a bowl letting out a stream of piss, not urinating over the side like she knows the sailors do. Perhaps it might be too windy, she thinks, but she watches, even though she knows she should turn away. Once Quill's shorts have been tugged back on, Eliza sees the apprentice pull the shirt off overhead. The action reveals skinny shoulders, slender arms, and a bound chest, the material thick and white. The surprised air escapes from Eliza's lungs. She knows what the material must conceal: Quill is not really a boy after all. Eliza's eyes dart to the left and she sees Axel stir. Quill does not notice, so Eliza steps up onto the deck, making her movements as loud as possible. Quill's head whips round, eyes flaring in alarm, but in a flurry of limbs the shirt is pulled back on, all before Axel has seen anything. Quill's eyes dart to hers, as if fearful she will give away the secret. But Eliza says nothing. She looks once more to the deckhand: shorn hair, bound chest, the big, brown eyes of a child. Axel never has to know.

He yawns and stretches his arms in the hammock, apologizing for his slumber. "I always sleep ever so deeply on ships," he says. "Something about the rocking, I suppose, like one is a baby again."

When Eliza eventually looks to the sky she is staggered by the sight on the horizon. It is the eerie green of a fish belly, lit by ghastly flashes of lightning.

"I do not like the look of this glass at all." Axel gives the barometer a tap as the low threat of thunder rolls toward them on the waves. "If it gets any lower we'll have to run for shelter."

Eliza looks fearfully at the piling clouds and the unsettling stillness of the water. Even the gulls have abandoned their ship.

They wait silently on deck, hearts in their throats, as *Moonlight* is smacked by intensifying squalls. Keeping her eyes fastened to the encroaching clouds, Eliza hugs herself to stay warm. She wishes they were safely tucked into a mangrove channel. On shore, storms can send five-hundred-gallon water tanks spinning through the air; there's no doubt they could smash a lugger like theirs to splinters. She shivers, pulls her arms tighter. The wind has teeth and they bite keenly through her cotton blouse.

None of those on board can peel their eyes away from the horizon. Even so, when it comes, it takes them by surprise, striking like something solid. The lugger begins to roll, crashing bow first through dark, churning swells.

"Let's douse the jib," Axel yells into the wind, as he and Quill set about hauling in the ropes. They hasten around Eliza as seawater sloshes across the deck, Axel giving orders to Quill, who carries them out without pause.

"Tell me what I can do to help." Eliza's voice is smothered by the wind. Before she can call out again, a huge wave smashes into the lugger. Her ears fill with water and she is confined to her own head. Immediately, the ringing starts. She shakes her skull, tipping it sideways and knocking her ear with a flat palm. When that doesn't work, she holds her hands up against the driving rain and looks again toward the horizon. Her stomach drops when she realizes she can no longer see it. The waves have taken over, towering like ancient unshackled beasts. The boat creaks and lurches, straining at the seams.

Around them, water thrums, hissing and seething under the old wooden boat. The bow plunges in and out of the waves, and Eliza's knuckles whiten as they beat into the mud-thick nor'wester.

After a time and without warning, she feels the boat change course, careening so dramatically she fears they will all tumble out and into the water. She looks up, the ringing still obnoxious in her ears, so obstructive that when Axel pulls himself across the deck and begins to talk, she can only make out half of what he is saying.

"We . . . way . . . sea." He gestures to the ocean with his outstretched arm. Water streams down his face and pools in the notch above his lip. "Run . . . shelter . . . Cockatoos." He sounds calm but his eyes are wide. Eliza's ears finally begin to drain. "I'm going to put her nose into the wind," she hears him shout as her hearing sharpens. "Just hold on, Eliza."

At that very moment another wave comes over the gunwale. It

rends and snarls around the deck. She groans. "I can't just *hold on*! Tell me what to do!"

"Quill, take the helm and point us into the squall. Eliza, come then. You help me take in the rest of the sheets." The boat lurches and the sails flap wildly. "We need to reef the main and the mizzen too." Her fingers are clumsy, agonizingly helpless. "Here." Axel shows her how and they haul in the ropes hand over hand. Her skin is pale and puckered with the wet, but she works relentlessly as her fingers ache. All the while the sea hisses and spits like a she-wolf, and it takes all of Eliza's effort not to go spilling across the deck. But eventually the sails are lashed down and each soul turns to face the blow.

For what feels like hours the ship stands into the racing tide, smashing into colliding seas, doing battle with colossal sheets of water. Waves lash around them, and from somewhere deep within the ship comes a moaning sound like a giant exhaling. The sky has darkened now but Axel must have lit a lamp—she can see him holding it aloft.

Then, abruptly and without warning, the rain stops. There comes upon the lugger a despicable lull. "It's the eye of the storm," says Axel quietly. They look to each other, chests heaving. The silence is monstrous; it squeezes them in its fist. Eliza looks up—a black funnel leads to a pocket of clear blue sky. It lasts just seconds and with a terrifying thunderclap the cyclone revolves around them, the wind howling furiously once more.

She hears Axel call, "We need to throw out the anchor!" His voice is strained, arm braced against the boom. "It's our only hope now. Let's get it down and hope for a change in the wind." Quill springs into action and down the chain rattles, each of them praying that the plunging bow will not split in two. The lugger lurches, creaks, and groans, the sound of splintering timber a torment in the air. Galloping waves tower above them. They are lost in a dark forest of water, surrounded by the anguished wailing of damned souls.

Eliza turns her head wildly from left to right; she cannot believe what is happening around them. Suddenly, with a furious shriek and the water-drowned roars of a rupturing ship, the sea breaks clean over the gunwale, taking Axel with it.

She looks on in horror, pulling herself to the rail and scanning the water. The waves course so violently, it's impossible to discern any shapes held within them. Panic swamps her limbs. She calls out for him.

"Quill! Help me find him!" She looks back across the ship but she can no longer see the deckhand. She cries out, scouring the ship's length. That's when she sees the body wedged behind the cabin top. Quill must have been knocked out by the boom. It's only temporary; she tells herself that this has to be true. She must find Axel in the water before it's too late. She knows he cannot swim well and his shoulder will make things even harder for him. She scans the surface again. It rages—nothing could exist inside such a temper, surely. The sound of it swarms around her like angry wasps and hornets. Her breath halts. There, she sees him: he's clinging on to a thick plank of wood. She looks behind her to see that the hatch to the hold has been ripped cleanly off by the storm. She tries not to think of the water that will be pouring in, to consider whether it could sink them. Among the waves, Axel's body is half-slumped across the hold door. His eyes are closed. She watches in desperation but he doesn't move, the water washing back and forth across him. She calls out to him again, screaming his name into the wind until she feels as if she might cough up her own lungs. Still, he does not open his eyes. His skin looks blue.

It doesn't take long to find what she's looking for. Still coiled in its position, braced stealthily against the waves, the rope is so heavy with water it is hard for her to shift. But with her face turned toward the storm she takes one end of it and feeds it through the fairlead, knotting tightly, fingers burning with every tug. She then loops the rope around her waist, pulls it tight, and secures it with a bowline–the one knot her father taught her as a child. She does not realize quite how much she is shaking until she climbs upon the gunwale and throws her legs over the side. They plunge in and out of the water with every roll of the lugger. But even though the boat is moving, she pauses stock still. For a moment, at least, she is not there. Instead, her mind goes to another boat resting in the shallows of Sixty Mile Beach. There is a body in the water, a small one, with fair hair that dances in the waves.

She takes a breath and her lungs fill with sea spray. She coughs. Tries again, and launches clear off the side of the ship. The water could be ice but she would still not feel it, warmed from the inside by something hotter than blood. She sinks until her body is submerged, suspended beneath barreling waves, silent, momentarily graceful. What's that she sees in the corner of her vision? Is that something moving through the water with the whip of a tail? The ocean pushes into her ears with unwelcome fingers; she feels the pain move into her jaw and pulls herself upward, breaking the surface and gasping for air. Looking desperately around her, she tries to find him, but the waves are so high she cannot see above them. She stills herself; she must stay calm. She tries to move in time with the water, keeping her chin above the surface, allowing herself to be tugged up and down with each wave. If she does not find him soon, he is going to be lost to the water. All it would take is one big wave to snatch him off that door.

She turns her head; the horizon lurches and falls. Then, she sees him again. Ten yards away. Can she make it with the rope? She pulls to find it still holding tight. She takes a breath and propels herself forward, not allowing herself to think of what patrols beneath. The water is so rough it takes all her energy just to advance a yard. She pauses, bobbing, then a clap of thunder rips through the sky over-head. It shocks her into movement, and she starts again to swim, Axel dipping in and out of sight with every spasm of the ocean.

Eventually, she reaches him, her throat scoured sore with gray seawater. By turns, his body nudges toward her, then pulls back again. It's a maddening cycle. She is not sure if he is breathing. His eyes remain closed.

With one last burst of strength she launches herself forward, legs kicking out behind her until she makes it and grasps hold of the door. It is slippery but she hauls her body weight onto it. She runs a quick hand over his face to try and rouse him, pulls at his shoulder, gives his cheek a sharp slap. She thinks she might have heard a gurgle from his lungs but the sound is smothered by the wind. With her eyes fixed on the lugger, she kicks out furiously behind her, propelling the hatch, and their bodies, slowly across the waves. It's a torturous movement—for every few yards they progress, the waves knock them back twofold. Perhaps the rope will be easier. She grabs it with one hand, and it slides fluidly from her grip. She tries again, reaching for it and clenching its sodden weave in her fist. Somehow she manages to hold on, and slowly she starts to put hand over hand to pull them in. Everything burns, every inch of her skin is on fire—but gradually, painfully, she pulls their makeshift raft toward the lugger.

She is close enough to touch the hull, but it's a balancing act—she doesn't want the door to smash into the lugger. She stays there a moment, keeping the boat at arm's length. Her mind empties of all logic. She hadn't thought of how she would get him back on the ship. For a while they float there and her hopes begin to sink beneath them. Perhaps she won't be able to save him after all. Maybe their story will end with the two of them drowned. She is still trying to wake him when the voice comes from above.

Quill leans over the gunwale, face set in determination. One eye is grotesquely obscured by a cabbage of swollen flesh.

"Take this." Quill tosses out another length of rope and Eliza ties it as best she can around Axel's middle.

"Eliza, come, then we'll pull him in."

"Take him first!" But she feels the tug of the rope. Quill is hauling the length in, hoisting her closer to the boat until, finally, she slams against its side. The force of it winds her.

"I can't pull your weight up here. You'll have to do it yourself." Quill strains, tugging hard on the rope. Eliza turns herself in the water, holding her breath as she waits for the crest of the next wave. Then, when it is at its highest arc, she reaches and grasps hold of the gunwale. The bruising pain is immediate but she starts to drag herself upward, fingers slipping from the slick wood. Quill launches halfway over the side, grabbing at her waist, trying to haul her body in. Eliza pulls with all the strength she can find, the sea grasping at her legs like greedy mangrove mud. Eventually, she edges over the gunwale and collapses onto the deck.

"Hurry." Her voice is hoarse, salt making her eyes stream. "Get him in." Together they wrench at the rope attached to Axel, his body swayed in a taunting waltz. When it reaches the side of the boat, they pull until their eyes bulge to get his limp weight up. When he eventually slips over the gunwale it is with a slither, the ocean spitting his body back out like gristled meat. He lies unseeing, unmoving, limbs splayed at awkward angles. She hurls herself toward him, falling hard onto her knees. She takes his face in her hands, turns it to her, calls his name, pulls open his cold eyelids with clumsy, frantic thumbs.

"You need to get the water out of his chest!" Quill's voice comes at a harsh pitch. Eliza cannot fail again. She puts her hands together—she is sure she has seen Blithe do this to drowned divers before—and places them firmly on his chest. Pools of water gully over her fingers. She leans her whole weight into it and pumps up and down. Fast. Fast. Fast. No response. She puts her mouth to his, ignoring the iciness of his lips. She pinches his nose and blows her breath into his lungs. She pleads with him to wake up, pounds again and again on his chest. The ship rolls, tipping the horizon upward, and they begin to slide down the deck until the lugger suddenly rights itself. Eliza grasps Axel by the shoulders, pinning him to the planks.

When it comes, eventually, it's like the sun. Axel coughs, turns his head as water spews from his throat. He creases in half, elbows meeting knees as his stomach clenches and spasms. His breath comes in heaves and his eyes widen, searching for something to latch on to. Eliza leans over him, reaching for his hand, and their fingers lace into one another's. Quill slumps back in exhaustion. Eliza tastes the sourness at the back of her cheeks. She turns, pushes the wet hair from her forehead, and vomits across the ruined deck.

CHAPTER 35

The storm subsides, as all storms do, and the three of them work to piece together the fallout. They move slowly around the deck, bailing water and repairing sails, weary fingers moving diligently to reweave ropes and sand off splinters. Quill's swollen eye has bloomed from black to green, weeping until the skin hardens and the sclera shows itself like an old, rotten clam. Axel is still weak. Bruises have appeared like riddles across his body and forehead, but he does what he can to aid with repairs.

They remain at sea for another two days, coaxing the lugger back on course after being thrown so wildly off path. They sleep and eat in a blurry lull, washing their faces with seawater, comforted by the needy rhythm of their own bodies. Before long, they are barreling toward the Rosellas; they'll have to rest there and ensure repairs to the boat have been successful. They cannot risk it in another storm.

The blow has robbed the sea of all its color, turquoise turned to pewter, its surface strewn with the bodies of near-dead fish. Quill claims a huge sailfish one morning and hauls it onto the deck. It flickers and dances as it dies and they all watch, eager eyes on its ugly, writhing body. They feast in silence like men after a battle, juice dripping slowly from chin to clavicle as the sunlight picks out the shape of ladders across the waves. At night they sleep together on deck, faces kissed by the clean white moon. By the time the final morning breaks they are reborn, drooped heads lifting toward the dawn.

When the Rosellas come into view, in the early hours of morning, they are nothing more than a smudge on the horizon. They don't trust their eyes at first, after days of only seabirds and winged fish for company. But Axel checks his compass again, spreads a map on the sun-bleached deck. He hovers a finger over a cluster of shapes. "This is them all right, see the distinctive horseshoe pattern?" The map shows one larger island at the center, with a series of smaller shards spreading upward from either side.

They make their way into the chain and drop anchor in the lee of the largest island; the lugger should be protected from the winds in here and the water is still enough to allow them to perform inspections to the hull.

It's a small distance to shore but they let loose the dinghy and take her in anyway.

Eliza surveys the island as they approach. She is surprised at its small size. It can be no longer from tip to tail than a few hundred yards. It appears almost entirely green, covered in dense rainforest, with just a thin strip of beach running around its perimeter. The reflection of the sand is blinding, the water the color of blue-green glass held up to the light.

Peering down into the shallows she sees small fish darting around the dinghy. They are so bold it startles her, and she bends to try and identify them. A cloud of surgeonfish passes in a blur of vivid blue and yellow. A few parrotfish sway carefully in the current. Then a slow, hulking dugong drifts clumsily into sight. Eliza shrinks back in shock. Its skin is gray and leathery against the weeds.

"Looks like a porpoise, tastes like a pig." Eliza looks up to see Quill peering into the water. "That's what they say anyway."

Her father would have found this fascinating. She pulls herself back onto the thwart and her shoulders sink. She wonders if they will find any sign of Thomas's visit ashore. He had promised her he'd come here, that he had scoured each of the Rosellas for signs of her father. Can she trust him? If he's telling the truth, perhaps he left behind some sort of shelter they can use tonight.

Together they pull the dinghy up the beach and Eliza frowns as she glances at her feet. There are strange patterns in the sand, thick lines covering the beach, as if a few hundred knotted ropes have been dragged up from the sea.

"What do you make of that?" Axel asks her.

"I've never seen anything like it before."

She casts her eyes along the beach for any sign that Thomas made a shelter here, but there's nothing—no hammock, no calico or swag. Although she knows the telltale footprints she seeks would have been long covered by the wind and tide by now.

With the dinghy safely stashed, Quill immediately sets about searching for firewood. Eliza peers into the forest: it is thick, dark, and damp. The eerie calls of unknown birds escape from it like smoke.

"Eliza, let's take a look around, yes?" says Axel.

She nods, eager for any signs of Thomas, or even—she allows herself to hope—of her father.

As they plow deep into the trees, the light takes on an unusual grainy quality. The ground is moist and riotously fecund, the branches displaying cheery white and pink flowers with yellow stamens that protrude like trumpets. In the slices of sunlight that cut through the canopy, she notices thousands of suspended spores that twirl and glitter. They seem to glow in a wash of purple, gold, and green. She cannot take her eyes off them, and Axel moves to scoop some into his palm. They shift like water but disappear entirely when removed from the light.

Around them, on the forest floor, unseen things scrabble and scurry. Every now and then an animal wail rings through the trees, raising the hairs on Eliza's forearms. Surrounding branches hang heavy with fragrant bloodred fruits, some of them so high they could never be reached by human fingers. As Axel presses ahead, Eliza plucks one from its stem and puts it to her lips, takes a bite. She sighs. It is the sweetest thing she has ever tasted. Axel turns just then, and she quickly tosses the remains of the flesh into the undergrowth, wipes her hands on her skirts, and follows.

She has never been in a forest like this before; it puts her in mind of something from a children's story. She half-expects the trees to come to life and wrap their gnarled roots around her body. She blinks away the thought and continues deeper into the gloom. The forest's breath is damp, but eventually they emerge into the stark sunlight, having scoured every tree and leaf they could reach. While they've been away, Quill has built a fire and walked the shoreline to see what could be found on the beaches.

"Nothing," they all agree, and Eliza feels her hope slacken.

"It's all right." Axel's tone is upbeat. "We knew he wasn't here; Thomas told you he wasn't. We'll check the other islands in the chain on the way out tomorrow, but we've come here to reach the Nevermores." He gestures with a straight arm in a vague southwesterly direction. "Then, if necessary, the De Vitts." He points to the northwest. "We have come so far but still have so much more to do. The best thing we can do now is rest."

By the light of the fire they eat: salted fish from the lugger and anything they have been able to forage from the shallows. They are quiet as embers flee upward into the arms of the stars that have emerged to greet them. Quill points out constellations in the shape of scorpions and hunters pulling back their neat bright bows. Eliza cannot be certain but she wonders if she feels the earth trembling beneath them. On the water the lugger patiently observes; she is grateful to have it there, standing guard against anything malevolent. When it is time to sleep, they do so on the beach. Axel had been satisfied that there would be no rain overnight, and it is warm enough to go without shelter. So each of them spreads out a small distance apart on the sand, doing their best to ignore the forest's unnatural noises that make sleep harder to grasp at. Are those voices Eliza hears coming from the trees? When she eventually succumbs, the dreams that limp in have the weighty quality of hallucinations: her father and mother slowly dancing atop a cliff at sunset, the sky around them ablaze with a bushfire orange; Eliza plucked from the ground and lifted to the heavens by a huge eagle with gold wings, its talons drawing blood from the skin at her shoulders. Then Thomas, in the most unnatural of positions: with Eliza in his lap, he tenderly strokes her hair and whispers a soft poem. The strangeness of the act is as unsettling as any corpse. His fingers twist her curls and run slowly down her face. But they are not soft anymore; instead, the nails scratch at her skin. They tear at her arms and legs and feet and, from under the blanket of sleep, she lets out a scream.

When she wakes with a start, the scratching sensation persists. Her skin itches and scuttles, and she wiggles her shoulders to try and rid herself of the discomfort. It does not abate. She lifts her head upward, pushes herself up to a seated position. Then, slowly and with a small sense of horror, she holds her arms in front of her. She cries out and jumps to her feet. There is a reason for the scratching—she is covered head to toe in crabs. They are tangled in her hair, their blindly waving legs caught in her collar. They claw and skitter across her chest, and as they fall they flounder like something abandoned. Casting her eyes around the beach, she is astonished by what she sees in the moonlight. Every single inch of sand is swarming with crabs. There must be thousands of them crammed into that small space, rippling like a vast, moving blanket. The moon has picked out every detail, each quick-moving leg, each shell—everything is illuminated. The crabs flee from the forest in a steady rush, making their way toward the sea as a grappling mass of bodies. *This* is what must have made the strange tracks in the sand, she realizes. Quill and Axel are stirring now. In turn they leap up and yell in alarm. Eliza plucks one of the creatures from her arm to inspect it; its shell is wholly translucent, and she can see its innards pulsing away within. Two huge pincers appear out of proportion to its body, and its hard black eyes sit on stalks that tremble.

"Fascinating," she whispers.

"Well, I've never seen anything quite like it in my lifetime." Axel shakes his legs one by one to dislodge the crabs. "Ouch."

"Why are they so desperate to leave the forest?" Quill asks, and they all peer nervously behind them into the darkness.

"Listen." Axel raises a finger to his ear. They hold their breaths. The mass of bodies emits a collective growl as it seethes.

It takes a while for them to collect their lanterns and scoop the crabs from the belly of the dinghy. Each step must be carefully taken so as not to crush the creatures. The moon is still bright and full, a polished silver plate, and as they row back to the lugger it casts its wrinkling glow across the sea. They climb aboard and from the deck they watch as the crabs continue their exodus. *What strange behavior,* Eliza thinks, *it's as if the trees are humans ridding themselves of lice.* She rushes below deck to grab her father's diary. She turns to a blank page and carefully sketches out what she sees. She includes a small diagram of the crabs, making a note of their translucence and that strange growling sound that seems to come from within their stomachs. Her father will adore that detail. She *has* to find him. She has to tell him what she's seen.

By morning there are no crabs left on the beach, as if they have dissolved into the sea like powder. Eliza and Axel ready themselves for the sail under a sky smeared with dawn. The wind is agreeable; the Nevermores, by Axel's calculations, less than a day's sail away. If they leave now they stand a chance of making it by sundown.

Their departure is slow as Eliza ensures they check every single island on the way out of the chain. The largest of those remaining is not even half the size of the first. Others are no bigger than a house, a low sand hill topped by a single tree. There is no sign of human life on any of them.

And so they speed toward the Nevermore islands, Eliza watching the water as they sail, sending her eyes skyward occasionally to monitor the behavior of the clouds. She pictures her father in that small boat out on this sea. Buffeted by waves. Nosed at by sharks.

"I know you will have held on," she whispers. "I'm coming to find you."

Must be them," says Axel. "See, they're scattered all around us here." He stands to take in the landmass before them, rising out of the water in a blaze of jagged ochre. "Uninhabited, by humans at least, I'm pretty sure of it. If your father was blown off course, and managed to survive in that dinghy, there's a chance he could have ended up here."

Eliza's mouth feels suddenly dry.

They hoist the sails and the lugger barrels toward the island. She grabs a scope and begins to inspect the landscape. Shrubby sand hills are set way back from the shoreline. The beach is littered with rocks, and mangroves speckle the island's outer fringes.

"We'll have to anchor here and take the dinghy in," says Axel, who sets about unfastening the boat. Birds skirl above them as they row steadily ashore. Eliza watches them carefully–glossy black frigates with bulbous bloodred throats.

When they reach the sand, they step out and drag the boat up the beach. They drop it and cast keen eyes around them, but Quill hangs back slightly.

"Everything all right?" Eliza shields her eyes against the white wall of sunlight.

"I've got a bad feeling, Eliza."

"What do you mean? Are you feeling unwell?" Her hands go to her hips.

"There's something wrong about this place," says Quill. "Can't explain it. Not something to be mucked around with."

Eliza takes in the silent sand hills, the breeze fingering its way along the tops of the bushes. In the distance, sprays of tawny spinifex grass sway; beyond them crimson cliffs are wrought with cracks and chasms.

"I think we need to have a look around at least," Axel says as he eyes Quill warily.

That's when they see them. On the hill. They arrive as one–as if they simply rose from the ground. A small, angular group of four. They stand abreast, silent and unmoving, the sinews of their pale bodies picked out by the sun's harsh rays. Their clothes are tattered, white limbs grizzled and stringy. Two males, two females. Still as stone.

Both groups inspect each other until Axel eventually steps forward. It has a disassembling effect and the group on the hill shifts apart. The younger male breaks off and starts to descend. Eliza swallows. "Who do you think they are?" she whispers to Quill. "A family of old convicts or something?"

They watch on as the two figures meet, shadows bold on the fine pale sand. Eliza cannot help but notice how this harsh landscape glows with garnet, amber, jade, and aquamarine.

Axel turns, beckons them forward. They go across the wind-whipped sand, and he comes to meet them halfway. The man behind him is lean and pensive. There is something wolfish about his face. Guarded eyes court the light as he blinks. He has an old revolver tucked into the waistband of his trousers.

"They're convicts of a type." Axel's voice is low. "The older ones ran this as a trading island for a while."

Eliza feels suddenly sick. "Trading what?" But she does not need the answer; she knows the early pearlers bought and sold native crews on remote islands like this. She looks to the rest of the group. A family certainly, she can see that now; a collection of thin limbs strengthened by exposure to the elements. She wonders how long they might have been here now. What sort of life they've scratched out. Whether it can be worth it to hide what they have done.

The man introduces himself with his family name, Kelly, and reluctantly leads them up a spiraling path to a hut. It is well made, strong enough to withstand the winds that send the grasses to a bow, every inch of it filled with black smoke from a fire. The mother and daughter sing quietly as they select pots to fill with water, and place a loaf of old damper in front of them. Eliza can't resist a bite, but it tastes bitter. Meanwhile, Kelly tells them the family has been out here for years; his father came out on one of the last convict ships, then was indentured with his family to help oversee an island for the trading of people. When things changed with the law, all the other workers escaped. His family stayed behind for fear of being captured and jailed on the mainland. Since then, they've been taking from an island that gives them everything they need: fish, bush meat, shelter, secrecy. The man's father watches on with old, gray eyes as he talks. Eliza swallows away the sour taste. "He's no good, that man," Quill had whispered to her. But she cannot let her disgust show. Not yet. These people might have something she needs.

As she goes to speak, another voice comes from outside. It is deep and commanding. There's a rustle and a man peers in through the doorway. He is strong limbed and scarred with sunburn. He has those same lupine eyes.

"This is my brother, Joseph," says Kelly, before launching a gob of spit to the ground. Joseph strides in and hurls a brace of dead lizards onto the tabletop. Their shiny eyes are fixed open, long tails stiff in death. The mother stands slowly and begins, with shaking hands, to unstring them. Joseph swings a sack off his shoulder and upturns it to deposit slick fish into a waiting bucket. The hut fills with the eye-watering reek of dead flesh.

"Who's this?" he asks suspiciously, nodding toward Quill.

"We've come from Bannin Bay." Eliza quickly stands.

"We're looking for someone," Axel adds with a protective glance at the deckhand.

"Mmmm." Joseph grunts as he takes a blade and begins to descale a skipjack. Eliza notices how the air in the hut has changed since he entered it. "You fellas got anything to do with this?" He stops his task, reaches into the front pocket of his shirt, and pulls out a compass.

Eliza's heart turns itself inside out. She has seen that compass before. She grabs for it and eventually he lets her take it. It has lost its lid; the glass is smeared with dull, gray fish scales, the brass blood warm from being kept next to Joseph's chest. Her ears swarm as she inspects it. She feels at once cold and hot. Carefully, she turns it over. There, engraved into the back: *Brightwell*.

Joseph had found the body on the shore of the next island.

"I moved him out of the shallows," he said clinically. "Didn't like to think of him being pulled apart by the sharks."

The women had looked to Eliza with pity, but she could not make out the details of their faces.

Now, through the doorframe, the blue of the sky hurts to look at.

"I dragged him back to the tree line. Covered the body with some sticks, some leaves; thought that'd keep away the worst of the predators."

"So, a drowning, you think?" Axel asks him tightly.

"I'd say so. The water here's wild as the devil's guts."

Axel swallows. "Was there anything else with him? Any*one* else around?"

"Just a dinghy, in the shallows. Beaten up bad. It'll be useful if I can repair it; I stashed it safe, couldn't get it back here on my own. Then the compass." He nods cautiously toward Eliza.

She is certain she will vomit, but if she starts it will surely all come up too—her stomach, her liver, her spleen. She wraps her arms around herself and sees Axel reaching for her. She sways away from him, everything blurred, as she makes her way out of the hut. Once outside, the air invades her lungs like poison. As Axel steps out behind her, she sinks to the sand with a howl of despair.

"You should drink."

The women have brought out a dish of water. She dismisses it; it could be champagne but it would still taste like mud. Axel settles next to her on the sand. The sun above is sharp as a slap.

"I need to see him." She says it through gritted teeth. She wants to crawl into a hole and stay there, not living, not dying. But if she doesn't see her father's body, she knows she will never truly accept it.

"Eliza." Axel looks haunted, eyes dull. "I don't think that's a good idea. A woman shouldn't see something like that. It won't help anything."

Her insides take light. She leaps to her feet. "And how do *you* know what is going to help me now?" Her fists are so tight they could shatter. "Are you the one who has lost his father? Are you the one who could not save him, after all this *mess*?"

He cannot look at her. "I won't let you see it. It is not appropriate; you have no idea."

"I am not some fragile woman!" Her limbs crackle. "I am a human being, just like you." There is no chance that she is leaving without seeing her father. "Just take me to him. I can handle it." She sets her jaw tight. "I have to see him."

CHAPTER 36

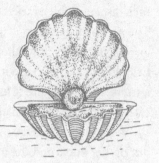

They are silent as Axel pulls on the oars, the dinghy inching toward the next island with solemn certainty. The boat sits heavy in the water with five of them in it. Joseph had reluctantly agreed to come in exchange for the dried food on the lugger. The other Kelly brother, Daniel, has come too, to help bring the stranded boat back for repairs. Eliza resents his presence. How can they possibly think of taking a boat from a dead man? From her father?

Joseph had briefly told her what to expect. "There may have been some animal activity," he muttered. The words had hung ugly in the air.

Once on shore, the brothers move nimbly. Eliza, Axel, and Quill follow behind, stumbling as they try to keep pace. Sandflies swarm and speargrass draws blood at their ankles. She is sure snakes must be lying in wait, but would she care if she was bitten? Would it matter if she fell from a rock and smashed her skull to shards?

The island flattens out and opens onto another beach. At the foot of red cliffs, gums sway softly; beside them eucalypts have been half-burned by lightning strikes. White birds lift gently from the branches, then disperse with a racket. The wind is so strong down here it wails. The air tastes like rain.

Joseph gestures to the treeline at the other end of the beach. Eliza lifts her chin to see it. There is something there at the base of a trunk, but from here it looks like nothing more than a pile of discarded firewood. The sea pulses and the wind moves around her, but she is surprised to realize that she feels nothing at all. She can see the dirt on her boots and the mud under her fingernails, but her mind is on another beach, watching whales spout in the distance, identifying birds by the shape of their wings in flight. As she slowly blinks, she can imagine the sun glancing off her father's spectacles. She can feel the warmth of his broad, dry hand on her shoulder.

"Eliza?" Axel's voice cuts through the haze. "I'll come over with you." But she shakes her head and makes her slow way across the beach alone. The sea watches on but the birds have ceased their singing. She reaches the tree and bends with shaking knees.

The mass in front of her is covered in leaves, each one seething with a thousand crawling insects. She looks down at the shape under veiled eyelids, snatching glances, saving herself from the fullness of it. Flies drift upward and find their way to the corners of her mouth. The smell in the air is obscene. It claws at her throat. Looking down again, she sees the flash of a button through the green. Again, she blinks: white cotton. Again: white skin. But it's not enough; she must see him, she has to see his face, his spectacles. She reaches down and pulls away the leaves.

The scream comes like that of an animal. Something caught in a trap. She does not see Axel take off at a run behind her, does not realize at first that it is her who is making the sound. When he reaches her she is on her knees, facing away from the body, nose thrust into her elbow.

"Come away from there, come on." He reaches out an arm and makes to move her off. He does not hear her speak because her voice is just a whisper. But she can see that in his bones he can sense what she has said. He bends, eyes wide, seizes her by the shoulder, commands her to say it again. Her words, this time, come louder than the wind.

"It's not him."

She did not cry out when she saw the first remains of the body. Not much left after the animals had had their fill but bone and sinew and hair the color of saffron. Her eyes were tearless as she knelt for a closer look, the stench of spoiled meat sullying her face with a creeping tongue. But her throat constricted when she saw them: finger joints flung about by the beaks of birds. And then she screamed when her gaze alighted on it—half hidden, wallowing in the orbital socket like a pearl in oyster flesh. It was gleaming there: a glass eye with a painted gray iris. Watching her.

Back on the beach, her stomach clenches with the horror. She had shown Axel. He had seen it too. They knew immediately who it was. "*Winters*," they whispered.

On the sand, the Kellys had kept their distance, but now Axel nods and they come cradling Winters's possessions, found in the wrecked dinghy: a white hat bent out of shape, a jacket, an empty flask. After a short while Joseph disappears again, then emerges from behind a rock with a pile of shells. They were in the dinghy too, he says. Each one is about the size of her palm. She takes one from him, turns it over in her hands. Its carapace is riddled with lugworm grooves and it's filled with a hard, gray-white substance inside. She picks at it with her thumbnail and wonders why it stirs something familiar inside her. Axel holds one to the sun and knocks on the compacted powder with his knuckles. Quill sniffs it, frowns. Eliza's thoughts are watery, swimming in her skull; she is reaching for something she cannot quite seem to grasp.

"Why was my father's compass with the body?" she asks quietly.

Axel leans in and lowers his voice. "Eliza." He places a hand on her arm. She shrugs it off. "Have you considered that your father might have been in the boat too?" He looks like he might be sick. But she is not listening; her mind races through the pages of her father's diary. "We know this is how he got off that lugger." Axel's voice is gentle, still. "Because Winters was there to help him. To row with him, and they ended up . . . here, evidently." He gestures to the wind-scoured cliffs.

"Yes, I know that." The words sound warped and distant.

"They must have gotten into trouble—a small dinghy like that out on the ocean. Maybe your father was lost to the— Well. There are crocodiles around here. Sharks." His eyes drop to the ground.

At that very moment Eliza's mind's eye lands on the passage it has been searching for. She holds her breath as she runs through the words again.

Gray and foul smelling when laid; powder white when it dries. White gold!

"It's . . . guano," she says. Axel is stunned into a short, confused silence beside her.

"I'm sorry. What?"

"This white substance"—she taps it—"it's guano." She scratches at the powder again. "Seabird excrement. It can be used for fertilizer. It's sought after, in the Americas particularly. Peru."

Axel looks at her pityingly. "Eliza, maybe you should sit down."

"Joseph, this is from birds, isn't it?" she calls out.

The man does not hear her question at first.

"Eliza." Axel encourages her to sit on the sand.

"These shells came from an island occupied by seabirds." She is certain now. "Flocks of them. In their thousands, probably. There are islands off the coast at which the deposits build up, undiscovered for years. There are some on Brolga Island; I read about them in my father's diary. There must be others very near here too. The excrement desiccates over time; it must have hardened into these shells." She shakes her head; the thoughts are fizzing like moths against a lantern.

"Eliza!" Axel's voice comes as a rebuke now. "*Sit down.*"

"Joseph, please–is there an island near here that's home to nesting seabirds?" She looks out to sea. "They must have seen the smoke on this island and brought the shells and the compass to try and trade," she murmurs. "They must have been so desperate. Delusional, even. In need of food and shelter . . ."

Axel looks at her as if she has truly turned mad. But it's all rushing in on her at once now. Clementine's words; perhaps she isn't a fraud after all. Perhaps she *had* seen a vision of her father surrounded by birds. What if Min had merely said that to try to protect her, to stop her coming out here? What if she was trying to keep Eliza safe?

"There is one, isn't there?" she asks as Joseph turns toward her. "There's an island near here where the seabirds gather?"

He nods, bewildered, and raises an arm to the horizon.

THE DIARY OF CHARLES J. G. BRIGHTWELL, MASTER PEARLER

Saltwater crocodiles

For all the creatures that stalk the waterways of Western Australia, there is one of which I will admit I am most afraid. It is a creature that haunts me in my sleep, one that circles my luggers in the soft lull of twilight. It has been known to ambush men while they wash shell in the shallows, or to haul fishermen clear out of the mangroves–leaving nothing but their battered hats on the tide.

The saltie is a large (I have seen them reach 20 feet long) and opportunistic carnivore. A veritable apex predator, this croc prevails over almost any animal that enters its territory: sharks, fish, reptiles, birds, and mammals–including, of course, we human beings. A crocodile will either drown its prey or simply swallow them whole. In the water, the creature performs what is referred to as a "death roll," where it revolves like a spinning turbine in order to tear chunks of meat from its victim. Young saltwater crocodiles are also capable of breaching their entire bodies into the air in a single upward motion to reach prey that may be perched on low-hanging branches.

The crocodile's body is broad and its skull thick. Its skin such a dark brackish green it appears near black. If swimming, the shadow of a submerged saltie charging toward you is a blood-chilling sight, its reptilian eyes hovering just above the surface as it powers easily through strong currents.

The saltwater crocodile has a long history of attacking humans. Oh, yes. Its bite is the strongest of any animal on this planet. Ransford got taken by a saltie a few years back; he'd been slurping squareface by the bucketload and was so pickled he took a wrong turn after leaving the Kingfish. Ended up splashing his way through the mangroves under the moonless sky, the reckless sod. The night-can collector found his body, or rather what was left of it the next morning. They scoured the area for clues. As it transpired, there was a huge saltie just yards away, tucking into what remained of his right arm.

CHAPTER 37

Axel had implored her to spend the night on the Kellys' island first. They should set off at first light, he'd said; they'd be far more useful once they had rested. She had gritted her teeth against the proposition. She must go right now, even though the sun has started to sink, a slice of orange dripping its thick juice across the sky.

As they make their way to the dinghy, she notices a figure lagging behind. She turns to see Quill stopped halfway along the beach.

"What's the matter?" she calls.

Quill approaches. "I'm scared."

She shakes her head, puts an arm on Quill's shoulder. "Don't be. We got through that storm, didn't we? This is nothing, we're just . . . taking a turn in the lugger. Think of it like that." She continues toward the water; Axel is already readying the dinghy.

"Ghosts," Quill calls out after her.

Eliza stops in her tracks.

"I am afraid your father will be a sea ghost now."

Her brow folds, but she cannot find the words to answer. Quill traces a winding snake's trail into the sand with a toe. "If we find him, it means the sea spat him out. It didn't want him. It means he's a bad spirit."

Eliza does not flinch. She does not shout. Instead, she gives the smallest of nods and sets off toward the dinghy, leaving Quill on the beach, watching her go.

The lugger creaks as it slips through the water, dog tired now. The low sun casts a sepia glow across the deck and the sails bloat with the rising wind. Without Quill to guide them, picking their way around the reefs is a dangerous duty. They could easily find themselves stricken. With every minute that passes, the light diminishes, the sun stepping one foot out of the door, then two, leaving it open enough for only a watery dribble of light. The air is swamp-thick, bristling with rain that needles the skin. Eliza thrusts herself against the rail, skirts billowing in the wind. She clutches at the scope, scouring every inch of sand they pass. When she lowers it, the brass leaves a perfect red ring around her eye.

The lugger swings westward, rounding the top of the island; that's when the orchestra starts. Rain drums on the deck and the wind comes in gasped percussion to the sea's roar.

When they come to the island Joseph had pointed out, the channel before them is choked with mangrove bushes. It is far too tight for the lugger to squeeze through.

"We'll have to take the dinghy." Her voice is half-lost to the wind.

"Eliza."

"The island is just through there." She wipes the rain from her face. "We need to check it. What if he stayed behind when Winters went on to trade? Or perhaps he was able to swim back if the storm hit them." The words die in her throat as she tries to picture her father, exhausted and terrified, being able to swim across such a stretch of water. She straightens against the doubt. "We have to keep going. Come on."

"No."

The word comes like a hammer stroke. She looks to him; his shoulders are slumped.

"There's no light left. We'll be lost in this weather." His tone is pleading now. "It's safer to wait here; we'll sleep back on the island." He sighs. "He's not here, Eliza! We tried. You are soaking wet; you'll be lucky not to catch your death. You're shaking. We did all we could. I mean, good God." His chest heaves. "He's gone, Eliza, can't you see that?"

She is surprised by her own calmness.

"If you are not prepared to look for him, then I will do it alone. I've said it more than once. I said it when we first met."

Axel scoffs. There is no more to be said. She turns to the dinghy and starts unbuckling the ties.

"Don't be so ridiculous, Eliza. You'll die if you go out on that thing on your own. It's dark. You'll be tipped overboard!"

"I didn't come this far to give up." She thinks of her mother, of Ned. Those who have already been taken from her. What does she have left? "He could still be alive." Axel shakes his head. "There is a chance of that. A *chance*." The wind sets up its plangent wail. "We found Winters, didn't we? And as long as there is a chance to find my father too, I *have* to try."

She pulls herself onto the gunwale, crouches with knees to her chin, and claws at the knots. Axel watches her as she tugs and heaves. She doesn't stop when a gust of wind threatens to topple her. She lets the rain drag the hair across her face. But the dinghy won't shift. Just as she is about to cry out in frustration, Axel marches over, reaches and easily loosens the buckles. It is fueled by annoyance but sets in action a string of motions. The dinghy plummets downward with a rattle and smacks the water. Without pause, Eliza pushes herself off the lugger and into the boat, landing messily. She staggers in the near darkness. The surrounding water sucks greedily at the wood.

"I won't go with you, Eliza. This is a terrible idea."

"I didn't ask you to. Pass me the lamp." Reluctantly he takes it from the cabin top and leans over to pass it down. It stutters and spits. She places it on the thwart.

"I'll be fine," she shouts as she pushes herself off. "Come and look for me at sunrise if I'm not back. Or perhaps Quill will decide to come." She strains to be heard above the thickening rain. Axel watches as she slots the oars into the rowlocks. He skirts the edge of the lugger, keeping her in his sights as she pulls slowly past. She rounds the front of the boat, her white dress a glowing ghost in the darkness. With a glance back at the island and an eye to the heavens, Axel shifts himself up onto the bow. But when the moment comes he cannot do it. Cannot summon the courage to push himself off the edge of that lugger. Instead, he watches her go, swallowed by the mangroves like an insect down a great bird's throat.

With a snap the rain comes on twice as strong, but Eliza's eyes are fixed firmly on the channel ahead. There she'll be sheltered from the wind, and beyond it she can already see the gray bodies of circling birds. Clumsily she tries to scoop out the water pooling at the boards. Clouds have snatched any light from the stars. Her teeth begin to chatter.

When she reaches the mouth of the channel, it's as if the wind has been snuffed out. Bushes whisper as she pulls on slowly past, sharp roots scraping noisily at the bottom of the boat. She hears the soft squelch of mud on the banks, thick enough to swallow her whole, and writhing with invisible things. A bird cries out in the mournful gloom, and a nearby splash signals something hurling itself into the water.

She picks up the lamp and holds it out in front of her. The channel is full of noises—ticks, creaks, and snaps. She can feel the scratch of biting animals, senses the weight of the things in the trees. With a trembling hand she holds the lamp out farther, its weak glow illuminating slick, oily roots. As she drifts, leaves glisten bright in the spotlight, so green and so glossy it makes her think of Bannin's bungalows. The tiny shapes of frogs leap with gentle plops into the water; flies descend on the lantern in a black, swarming cloud. Then she starts to see them. Here and there, low in the water. Eyes. Unblinking and inhuman, they drift away as the dinghy gets closer, each set slipping under the surface like two tiny falling moons.

She doesn't see anything approach the dinghy, but she senses its large presence in the darkness. In an instant, and with a rush of water, something propels itself upward near to her elbow. She cries out. It sets the dinghy rocking. She thinks only of the lamp, her sole light. She looks frantically around the surface, the lantern picking out laddered ripples. Something flaps from a tree and her eyes leap upward. Another splash comes near her arm and she half-stands in fear. She has stopped rowing now and the boat begins to turn in slow circles. Somewhere in her mind an image is materializing. Showing itself through the shadows. A rose, a white one. She remembers crushing its petals between her fingers as her father had talked, his words seeping back to her through time.

"There's only one thing you should do if you find yourself alone in saltie territory," he said. She'd only half-listened as she thumbed white confetti into her palm. "Eliza." She had looked at him, framed from behind by the sun. "One thing, Eliza. Keep as still as you possibly can."

Slowly she reaches for the oars and holds them still so there's enough resistance to calm the boat. Her muscles are coiled so tight they quiver. In this position she can slowly drift in the current. But the inertia is excruciating; her skin screams out for movement. Every inch of her wants to charge through the channel and get to the island as quickly as she can. But she forces herself to remain still. After a time she allows herself to turn her head slowly left to right.

Above her, heavy clouds part to reveal a bright full moon. She can see its dark spots like watching spirits. The air shimmers. She can see more clearly now. The banks are alive with spindly mangrove trees. The planets come out to watch now too, and stars in the shape of a fiery cross. Their light gives a strange clarity to the surroundings. Time hangs suspended as the boat drifts along the swamp. A breeze whispers over the water. Eliza's eyes follow its path and land on something peculiar.

There is a shape there.

In the trees.

Something that should not be there at all.

It is unmoving, solid, high above the waterline. She cannot bring herself to breathe. The water around her ceases to move. There is no longer darkness, just a river of light. Something has set fire to the air and it burns so bright she can see that, finally, she is where she was supposed to be all along. Memories tear through her, passing fast like playing children. She's on the beach with him, searching for empty crab shells; she is in his arms, shrieking with excited glee. After a flash in her mind that leaves bright marks on the insides of her eyelids, she sees him returning from sea, stepping off the *Starling* with a clear smile and open arms.

Her ears roar as she pulls on the oars now, sending the boat clumsily toward the bank. Is that movement she sees? Can it be? She is thankful for the moonlight, bright as the sun, picking out branches slicked with algae, illuminating something pale and out of place among shadows. A loud splash announces itself nearby but it is easy to ignore. She raises her eyes until the moon unveils something else: skin, human skin, fleshy like the inside of an old peach. She wants to spit the bitter taste from her mouth, but slowly, painfully, she moves her eyes farther upward. She feels as if her heart has been ripped from her chest and beats in the air before her. There is a leg. There: a booted foot. Upward still, something once white. Dull buttons clinging to sodden cloth. And there! An arm wrapped tightly around a branch, and at the end of that: a hand, one finger encircled by a ring. She feels herself begin to fall away but tries with all her strength to hold herself there. Farther still, her eyes meet a black mass of hair, scorched skin, and two eyes, owl-like behind smashed spectacles. Blinking back at her. Alive.

CHAPTER 38

The man is on the move. He awoke before sunrise to start his steady climb; from a higher vantage point, he will better see what, or who, is coming for him. His eyes rake the soil, finding roots and tubers. At his feet the displaced earth signals the messy diggings of a bilby.

The trees crane to watch him as he passes. Above, the bluff saws against the stark sky. As he picks his way up it, his broad hands brace the weight of his whole body. His feet grip the earth as scree tumbles away beneath them. He is high enough now to see the backs of the eagles. The sun is fierce and the air thick, but he has been able to whittle a weapon in the nights' solid darkness. He carries it with him, finds purchase in the landscape, rests with it in the shade when that comfort comes. But mostly, under the glare of the sun, he puts his head down and he continues to climb.

Down below, Parker's head weighs heavy on his shoulders. It has been weeks now without cooked food, without the safeguard of the constables' station. But he must continue; his is the civilizing force in this landscape. He is well used to flushing out those who dare elude him. Any buggers around these parts must yield to that or pay the price.

He rests with his tracker for a short while at a creek. The water runs weak as piss. Stagnant pools shelter the occasional armored predator. A struggling posse of gums is strung along the bank, but the men find shade under the branches of an old, dry boab. The horses bray and twitch, fat flies clinging to quivering eyelashes. The tree is so wide at the trunk it would take a hundred steps to make your way around it. Parker daren't try, daren't trudge with heavy dirt-caked boots, for he is not sure his legs would carry him back again. He is a man who likes to be sure.

His lips are boiling with blisters now, his skin so fiercely red, his nostrils engulfed with the fetid stench of his own body. He slumps against the tree's coolness, mad with thirst.

"Mister!" The tracker's voice comes as an urgent hiss.

Parker shoulders his rifle on the strap and walks to the tracker, follows the crane of his neck upward. The bluff is studded with spinifex but he cannot see much else amid the glare. The sun is blazing directly into his eyes and he has to squeeze them almost shut to counter it. Something is moving up there, though, he's sure of it now, and his fingers twitch toward the weapon, grasping cleanly for it when he sees the dark figure emerge. With a thumping chest and watery guts, he shoulders the stock and takes aim at the silhouette. The figure is backed by the lowering sun and a bright light spills out all around it. Parker squints, pulls his trigger finger back ever so slowly, then blinks the bloody flies away, just in time to see that the figure has raised a spear in return.

CHAPTER 39

Axel was astonished to see Eliza return to the waiting lugger with her father's body slumped against the stern sheets. But he was aghast when he realized that the man was still breathing. There was little time for explanation as they clamored to get his body onboard, as they muttered hurriedly to each other, making an assessment of his injuries. Frantically they tipped water into his mouth as his throat gulped in noisy panicked breaths. Once back on their island, Quill was able to barter with the Kellys for any medical supplies, coming away with iodine, bandages, needles, thread, some dry antiseptic, and a vial of laudanum.

They did not wait until morning to begin their journey back to Bannin. As soon as they were certain they had everything they needed, they hoisted the sails and nosed the lugger out of the Nevermore chain. The air was wet and the moon had started its slow retreat, and it was only when the boat was coasting, when Quill had collapsed into hot sleep, when Axel had assessed every wound on her father's body, that Eliza allowed herself to breathe properly again. With shaking hands she picked up a tin plate and turned it to see her warped reflection in the lanternlight. Her father's blood was smeared across her cheeks, caked into the creases of her neck. She dragged her fingers roughly across her lips and tasted the iron, tugged at skirts stained with crimson and felt for the places where the branches had broken her own skin too.

"He's got deep flesh wounds in his legs and his hands are badly torn up," Axel had said as they spoke in whispers outside the cabin. "It'll all need disinfecting and stitching, but he's dangerously dehydrated. That could prove fatal." He had looked in through the doorframe and then back to Eliza. "How on *earth* did he get up there into those trees in the first place? What in God's name was he doing?"

She shook her head and peered in at her father.

"We won't know until he's strong enough to talk. We'll just have to wait. Let him rest now." Her words were calm but her heart was aflame.

She does not leave her father's side for the next three days. Taking her meals at his bedside, holding a cloth to his forehead to try and break the fever. Waiting and waiting for him to regain his lucidity. Waiting for him to talk.

When he finally opens his eyes, when he groans and pulls himself upward with a face full of agony, Eliza is so relieved she feels as if she could scream. Everything inside her alights. Her father is alive. He is *alive*.

For a while they stare silently at each other, Eliza not knowing whether to curse or to cry. His face is thin, excavated by the sun. His lips are raw and shiny-wet with blisters. His mustache is wiry and long. He seems so lost without his spectacles. She glances at what remains of them now on the chest next to the bunk. He gulps and she can hear the scratchiness of it in his throat.

"How much do you know?" he asks her, hoarsely. There is something in his voice she can't decipher.

She watches as he gingerly turns his palms to study Axel's needlework. The flesh has been crudely stitched together, but she can see none of the leeching redness that Axel had warned would come with infection.

She shifts on the deck stool.

"All of it, I believe. If Thomas was telling the truth."

Her father nods; through his weakness he seems . . . impressed? "So you followed him."

Is it amusement behind his words? His face does not imply it, but there is something playful in how he speaks. It makes her momentarily furious.

"Was this a game to you? Another reckless venture? Because people have died."

His head whips up too fast and he clutches his neck in agony. "Not Thomas. *Please.*" His eyes are unhinged.

She shakes her head, feels a stab of regret. She looks at his arm, sewn up like patchwork. "No," she says, softer now, "not Thomas; Winters. His body washed up on one of the larger Nevermores."

His eyes drop to the boards, and she sees his shoulder slacken.

"We should never have tried it in the storm," he murmurs. "The poor soul. We just had to get off that island. We thought Thomas would come. We waited. We did." He puts his fingers to his brow. She wonders if the storm is the same that almost took Axel.

"Balarri too," she whispers. Her father looks up, then crumples again in grief.

"Not dead. Jailed." She corrects herself quickly. "For *your* murder. He escaped, unsurprisingly. Last thing I heard, Parker was still out in the bush searching for him."

Her father is shaking his head quickly. "We sent him back early so that wouldn't happen. Damned Parker!" His voice is sharp now, his face pinched. He must still be in pain. She offers him the vial but he refuses it. She shifts the stool forward and puts a hand on his arm. It has an extinguishing effect on her anger and tears come in its place. She bends to rest her head on her father's chest. He flinches in pain but he holds her there as she cries, her tears spiked with sorrow and fear for men who've become pawns in a game not of their own. But she knows, there's relief there too. However guilty that might make her feel. In her darkest moments, she was sure she would never see her father again. But here he is. Here is his smell, here is his low, rumbling voice. Here are his spectacles and his ring and all the objects she had believed forever lost. When there are no tears left, she lifts her head and wipes her eyes.

He tells her then, just as Thomas had told her, of the blackmail letter. How he and Thomas had clashed before a plan was eventually agreed on. He explains how, under a veil of darkness, Winters had collected him silently from the *Starling*. They had intended to make their way to the Rosellas, to wait for Thomas, as had been agreed.

"There were winds that night far stronger than we had anticipated," he says. "The day had been still, no problem at all. Matter of fact, it was absurd how clement the conditions were. But when the moon emerged it brought with it a howling wind from the nor'west. We were soon thrown far off course, no matter how hard we rowed or attempted to correct our path. We found ourselves at sea for two days with nothing—no water, no food, just the sharks that started to circle. I was convinced we'd die there. That we'd be drowned by a blow or succumb to the heat. But on that third morning, as we blinked into the sun, a mangrove channel came into view and beyond it, the green hump of an island. We were certain it was a mirage, Eliza!" He almost laughs. "We were astonished; the air above it was simply teeming with birds. As we neared, we could see that this could be a place we could shelter. We made our way down the channel, reached the island and scoured it: no human inhabitants, just a stinking gannet colony on its eastern edge. We fashioned a shelter, found a small stream inland to provide us with a water source. We could scavenge in the shallows for just enough food to keep us alive, we simply had to hang tight and wait for Thomas to come. Surely, we thought, when he found that we had overshot the Rosellas, he would widen his search. But"—he frowns—"you know your brother, the inveterate pessimist. He's not like you or me, or your mother, even. He must have found the Rosellas empty and believed us drowned. Oh, the poor boy. What anguish he must have been going through."

Eliza blinks, astonished. She cannot believe her father has such compassion for her brother. How, when faced with the truth that his own son did not believe enough in him to search for him, he extends sorrow and empathy, not fury. How he does not share her suspicion that this is merely what Thomas intended to happen all along.

"So we waited," he continues. "For over two weeks, until it became clear that unless we acted for ourselves, we could die on that island. So each day we began to take the dinghy out farther and circle every island in the chain. Looking for signs of native settlement, passing boats, anything that could help us. That's when we saw the smoke."

She thinks of the Kellys' fire, their ramshackle hut on the hill near the sun. She *knew* that must have been visible to them. "And you went there with the guano and compass to try and trade."

He looks at her, blinks in incredulity, before his mouth curls into a small smile. "That's exactly correct. Yes. We knew then that there were humans on that island. We didn't know who they were or, indeed, how they might receive us. But we had to try, and that's all we had to trade. As unusual as it was." He lifts his eyes to scour the pipe-blackened rafters. He seems to be working himself up to what he has to say.

"The sky looked grubby the day we went out; we weren't happy with it, but we had waited long enough. We were desperate to get off that island, particularly now we knew there was somewhere that might have supplies, food, even a boat to get us back to the mainland, perhaps. So we set out rowing." His damaged hands flicker to his mouth. "It was a reckless decision, made by addled minds. We weren't out on the water long before the blow hit us, crushed us like a fist would. We could still see the mouth of the channel behind us and the island on which we'd seen the smoke some distance ahead. We discussed whether to turn back. But soon enough it wasn't our decision. The waves began to rise. I've seen many furies, Eliza, but let me tell you, they look quite different when you're two men in a dinghy." She thinks of Axel in the water, how she was so sure it would take him too. "The waves were high as houses. We never stood a chance." She tightens her grip on her father's arm. "I was tipped out of the boat. I never saw what happened to poor Winters. I just swam and swam and swam for what seemed like hours. I was certain I would drown, Eliza. After everything that had happened, I was sure I would drown out there. I almost surrendered. Nearly allowed my body to be swallowed by the sea. But then I thought of you."

Her breath catches.

"I thought of you and all that you have been through. My daughter. My poor daughter. How you still are so wonderful after everything that has been sent your way." She swallows. "I thought of how you lost your mother and then you lost Ned," he continues. "The tragedy of it, and then Thomas and I had simply disappeared. We left you alone. I was disgusted with myself. I knew I had to get back to that island and get back to you, somehow."

She does not ask him then why he found it so easy to leave her in the first place. Not now. Not yet.

"Somehow, by the grace of God, I made it back to that channel. The water was not as rough there, but I was also not the only one in it." She feels a chill pass over her; she remembers being almost upturned in that water. "As I pulled my way through, I could see the armored tails of salties. Just the tops of them, on the surface. I panicked. I knew I had to get out of there, so I scrambled for the bank and pulled myself up the nearest thing that would hold me. Its roots were so sharp, they tore at my skin. The branches cut my hands and ripped out my flesh. I remember looking down and seeing blood had stained the water red. I had to get as high as I could if I was going to be safe."

She thinks of the storm that hit their lugger. It had been two days before they arrived at the Kellys' island in the Nevermores.

"How long had you been there when I found you?"

"Must have been three nights," he says. "The crocs never left. They waited, swaying in the current at the bottom of that tree. I couldn't descend to find water or food, couldn't do anything but try and outwait them. When you arrived, like an angel floating into sight, my Lord, I was sure then that I had died. No doubt about it."

"But here you are." She smiles but her mind is weary. She wants so very much to lie down and succumb to it all, but she knows that if she does not ask now she never will.

"Why didn't you tell me?"

He looks up at her, eyes searching hers.

"Why didn't you tell me what you and Thomas were going to do? How could you let me think that you were *dead*, even temporarily?"

He is quiet for a while and she scrutinizes his face.

"Because I knew I didn't have to tell you," he eventually says, carefully.

She frowns.

"It was simply safer at first for you not to know what we were planning. That lack of knowledge, initially, would protect you from yourself, from any rash action you might take."

She keeps her jaw set.

"But I also knew that, if something went wrong, you would find me." He blinks and lets it settle. "I knew that if something fell out of the chain, if something pushed the plan awry, you would stop at absolutely nothing to find me. I have never been more certain of anything."

She glares at him. She cannot seem to order the words.

"You had the diary; I made sure of that. And here you are."

She lowers her eyes to the boards. She thinks of all the times her father had planted clues for her. The mermaid charms, the dragonfly task. The mysteries that trailed like bread crumbs when he left. Had his diary been the biggest clue after all?

"You didn't trust Thomas to come and get you?"

"No, no, that's not what I'm saying." She is sure she sees a flicker of doubt ripple across his skin. "That's not what I mean at all." He clears his throat. "I wanted to give you the chance to do something to forgive yourself."

She shifts. A hotness builds in her chest.

"You saved me. Without you, I would undoubtedly be dead. I would have succumbed halfway up a bloodied mangrove tree. But you have *saved* me. There shall be no guilt now. No shame, Eliza. I will not have you blaming yourself for anything anymore."

His hands have started to shake now. She is confused, afraid. It takes a moment for her to realize what he is trying to say. Her mind goes back to that hot day. A boat in the shallows. A child floating on the tide. How she had tortured herself for years.

"Forgive yourself, Eliza." He reaches for her hand. "I want you to let go of that torment. Please."

She feels her temper flare.

"No." Her head swims. "I never asked you to do any of this. I never asked—" She pulls her hand away from his arm.

He shakes his head as if she has misunderstood. "I know that, but I just meant—"

"What will you do if Parker finds Balarri?"

"He'll be running rings around them out there."

"That's really not the point!" Her voice is high and sharp. "He wouldn't be out there in the first place were it not for you and this *ridiculous* plan." Her thoughts swerve and pitch. She knows everything her father has done he has done to help his children. But the chaos it has caused. The sheer *damage* to others.

"This was the only way I could protect you and Thomas. My family. I had to do that."

"What about Winters's family then? Or was he just dispensable to you?"

He drops his head into his hands. "That wasn't meant to happen, of course it wasn't, and I wish it hadn't ended up like this."

She looks at him, his body ruined, his face branded by grief. She doesn't have the strength to talk anymore, and so she fills his water jug and tells him to sleep. Closing the cabin door, she leans back and rests her head against its hardness. She shuts her eyes, the lids heavy and sore. In the darkness the image is faint: the boy she was never able to save.

CHAPTER 40

Bannin, two days later

Her father cannot be seen back in Bannin. They must be careful; until they can determine who wrote the letter, her family and others are still in danger. So Axel had agreed to take him on to Cossack in the lugger. He'll recuperate with Thomas until she sends word it's safe to return, although Eliza tries to ignore the needling possibility that might never happen.

She is short of breath when she reaches the jailhouse. Above her, brooding clouds jostle for space in the sky. She does not know how the heat finds such strength to persist. Even the sandflies have sought the shade now.

She is surprised to find the jail unattended and beats hard on the door for attention. After a while the jailer emerges from its innards, extracting himself from the shadows and shielding his eyes from the sun. He grunts in acknowledgment.

"Has a man named Balarri, from the *White Starling*, been taken in here?" she asks quickly, watching as a line of ants streams out from the doorway. A retching cough sounds from one of the cells. From another, a prisoner wails gently then launches into loud, inebriated song. "Has a man been brought in by Parker?" she asks again.

The jailer lets out a whistle of air through his lips, stuffs his hands into his pockets. "Haven't seen Parker for weeks now." He leans crookedly against the doorjamb, then pushes himself off it to stamp on the ants. "His wife sent a posse out to look for him, that much I know. Came back with nothing but sore arses and sunburn. Ask me, he's pissed off to one of the stations. Living an easy life, sure as anything, drinking himself silly, I'd wager."

She considers it but cannot imagine Parker abandoning his station, the power it affords him, like that. If he has not returned, then does that mean he has not yet found Balarri? Does that mean she might allow herself a shred of hope?

She leaves and makes for town, the paper hot in her restless fingers. There are barely any legible words remaining, but she holds it close to her chest as if it is something that needs protecting. She had taken it from her father's pocket, gently unfolded it and laid what remained on the deck. It was a mess of blotted ink and congealed matter, barely even discernible as paper. But she had managed to dry it in the sun, salvage a small sample of the handwriting: distinctive long, looping letters among the disintegrating mess.

People watch her with sharp eyes as she passes through town. All around her are a blur of faces where only the smallest details show themselves—a sideways eye; a snag-toothed grin. Their glares bounce off her like pebbles. She is focused solely on the boy she must speak to.

He is standing at his counter as usual. As she enters, the bell trills loudly. Above, a slow fan struggles to turn the stagnant air. The post boy's pale eyes are immediately anywhere but on her, skittering around the room. She smooths her skirts and fixes her face into a smile; the way her cheeks crease makes her think of her mother. She glides toward him, just a few smooth paces to the counter.

"Good morning." The softness in her voice surprises her. "Are you . . . having a pleasant day?" The boy is alarmed. His Adam's apple bobs up and down behind his freckled throat.

"Very good, miss," he manages to splutter. "Weather should be cooling down soon." They both look about the room, ignoring the fact that even the walls seem to be sweating.

She launches directly into her inquiry, keeping her tone pleasant so as not to draw the attention of other customers.

"Would you be so kind as to tell me why I did not receive a letter that was sent here for me a couple of weeks ago? An important letter. It would have been marked for me—Eliza Brightwell. Postmark Cossack."

She had thought of this on the lugger back to Bannin. Remembering her strained conversation with Thomas. How, when he first saw her, he had asked if she had received his letter. She'd allowed it to pass her by and hadn't asked him what it said; if he had attempted to write, to tell her of his plan and his failure to find their father. She cannot believe she allowed it all to slip through her fingers.

The boy moves from foot to foot. Sticks two fingers underneath his collar.

"It would be in your best interests to tell me the truth," she says, hoping the vague threat sounds convincing.

"I apologize, miss." The boy's eyes are frantic. He glances over his shoulder into the back room where the postmaster hovers halfway up a ladder. "I didn't think I was doing nothing wrong."

Her glare is enough to make him continue.

"She said she knew you. Said she'd take it to you. She only offered paying so I wouldn't tell anyone I'd given it to her."

"Who did?" Eliza is stunned.

"Just a woman. Don't know her name, miss. Plain as anything, nothing much about her. I guessed she was family."

"Was she a pearler's wife or a working woman?"

"The pearlers' wives don't often come here, miss; they send their servants in their place. I'm sorry, miss. Really. I'll do anything. Please, just don't report me." He looks back again at the ladder. "I need this job. I need the wage."

Without pause she takes the scrap of paper and places it on the counter in front of him. "Well then, I need you to tell me who wrote this letter. I presume you are familiar with the handwriting of most people in this town. There aren't that many who are able to read and write."

He looks confused and bends to inspect the sorry mess.

"There's been severe water damage here, miss. I'm not sure—"

"I know that but, look, there's still some writing preserved. See here, and here." She taps what remains of the ink.

He runs his fingers across the paper, reluctantly picks it up and holds it to the light.

"There's no watermark remaining; I've already checked. It's been scored off."

"You're wrong there."

"Excuse me?" She is taken aback by his tone.

"The mark has been scored off, but if you look closely, you'll see that the tops of the letters remain, here. They are somewhat spoiled but . . ." He traces the very bottom edge of the paper gently with his finger.

"B-R-I-G-H-T-W-E-L-L."

Her eyes whip to him. "Yes, Eliza Brightwell. That's me."

"No. I mean, this is Brightwell paper, this is. Seen that mark many times."

It is as if she has been hit. The room dissolves into smears. Surely not. Her father cannot have constructed *all* of this, just for her sake?

He cannot have gone that far. Her tongue feels as if it is fastened to the roof of her mouth.

"That's just not possible, I'm afraid. Look again. Perhaps somebody uses a similar watermark?"

The boy frowns. He fingers his shirt buttons and reluctantly puts the letter back up to the light.

"Miss, if you'd come here, you'll see it." He leans forward with the paper in his hands, eyes trained on Eliza's face. "See the very tops of the letters here. Just the slivers." He grabs a blotter and a pen and begins to slowly write the letters.

"There you have it," he says with a satisfied nod when finished. "W. E. BRIGHTWELL."

She drops her hands as if she has been burned.

CHAPTER 41

S hell grit crunches underfoot as Eliza approaches the bungalow. Drapes sag out of windows propped open with old timber
struts. The lilies in the garden are pristine and look alarmingly bold
against the rusting sheet iron.

She had thought perhaps she might be more afraid. She feels
nothing now but numb.

When he comes to the door he appears surprised to see her,
but he cannot be. He invites her inside and she follows him. The
air is stale but clinically bright, the sun slicing in through the open
windows.

He offers her tea. She does not take it. For a while they say nothing, the silence a thread pulled taut.

"How are you feeling, Eliza? I have been thinking of you often."

It floors her, but her throat is stopped by something. Her eyes scurry across his body, as if hovering too long on any part of him will blind her. He looks so weak there, his thin limbs all sharp angles and shadows. What a fine ruse.

She takes in the room: a moon-phase bracket clock beating out the time; once-gleaming ornaments solemn under dust. In the corner, a gun sits patiently on its pegs. Below it, a picture of her father, smiling through spectacles. Before she can think, she has crossed the room. She takes the frame, raises it above her head, and brings it down with a crash. Willem half-rises from his chair but freezes, confused, watching to see what she will do next. Her boots scrape against shards of glass. She bends, skirts gathering the filaments in their folds, and reaches for the photograph. Pulling it clear from the debris she puts it to her mouth, purses her lips and blows the splinters from its surface.

She takes the letter from her pocket, pauses, and then places it on the floor at Willem's feet. It's a cruel gesture and she knows it. He looks up at her, and then to the floor. She takes a step back and folds her arms. She watches as her uncle slowly starts to bend, his good knee taking the weight of his whole body. It is an awkward movement, and his knuckles whiten as he grasps the edge of the chair. His wooden leg begins to splay outward. His face reddens as he reaches. He inches closer until she can take it no longer; she bends and snatches it away so his fingers grasp at nothing. He sinks back down onto the chair with exhausted alarm, and Eliza thrusts the letter into his hands. He takes it, studies the remains of the matted paper.

"May I ask what it is?"

She could spit.

"You know what it is, Willem."

"Eliza, I really d–"

"*Enough.*" The steel in it cuts him; she can see it does.

"He almost died because of you. Others have died. All because of your–your greed." The words tumble out clumsily. "But blackmail; how could you? How could you go so far?"

He quickly reads what sparse words remain on the page. The shift in his face is subtle: a reassembling of lines; a tightening of the jaw.

"This is blackmail?" he asks. When he raises his eyes, Eliza sees in them something she has never before observed in her uncle. He rises, pushing himself upward with bony arms. Without a word he crosses the room, glass shards crunching underfoot. He does not look at her as he passes and soon she is alone with the shadows. Her limbs twitch with uncertainty. Should she follow him? No, she'll wait. She scans the room again, her gaze gliding over enamel boxes, the sunlight glinting from empty glass jars. She blinks but the image of her uncle's expression is burned into her mind, how his brows stitched themselves together. She hears him clear his throat and call to the back of the bungalow. There's a long silence, then muffled sounds follow at an agonizing beat.

When he passes back through the doorframe, he has one arm on his wife's shoulder. It appears to be a propulsive rather than protective gesture, and he steers Martha slowly to the center of the room.

"I think there's been some sort of mistake," he announces. "Perhaps we can discuss this, try and get to the bottom of everything."

Disgust sits in Eliza's throat, pinches the very top of her nasal passage. But she is not surprised that, even when collared, her uncle relies on the pandering support of his wife. Beside him, Martha's face is unreadable, but her presence has a blunting effect in the room. Willem looks at the paper, then passes it to his wife, who barely glances at it. He moves toward the escritoire at the side of the room, reaches for the clasp, flicks it open, and down drops the door. Behind it, an inkwell waits alongside a fountain pen in a silvered stand. Papers are stacked in a neat pile and tied with ribbon. He undoes the silk, reaches for the top sheet, and studies it intently.

"What we must first establish is how someone might have stolen our correspondence in order to copy your hand," he mutters.

Eliza sucks in a furious breath. How can he *still* be trying to weasel his way out of this? She has presented him with the evidence of his deed. It is written there, quite plainly in ink. And. And. She pauses. Blinks. He'd said *your* hand. She looks up at him.

Her uncle is glaring at his wife. His teeth are clenched, and she can see the muscles in his jaw twitching.

"Can you think of an explanation for this, Martha? Anyone who might want to finger you for such a thing?" Eliza sees the paper shaking in her uncle's hand. She steps forward and reaches for it. It takes less than a breath for her to recognize the long, elegant scrawl. *Dearest Willem.* The fine loops and sloping lengths have been seared into her vision by now. She does not have to read the contents to see that the hand is the same as her scrap of paper. Instead, she raises it slowly above her, lets the light pass through, sees the watermark she is expecting, clear and crisp. She lowers it. At the bottom of the letter, in writing Eliza knows so well now: *Your loving wife, Martha.*

She raises her head to study her aunt's face: chin thrust forward, eyes unblinking. She recognizes its meaning, but it is not the one she had expected to find. It is defiance.

The woman in front of her could look no less like someone capable of blackmail. How could such plainness send a man to the limits, out onto the ocean to protect his family? Her face is unlined by weather or work. Her body is soft and unremarkable, her hair the most perfunctory light brown. She blinks back at Eliza as if she is nothing more than a dog.

"How could you?" Eliza whispers, and in that moment she realizes it must have been Martha who intercepted the letter from Thomas too.

"Martha. *Tell her.* Explain, go on." Her uncle's breathing is ragged. "Tell her someone must have done this. You must have been careless with one of your letters at the Circle."

Silence.

"Martha, speak!" Willem barks. Her uncle's alarmed rage is shocking. But Martha still does not respond. Instead, she appraises them, eyes small and hard. Eliza's mind goes to words she'd read in her father's diary—a note about sharks: *a black, dead eye that chills the soul of any sailor.*

"He made it so easy to do," she eventually says. Willem's eyes close in horror. "Your father is a weak man. His family has always been his downfall."

Eliza struggles to marry the woman in front of her—the woman who led meetings about morals and godliness and decorum—with the words that are coming from her lips. An insect's buzz sounds from somewhere in the room. Outside, the sea hums its melancholic tune.

"He is pathetic, really. Undeserving of all that he has been given." Martha's face is taut. "It started with your mother. Not fit to bring another child into this world. But she insisted on that baby and your father was too weak to change her mind on it. Her death is his fault, really, when you consider all things." Eliza feels the contents of her stomach swill. "I have watched your family, greedy with children, blinded by pearls, coasting on the profits of things that should have been ours."

For the briefest moment Eliza eyes the shelves at the side of the room. There are no frames, no crinkle-eyed children captured in paint.

"*We* paid for your passage here. *We* did. We are the ones who facilitated your father into a position that made him filthy rich. Yet when he lost his leg"—she gestures to her husband—"where was your father then?" Willem's fists clench. "All he was concerned with was his wife. Half that fleet should have been ours, and we would be running this town with the sorts of profits that could bring. Instead, we're given a paltry cut and left to scrabble for scraps in the dirt while your father's debts spiral. When I saw what your brother is really capable of doing too, it confirmed it. A man like that cannot inherit a fleet."

Eliza's fingers tense and she steps forward. Martha doesn't flinch.

"Oh, Eliza, he's a menace." Her voice is flat and plain. "His lust is a blight upon the bay and he must pay for that sin."

Martha's body lurches forward and she almost falls to her knees. Behind her, Willem stands with a raised arm, hands shaking with the arrow-quiver of anger.

"Get out." His voice is flat yet commanding, but Martha does not even lift her head. Her shoulders shake as she laughs bitterly. She does not see her husband slowly cross the floor and remove the Webley from its pegs.

"Leave," he orders. The word is harsh but heavy with sorrow. He cannot look at his wife but he holds the gun reluctantly out in front of him. "Leave this house. Leave Bannin, and if you try anything involving my family again, if I hear anything of any blackmail, I will send somebody to find you and kill you, so help me God." Willem's fury crackles. There are tears on his cheeks. "I will not hesitate to do it."

Slowly, Martha stands taller.

"I wouldn't stay in this town anyway. The devil has this dirt in his grip." She wipes spittle from her mouth, gathers her skirts, and moves toward the doorway. "I'll send a boy to collect my things." Willem's teeth are gritted so tight Eliza fears they will crumble. He does not turn to watch his wife go.

CHAPTER 42

The clouds have opened, spilling their bellies over Bannin Bay. The sound of it is animal, as if the earth is being gutted by grief. Eliza holds her hat against the wind as she battles toward Axel's hut. He should be returned from Cossack by now and she wants to tell him it is safe for her father and brother to come too.

The shacks on the foreshore vibrate with the stoniness of the rain. When she arrives, boots coated in wet sand, she finds Axel slack-jawed with a book balanced on his chest. He startles when she quietly lets herself in.

"Good God." He leaps up from the bunk. "You're soaked through; are you quite mad?"

She removes her hat and places it on an upturned barrel, squeezing the water from her hair. "A little rain never hurt anyone." She looks down at her bedraggled skirts and they both laugh.

"Here, let's warm you up." He takes a blanket and wraps it around her shoulders. "Perhaps I could light a fire, although I fear the wood would not take in this weather." She assures him she is fine and takes a seat on the stool in the corner.

They discuss what happened in Willem's bungalow, how they are sure now that Martha had left town for good.

"Have you been able to check on Quill?" she asks.

"Quill is very well." He nods. "McVeigh was delighted to have him back. I think the old fellow was a little lonely."

Eliza smiles inwardly at Quill's secret. She still treasures it, although it's hard to stifle the fear of what the future might hold.

"I'm glad you came here," Axel says, steepling his fingers before moving his hands to his knees. It's an odd movement and she wonders if he might, for some reason, be nervous.

Her shoulders sink. "No, don't tell me you are leaving," she groans. "Stay awhile, stay here in Bannin Bay. Please. I promise you'll like it." She looks around doubtfully.

He laughs. "It's not that. Well, in part it's that—I will have to move on eventually—but there is something I wanted to discuss with you first."

"So formal," she jibes. But then she sees that he is blushing. "What is it?"

"Well, the matter is . . ." He stutters and starts. The rain falls hard onto the beach outside. "I should think it entirely impossible that it has escaped your attention that I am in love with you."

She holds her breath. She is not sure what to do.

He takes her silence for encouragement.

"I have traveled to many parts of this earth but I have never met anyone quite like you, Eliza Brightwell."

She looks at him, willing him to stop.

"I have never met a woman who behaves as you behave. And, believe me, I mean that as a compliment."

She shifts in her seat.

"You astonish me and it—oh, what is the phrase—it makes my heart *sing* to be around you." She has never seen him quite this animated before, and that's saying something. "And not only are you beautiful—"

"I am not beautiful." She says it as if he has accused her of theft. But she knows she is not beautiful. Therefore, his words must be empty.

"You are *exquisite*, Eliza. A woman does not have to be done out like these society women to be beautiful. Your *soul* is beautiful and your spirit is-is—" He moves across the hut toward her. "I would never forgive myself if I did not ask you to be my wife."

She looks up at him: his handsome face, his clear, earnest eyes. She considers the prospect; she has never met a man like Axel Kramer before either. Someone so untroubled by the constraints of what a man is meant to be. His chest rises; she can sense the anticipation coming off him.

She shatters it. "I'm afraid I cannot do that."

His face slackens, then he moves away from her, eyes to the ground. "Of course, yes, I should never have presumed."

"I would not satisfy you."

His head whips up. "Yes, you would, Eliza, I know for certain that you would."

"And you would not satisfy me."

The wind moans outside. Axel has frozen still.

"I have no interest in acting as a wife to a husband, and when I travel I would not be content to do it on the arm of a man. An arrangement like this, however charming it is, would therefore not satisfy me at all."

He nods, laughs mirthlessly. "I should never have let you go alone into that channel," he says.

"What do you mean?" She frowns.

"Perhaps if I'd gone with you, your answer would be different."

He sighs. "I gave up; you cannot *abide* giving up. I know that well enough now." He smiles bitterly and she goes to him. Puts an arm around his shoulder.

"You are truly one of the greatest people I have met," she says. "And I do not want you to leave. I think you should stay here." She points to the ground. "I'm sure there are many women in this bay who would leap at the chance to be your wife. A dashing German adventurer?" She raises an eyebrow.

His smile is sanguine.

"Well, while you might not be fulfilled as a wife, I am afraid I cannot be fulfilled by a life spent in one place," he says. "I'm itinerant by nature; I will have to move on soon. Perhaps I shall see what's what in New Zealand, what might occupy me at the ports of the Orient. Maybe I'll even make my way over to London."

She smiles at him then. "Promise you'll come back eventually, even just to visit," she says.

"Of course I will, Eliza." Although she knows he does not mean it. "Nothing could keep me away from Bannin Bay."

CHAPTER 43

Two weeks later

As she walks, wheeling rosellas turn rose pink against the sky. The air above the mudflats is less sluggish now the rains have finally come. Beyond them, in the distance, the sea inhales and exhales like a beast.

When she reaches the dune, she sits and pushes her fingers into the sand. It is cooler under the surface and she pulls out her hands to let the sand flow from her palms. She remembers clearly that moment, years ago, with Balarri. How the clouds had sat engorged on the horizon, the sky blotchy like bruised flesh. There's a familiar dryness in her mouth. She's not sure she will ever be rid of it now. But she will make it her duty to wait for her friend, wherever he may be. She has still heard nothing of Parker's quest. She has begun to ask around about Winters's family too, although she has not yet been able to locate any. She will always hold that discomfort inside her. Sorrow for a boy coaxed to make a sacrifice that can never be repaid.

As she makes her way back to town, thunder tumbles from the sky. In the distance she pictures the Brahminy kites poised on mangrove branches and skippers writhing across the mud in their strange sort of ecstasy. She watches birds, bright as pins with their long, sharp bills, stalking the flats on stringy legs, searching for worms as the world keeps slowly turning.

On the fringes of town the smells and sounds whip around her. She takes a breath, tips her face to the sky, and allows herself a brief moment of calm. It's sliced in half by a whistle.

"Brightwell!" Min stands in the middle of the road, beaming. She's carrying buckets from the soaks and drops them in the shade before making her way toward her.

"Just . . . wandering about, are you?" Her tone is only mildly mocking. "What on earth are you doing?"

"I was just–paying my respects to somebody."

Min raises her eyebrows but doesn't push it.

They stand inspecting each other for a while, saying nothing, but their tight smiles speak of shyness.

"I've been meaning to talk to you," Min finally says.

"Axel's already told me." Eliza speaks quickly and raises her palm. "There's really no need to explain. It's wonderful news."

"I feel I do need to explain."

"Please be assured that you do not. I couldn't be happier for you both."

Min tilts her head; Eliza can see the amusement in her eyes.

"Look," Min says, "I know I wasn't his first choice." Eliza begins to hold her hand up again. "And, well, if we're honest, he's not mine either." Eliza closes her eyes and they both laugh. "But he's kind and handsome and gentle–and he'd never lay a finger on a woman."

Eliza shakes her head. "Never."

"He can give me something I wouldn't have been granted otherwise." Min reaches for Eliza's hand. "I can leave this place; see parts of the world I've only ever dreamed about. All those places we used to talk about, Eliza? And I know what you'll say—you'll say, "You don't need a man to do that." But I *do* need a man to get what I've always truly desired. That's the truth. I want children—you know that's all I've ever really wanted—plus, this man seems willing to look beyond the things I have had to do in order to get by here. As he likes to remind us." They chuckle. "And the money I've saved will help us settle down somewhere . . . else. Somewhere different."

Eliza tries to push away the idea of Min and Axel leaving. She may never see them again. But her friend deserves this happiness.

She pulls Min's hand to her chest. "You could not wish for a purer sou—"

The clatter of wheels comes tearing down the road.

They leap into the shadows as the dray bombs past, carrying on its bed a wooden pallet and the enormous body of a dead crocodile.

They frown, make the silent decision to follow it down the way, and watch as it turns into a side street where it is met by a waiting group of men. She can see Doctor Blithe and a handful of troopers, Snider–Enfields balanced neatly against their thighs. They're gathered outside the Chinese butcher's.

Eliza and Min glance quickly at each other as the butcher emerges in his leather apron and elbow gloves. He nods a quiet greeting and raises his hand to show a cleaver.

They watch in astonished silence as the men heave the crocodile off the pallet. It takes eight of them to lift its weight and maneuver it onto the hook on the wall. It hangs there, swaying gently like a pendulum. The beast is simply enormous, its body swollen and stretched in all angles from the inside. Eliza feels her pulse thicken. Min puts her fingers over her eyes, then parts them.

"Let's get on with it, then," they hear Blithe call. "Quick now or we'll draw a crowd, chop-chop." She can already see curious shop-keepers poking their heads out of their porchways.

The butcher strides back into the shop, then returns with a foot-stool that he places underneath the crocodile. He steps onto it and with a single fluid motion, like peeling a piece of fruit, he slits open the animal's belly and a body sluices out.

Well, part of a body at least: the top half, Eliza can discern, for it is still clad in blue.

The men raise their forearms to their noses and peer down at the grisly corpse. It's a man—that much Eliza can tell from this distance—and she watches as a trooper takes his boot and pushes the chin slowly upward. The corpse's eyes are fixed open, and as the head tilts back they lock onto Eliza's with chilling finality. Her breath catches. She half-expects those eyes to blink. She sees the rest of him now: the cruel nostrils, the heavy brow, skin tough as a bootstrap. Parker.

"That's that, then," Blithe announces through his elbow. "I think I can safely pronounce him dead, wouldn't you say so, chaps?"

"Poor sod," some of the troopers mutter, but others are already walking away. The shopkeepers have returned to their business.

"Hold on a jot," one of the men says. "What's that sticking out his chest?"

He bends toward the torso, shielding his nose with his shirt-sleeve. With the other hand he reaches for Parker's jacket, just above the heart. He wiggles something loose, then comes away with a small, hard object in his fingers. He holds it close to his face to in-spect it, then with a click of the tongue he tosses it aside. It skitters toward where Eliza and Min wait in the shadows. Eliza looks down at the thing nudging the toe of her boot. Its form is unmistakable: the sharp, bloodied head of a spear.

A NATURALIST'S LOGBOOK–
ELIZA M. BRIGHTWELL

17 May 1898

The swell was steady today and there was a good wind behind us, so we charted course and headed east to the reefs surrounding the Cockatoos. Quill was on scouting duty and while I hoisted the sails, a good few spots were identified at which we could try our luck for specimens.

From the surface, these reefs look like nothing more than a dun smear. But, as Quill likes to tell me, dive down and you'll find them alive with beasts. Occasionally I'll be presented with a fistful of creatures–writhing, coiling, and wriggling in a palm. It's enough to make squeamish sorts wince, but of course, to us, what can be found below these waters is truly captivating. Often these specimens are simply so strange–a wholly translucent worm perhaps, or a flabby monster, part plant, part animal–that I'll plop them into the bucket to take home for the microscope. Our diaries are becoming really quite detailed now, and Father tells us there's a publisher back in London who has expressed interest in a small print run.

While I usually work up on deck, today I was not content being shown these creatures like a queen at court. Today I had to see them for myself. So after a thorough scout for sharks, I stripped off and plunged right in. Oh, it was heaven. As the sun set, my body was stroked by the ocean. I dived down into the darkness until my ears could go no farther. Through glass lenses what I saw was truly spectacular: thick carpets of moss alive with turtles, spiders, and centipedes; many-legged sea insects that danced through the water in a ripple of limbs; glowing sea worms, things with tassels; a sea floor that pulses as if it itself is a creature too.

The evening was approaching, warm and calm, and the water was filled with flecks of phosphorus; fish charged past leaving trails of stars. It made me think of Balarri and how we used to marvel at sparkling fish scales. It made me think of the thing I found on the veranda last December: a seahorse. Dried out and stiff. Hooked onto its coiled tail was a string of small green shells. Quite astonishing, as if they'd been threaded onto a necklace. It was one of the most beautiful natural curiosities I have ever seen. Father assured me he had no knowledge of it, and sometimes I allow myself to wonder whether it might have been left there for me to find.

As I dived, other lights came floating down too, passing like silk parachutes in the half light. I looked up and I could see a whole ensemble of jellyfish there, fiery tentacles long and swaying in the current.

When my lungs could take it no longer, I shifted my body and pulled myself slowly upward. With a heaving breath I broke the surface and looked about me at an ocean ablaze with the sinking sun. Then I turned to the lugger, its steady masts kissed by amber, waiting patiently on the waves.

HISTORICAL AND
CULTURAL NOTE

I'd like to thank Bart Pigram for acting as a cultural consultant on this novel. I am also hugely grateful to Steve Kinnane and the Kimberley Aboriginal Law and Cultural Centre for their generous consultation and feedback.

Bannin Bay is fictional, as are its inhabitants, but its geography is modeled on parts of the northwest Kimberley coastline. I therefore acknowledge the traditional owners of this Saltwater Country.

I took my inspiration for Bannin Bay from Australia's early pearling hubs, which came to sweltering, stinking life in the nineteenth century. These include Shark Bay in Gascoyne, Cossack near Roebourne and Broome—a beguiling place, which thunders into the sea in the far reaches of the Kimberley. The geography of the islands surrounding Bannin Bay is also mostly fictional, but I have taken my cue from the landmasses that rise from the ocean off the northwest coastline, particularly Barrow Island, the Lacepedes, and the Burrup Peninsula.

The pearl oyster, *Pinctada albina*, was first commercially harvested at Shark Bay in 1850, but it was the 1861 discovery of the far larger *Pinctada maxima* shell beds at Nickol Bay that had prospectors flocking to Western Australia. By 1898, Broome was the principal cargo port in Australia's northwest, and it would go on to produce 80 percent of the world's mother-of-pearl shell. By 1900 pearling was the fourth largest export industry after gold, timber, and wool. This boom lasted until the emergence of cultured pearling and the mass production of plastic buttons, as well as the onset of the Second World War, which changed the fabric of multicultural Broome irrevocably.

I wouldn't have been able to write this book had it not been for the work of dedicated chroniclers of early Broome and its inhabitants, including Hugh Edwards and Susan Sickert, whose books *Port of Pearls* and *Beyond the Lattice* proved invaluable during my research process, and whose real-life anecdotes directly inspired Charles's diaries. I'm also grateful to the staff at the Broome Historical Society, who allowed me to trawl through their archives one unimaginably hot day in May. In addition to these resources, I relied on the comprehensive exhibition slides and accompanying printed text from *Lustre: Pearling and Australia*, a collaboration between the Western Australian Museum, Nyamba Buru Yawuru, and peoples of the West Kimberley, curated by Sarah Yu and Bart Pigram. I pay my respects particularly to the Yawuru, Karajarri, Bardi, Jawi, and Mayala Elders who contributed to those projects.

This novel is not history, but many of its characters are inspired by real people, including Conrad Gill—an enigmatic boatswain from the West Indies, who patrolled the streets of Broome with a gold earring and a talking parrot on his shoulder (in reality Gill did not arrive in Broome until 1900, but his cockatoo *was* something of a kleptomaniac)—and a dashing Japanese lead diver called Masajiro Sakaguchi, who was held up as a celebrity in the town on account of the vast amounts of pearl shell he hauled in each season. I used a variety of settlers as the starting point for my Brightwells, including British-born Eliza Broadhurst, an early feminist who survived famine and shipwrecks and established a school in the unforgiving outback; on returning to London, her daughter Katherine became a key part of the suffragette movement, tying herself to the railings of Parliament and embarking on a hunger strike in prison. I relied on diaries kept by the Broome Master Pearlers when it came to details on ships and "stones," while old adventurers' accounts of the rampant seas around Western Australia provided crucial background when it came to Charles's diaries. I must acknowledge, in particular, Ion Idriess's *Forty Fathoms Deep*, from which I drew greedily for Charles's encounters with whales and sharks. I have taken a novelist's liberties with some timelines. The Northwest's actual Master Pearlers' Association was formed in 1902, several years after my story takes place.

In 1883 Robert A. Cunningham, a recruiter for Barnum and Bailey's Circus, traveled not to Broome but to far north Queensland to find subjects for his next "show-stopping" exhibition. For *Ethnological Congress of Strange Tribes*, he sought to add to his "collection" of Indigenous people, and so he "recruited" six Aboriginal men, two women, and a boy from Wulguru country on Palm Island and Hinchinbrook, and shipped them to America where they were promoted as "Australian cannibals" and forced to perform alongside an elephant—singing, dancing, and throwing boomerangs to entertain the crowds. Throughout the 1880s and 1890s, this happened across Australia and other parts of the world, to children just like Alfred.

Father McVeigh's fledgling mission was inspired by the story of fellow Scot Father Duncan McNab. After serving as chaplain to Rottnest Island penitentiary, the call from above inspired McNab to begin a mission for Aboriginal people in the Kimberley. In June 1885, he set out in his mission lugger on an exploratory journey to the Dampier Peninsula, landing at Swan Point, northwest of Derby, in Bardi Country. He had no training, no knowledge of local languages, and no real plan. He had just turned sixty-five years of age. Over the years he traveled extensively in the area, observing and mixing with local people, building a bush timber church, and establishing a garden and cottages for the Bardi to utilize. He also began to compile a dictionary of the Bardi language and met a young Aboriginal boy called Nybe (known as Knife) who acted as his interpreter.

But regardless of the missionaries' intentions, their presence had a catastrophic effect on the country's Aboriginal population. Many churches banned or discouraged the use of Aboriginal languages and forcibly removed children from their families, where they were taken into missions and institutions in order to be "educated" and expunged of their Indigenous culture.

It was during one research trip to Broome that I came across a powerful monument overlooking the waters of Roebuck Bay. It depicts a pregnant Aboriginal pearl diver bursting from the ocean with a shell in her palms. The inscription reads:

And precious the tear as that rain from the sky,
Which turns into pearls as it falls in the sea.

–Thomas Moore

Pregnant divers were favored by the early pearlers because of their supposedly increased lung capacity. This was, of course, not the only way in which Indigenous communities have been exploited throughout Australia. British colonial forces arrived on the west coast of Australia in 1826. But, given the harshness of the land, population growth beyond the Swan River Colony, on the site of present-day Perth, was minimal. That was, until the discovery of gold in the 1880s, which triggered mass movement alongside the concomitant boom in the pearl shell industry. What had already begun, however, was a brutal dispossession of Aboriginal communities throughout Australia, and a reimagining of the land into a "frontier."

Many of the events this novel makes reference to, including police brutality, the use of chain gangs, and the practice of "blackbirding"–where Aboriginal men, women, and children were kidnapped, traded, and forced to work on early pearling vessels–are based on real-life accounts. Passages of "an open letter from Mr. David Carley to the Secretary of State direct," calling for intervention from the government in response to the enslavement of Aboriginal people and police brutality in northwestern Australia, are reproduced almost verbatim (only some names have been changed). The State Records Office of Western Australia holds numerous records detailing blackbirding activities, and for anyone interested in learning more about the police force's involvement in the colonial expansion into the Kimberley frontier, I would recommend tracking down a copy of the book "*Every Mother's Son is Guilty*" by Chris Owen.

Owen's book also makes reference to the practice of "komboism"– where Aboriginal women, and sometimes children, were taken, traded, and prostituted to pearlers. In some cases, these women were dressed as male stockmen against their will in order to disguise them from the authorities. I'd like to acknowledge that while my character Quill chooses to dress a certain way in order to navigate a male-dominated industry, historically many Aboriginal women of the Kimberley were not afforded such choice.

In Broome there also stands a cemetery where more than nine hundred Japanese men are buried. Similar cemeteries exist in pearling towns across the north of Australia. Hard-hat diving was and still is considered to be one of the world's most dangerous occupations. Many indentured workers–from Japan, China, Malaysia, Timor, the Philippines, and beyond–lost their lives to disease, divers' paralysis (the bends), and drowning. Official inquiries into the industry have not adequately addressed the high mortality rates of pearling workers, and their families have never been compensated. This book acknowledges all those who gave their lives to the industry as divers, skippers, tenders, and crew.

ACKNOWLEDGMENTS

Thank you to my brilliant editors–Carina Guiterman, Sarah St. Pierre, Sam Humphreys, Bev Cousins, and Kalhari Jayaweera. I am amazed at the care, patience, and dedication you have shown me and this book. I couldn't have wished for a better (or more enthusiastic) team of women to have by my side. Thank you also to Lashanda Anakwah, Alice Gray, and the amazing design, production, sales, publicity, and marketing teams at Simon & Schuster, Mantle, and Penguin Random House Australia. I am so grateful for everything.

Maddy–agent, cheerleader, mighty protector of authors. Thank you for sending me the best email I have ever received and for changing my life. Thank you also to Rachel Yeoh, Liv Maidment, Georgia McVeigh, Georgina Simmonds, Liane-Louise Smith, Giles Milburn, Vanessa Browne, Ursula Buston, and the rest of the team at the Madeleine Milburn Agency for all the kindness, support, and invaluable manuscript feedback.

I owe a huge debt of gratitude to those who lent me their expertise for *Moonlight*, particularly (Broome legend) Bart Pigram, mentioned in the previous Historical and Cultural Note, whose extensive knowledge of the early pearling era helped shape this book and the character of Balarri. Any errors in this respect are entirely my own. Thank you to Vinnie Antony for your generous advice on Kimberley flora and fauna (next time we'll find the dingo pups, eh?), to Barry Kirkham for sharing your much-needed maritime nous, to Xiaolan

Sha for your help with Hong Yen and Laura-Min, and to Graham Kenyon for the crocodile anecdotes; I hope to revisit LimilngaWulna land and share ghost stories with you again some time.

Thank you to the friends, family members, and colleagues who read early versions of this novel and were kind enough to encourage me to keep going—particularly Iona Sweeney and Kate Burke. Thank you to the early supporters of my creative writing and journalism, specifically Mr. Palmer of St. Mark's Primary School in Salisbury, and Lisa Smosarski at *Stylist* magazine—a true women's-mag hero who let me do *all* the weird stories.

Thank you to Richard Mellor and Joe Minihane for keeping me positive and accountable during the Great Lockdown of 2020. To Laura Adams and Robin Miller for the lifetime of laughter and friendship, and to Anita Bhagwandas, Nikki May, and Collette Lyons for the enduring moral support during this mad publication journey. I feel very privileged to have met so many talented debut authors via Twitter and Facebook along the way, too. We made it! Here's to you all.

Finally, to my family—Tom, Lucy, Martha, Rufus, Phoebe, Max, and Sam—and all other Pooks, Kirbys, Gardiners, and Arnotts. I am so grateful to have your support and I am very sorry for stealing your names and gifting them to morally dubious characters. Thank you to my mum, the strongest woman I know and the one person who will never tell me it's good when it's not. I am grateful for everything you do. To Bobby, the kindest, most supportive soul around; I love you, always. To Rose, the other half of me (I could never put it into a sentence so here are eighty thousand words instead). And to my dad, no longer with us, but whose influence can be felt on every page of this book. I wish you could have seen it.

ABOUT THE AUTHOR

Lizzie Pook is an award-winning journalist and travel writer who has contributed to the *Sunday Times*, *Lonely Planet*, *National Geographic*, *Condé Nast Traveller*, and more. Her assignments have taken her to some of the most remote parts of the world, from the uninhabited east coast of Greenland in search of roaming polar bears to the trans-Himalayas to track snow leopards. She was inspired to write *Moonlight and the Pearler's Daughter*, her debut novel, after spending time in northwest Australia researching the dangerous pearl-diving industry. She lives in London.